Upon This Rock

FEB 2011

Upon This Rock

Kendra Norman-Bellamy

www.urbanchristianonline.net

Urban Books, LLC
78 East Industry Court
Deer Park, NY 11729

ISBN 13: 978-1-60162-893-0
ISBN 10: 1-60162-893-5

First Printing March 2011
Printed in the United States of America

10 9 8 7 6 5 4 3 2 1

This is a work of fiction. Any references or similarities to actual events, real people, living, or dead, or to real locales are intended to give the novel a sense of reality. Any similarity in other names, characters, places, and incidents is entirely coincidental.

Distributed by Kensington Corp.
Submit Wholesale Orders to:
Kensington Publishing Corp.
C/O Penguin Group (USA) Inc.
Attention: Order Processing
405 Murray Hill Parkway
East Rutherford, NJ 07073-2316
Phone: 1-800-526-0275
Fax: 1-800-227-9604

Dedication

In memory of Marquitta ("Kita") Rogers
You were one of my greatest supporters. I still miss
you, my friend . . .

Acknowledgments

In everything give thanks for this
is the will of God concerning you.
(I Thessalonians 5:18)

Heavenly Father, thank you for the unmerited favor that you have extended to me. Because of you, I am able to live with passion and walk in purpose. For every achievement that I attain, I will give you the glory. It is all because of YOU.

To **Jonathan**, **Brittney**, and **Crystal**: thank you for being my home based cheerleaders. The many obligations that come with this God-given calling that has been bestowed upon me would seem much more taxing if it were not for your support.

Bishop & Mrs. Harold Norman Sr., I am abundantly blessed to have you for parents. Thank you for teaching me the ways of the Lord and for preparing me, even as a child, for the divine appointment that awaited me.

To my siblings, **Crystal**, **Harold Jr.**, **Cynthia**, and **Kimberly**: Thank you all for the priceless nuggets of blessings that you have added to my life over the years. You all are the greatest.

To **Jimmy** (1968–1995): Thank you for memories that never fade, and for the inspiration that birthed "I Shall Not Die" and The I.S.L.A.N.D. (**I S**hall **L**ive **A**nd

Not **D**ie) Movement. May your example continue to inspire others to live.

Terrance, I honestly don't know what I'd do without you. You believed in my writing ministry from day one, and have always assisted wherever needed. Thank you, cuz. I don't take any of it for granted.

Bridget, here is an early thank you for the increase that I have the faith to believe that you are already adding to this ministry. I'm glad to have you on my team.

To **Rhonda**: Thank you for promoting me even when I don't know you're promoting me.

Carlton, from the very beginning, you have looked out for me as an agent and an attorney. You're the best behind-the-scenes man ever.

To my godparents, **Uncle Irvin** and **Aunt Joyce**: It means a lot to have both of you in my corner. Thank you for your continued support.

To **Heather**, **Gloria**, **Deborah**, **Dwan**, **Sherry**, **Lizz**, and **TaShonne**: Thank you for being my confidants, my prayer partners, and my most cherished sister-friends.

To **Bishop Johnathan & Dr. Toni Alvarado** and my entire **Total Grace Christian Center** family: I continue to thank the Lord for you. There is no place... like Total Grace.

Thank you to **"Papa Vince & Mama Flo"** for always saving a seat for me in "our section" for Sunday morning worship. Also to my spiritual sisters, **Geri** and **Annette** for always offering words of support and encouragement regarding my writing ministry.

A special thank you to all of the members of the following groups of which I am blessed to be an active part: **The I.S.L.A.N.D. Movement, Iota Phi Lambda Sorority, Inc., Bossettes, Anointed Authors on Tour (AAOT), Pages of Grace Book**

Club, **The Writer's Hut**, and **The Writer's Cocoon Focus Group**.

Finally, to **Melvin Williams**, **Fred Hammond**, **Brian McKnight**, **BeBe & CeCe Winans**, **Antonio Allen**, **Vanessa Bell Armstrong**, **Lowell Pye**, **Marcus Cole**, **Fantasia**, **The Williams Brothers**, **James Fortune**, and **J. Moss**: Thank you for providing the delightful music that played continuously as I wrote this novel.

Prologue

Our Father, who art in heaven, hallowed be thy name...

Rocky shouldn't have been too surprised. He'd always known that there was a possibility that his past would eventually catch up with his present. He hoped it wouldn't—even prayed that it wouldn't—but realistically, what were the chances that he'd die a good man's death when he'd spent so many years living a bad man's life? Death was only seconds away. It was so close that he could smell it . . . the scent of blood as it oozed from a gun-inflicted fresh wound. He'd smelled it before on more than one occasion. But until now—until it was his own blood that reeked in his nostrils—he'd never known how much death stank.

Thy Kingdom come, thy will be done, on earth as it is in heaven...

Rocky's mind wandered in the midst of his silent prayer. What would his funeral be like? He could envision the crowd of people who would fill the church to witness his final farewell. Old friends, new friends, old enemies, new enemies, old lovers, new . . . Well, he hadn't had any of those lately. But Lord knows he'd had more than his share in the past, and whether their parting of ways had been amicable or bitter, they would make his funeral their Broadway pitch. He guessed that would be his reward for being attracted to the drama queen type. Rocky could see them now—falling out onto the floor and needing church attendants to drape sheets over their scantily clad bodies so that the funeral wouldn't come with an R rating. If he hadn't been looking down the barrel of a revolver, Rocky would have laughed at the footage of the film that played itself in his mind.

Give us this day our daily bread . . .

And then there would be all the troublemakers and drug pushers with whom he'd either run the streets or fought in the alleys. One would think their type would keep as low a profile as possible—but not the rebels with whom Rocky used to associate. Some had rap sheets as long as the eyes could see. A few of them, no doubt, were on the wanted list for parole violations. But Rocky would bet anything that they'd bravely roll up to his funeral in their custom-wheeled, tricked-out cars and dare the police to try and step to them in their official capacity. Guys like the ones Rocky knew would turn the church's holy grounds into battlegrounds without a second thought or a smidgen of conviction.

And forgive us our debts as we forgive our debtors. . .

How could it all end like this? Yes, he had been a menace to society and had spent more than half of his forty-one years behind prison bars, but after the overturn of the murder charge that had earned him a sentence of twenty-five years to life, Rocky had turned over a new leaf. Well . . . not *immediately* afterward. Hey . . . he had spent twenty-two consecutive years in prison. He wasn't about to give God or anybody else his heart right off the bat. He had to make up for lost time. He had ravenous hungers to feed. Hungers that Phillips State Prison had prevented him from satisfying. And if he handed his life over to Christ, God wouldn't have let him satisfy them either. Rocky wasn't willing to go from one solitary confinement to another . . . his promises to the Lord notwithstanding.

So the first six months of his newfound freedom had been spent at the buffet. Not feeding on an all-you-can-eat spread of food, but rather a smorgasbord of women. Black, white, Asian, or Latino . . . Thick, thin, short, or tall . . . Intelligent, ignorant, graceful, or ghetto . . . Married, single, or anywhere in between—it didn't matter to Rocky. After that many years on lockdown, he was an equal opportunity kind of guy. All women were fair game, as long as they were born female, easy on the eyes, and over eighteen (because nothing was worth going back to prison).

And lead us not into temptation . . .

Finding willing participants wasn't a challenge. Rocky had nothing but time on his hands for over two decades. In that span, he'd spent countless hours in the prison gym. Punching bags and pumping iron had become his favorite recreation. The results had made him the fear of many of his fellow inmates, but as a free man, they had made him the desire of many women. The opposite sex found his muscular arms, sculpted calves, and rock-hard abs, which were covered by a layer of smooth chocolate skin, irresistible. And thanks to his paternal grandfather (or so he'd been told), he had the chiseled, handsome face to top it all off.

After his release, Rocky put the auto mechanic skills he'd learned in prison to work as a shade tree mechanic. By the droves, women paid good money to watch his tattoos glisten under the sun while he worked on their vehicles. Tune-ups, oil changes, shock replacements, tire rotations, brake repairs, lube jobs—sometimes they'd just show up with a bucket and a sponge and pay him to wash their cars. Rocky knew what they were up to. In essence, when they paid him for his services, they were really hoping that their dollars would also buy his affections. Knowing that didn't bother Rocky one bit.

As far as he was concerned, if they were buying, he was selling . . . or at least he'd make them think so. When he looked at the bottom line, he was getting the better end of the bargain. They were hoping to play the role of his lady. He was hoping for a roll in the hay. In the end, he was the one who got what he wanted. For Rocky, life on the outside was going pretty darn well.

But deliver us from evil. . .

As a matter of fact, life was bordering on his dictionary's definition of "perfection" until he got that life-altering call from Rev. B. T. Tides, pastor of New Hope Church. When he walked out of Phillips State Prison, Rocky escaped to Calhoun, Georgia, a city about eighty-five miles away from Stone Mountain, where Reverend Tides and his church were located. How that preacher tracked him down, he still didn't know. The highly respected pastor and his men's ministry had been frequent visitors at Phillips. For many months, they had prayed for and ministered to Rocky and the other men who were held captive there. Theirs were the prayers and spiritual guidance that had led to the overturn of Rocky's sentence. For all those years, he had sat behind bars with no hope in sight, convicted of a crime he hadn't committed. But when the prayers of the righteous were sent up on his behalf, God heard and honored them, and it resulted in his freedom. Reverend Tides reminded him of that—not so subtly—in their hour-long telephone chat that day. He said that it was time for Rocky to stop running from God and honor the promises he'd made behind prison walls: the promise to turn over a new leaf, the promise to be a better man than his biological father had ever been, the promise to be a better man than his stepfather had ever been, and the promise to give his heart to God.

For thine is the Kingdom . . .

And so he did. For the first time since the Easter program he attended with his mother when he was eight and a half years old, Rocky made his way to the house of God and sat through an entire Sunday morning service. The Word pricked his heart that day. Reverend Tides had been nowhere around when Rocky was living scandalously, entertaining one woman after the other, but the sermon that was preached proved to Rocky that God really did have all-seeing eyes. It felt as though every word Reverend Tides spoke had been earmarked for him, and no matter how hard he tried, Rocky couldn't ignore the call. He didn't make his way to the altar that day, but two Sundays later, he did. And Rocky had been serving God ever since.

And the power . . .

It had been more than six months since his last salacious encounter. Females had been Rocky's struggle ever since he was fourteen years old and went "all the way" for the first time. Hands down, they were his strongest weakness before he got saved, and even with his life change, women were still the reigning champions. Salvation didn't make them any less of an enticement, but it gave him the fortitude not to succumb to the temptation that the opposite sex presented. It also changed his mind-set so that he didn't use them for his own indulgence. So why had judgment waited until he was walking the straight and narrow? If he were going to get shot between the eyes like a mangy dog, why hadn't it happened while he was living like one? Was this really payback for all the evil he'd done in his life? Or was this death sentence linked to the fact that he'd made the mistake of not only relocating to Stone Mountain, but also had taken advantage of the affordable rates that the lavish housing in the Shelton Heights subdivision provided? Rocky had heard the horror stories that linked themselves to the infamous neighborhood, and initially he'd avoided the neighborhood like the plague. Eventually he'd stupidly listened to his new church friends who assured him that it was all unfounded. So now here he sat in his own *lavish* bedroom, with a Colt .45—the gun, not the beer—aimed at his head.

And the glory . . .

Rocky wasn't afraid of dying. Maybe that was the one good thing he'd gotten from his stint as a hellion. One couldn't live the rowdy life that Rocky had lived and be fearful of death. Rocky had been shot once and stabbed twice, all before the age of eighteen. In prison, he was shanked once, but the retaliation he delivered to his attacker sent a loud and clear message that made that one incident his only. The likelihood of death hadn't activated Rocky's sweat glands in his corrupt years, so now that he knew the Lord, the probability that moisture would line his brow was even less. But just because he didn't fear death didn't mean he *wanted* to die. How could he die now, when it felt like he'd just begun to live? For the first time, he had friends; they were *real* friends who felt more like brothers and sisters than his biological siblings ever had. He'd never told them how much they meant to him, and if he died now, they'd never know.

Forever. . .

And what about *her?* For the first time in Rocky's life, he knew what it felt like to be in love. Lust, he knew all too well, but she was his introduction to love. She was a smart, beautiful, and self-confident Christian. She was also an outspoken, flippant queen of drama queens. She was the *package,* and he couldn't get enough of her. He'd told her that he couldn't stand her. He'd told her that he'd known murderers who weren't as cold-blooded as she. He'd told her that she could drive Pope John Paul to kill and Mother Teresa to cuss, but he'd never told her that he loved her, and now, she'd never know. If given a second chance, he thought that would be the first thing he'd do. Tell her he loved her. No . . . scratch that. It would be the *second* thing he'd do. His first order of business would be to move out of the godforsaken community called Shelton Heights.

When Rocky saw his killer's trigger finger make a move in preparation to close the deal, Rocky shut his eyes and held his last breath. He wasn't afraid of death, but he certainly didn't care to see the ejection of the bullet that would introduce him to it. In his years of drug dealing, alley brawling, grand larceny, and cop dodging, Rocky had heard many a gunshot, but none had ever been as piercing to his ears as the one that drowned out the sound of the prayer ending *"Amen"* in his head.

That was how it all ended. Here is how it all started . . .

Chapter One

"Happy birthday to you. Happy birthday to you. Happy birthday, dear Kyla. Happy birthday to you!"

Rocky sat on a corner stool, not even tempted to cover his ears as the song was rendered for the stylishly dressed honoree. The teenage friends that sang it to her were surprisingly on key, but the whoops and hollers that followed were deafening. The spontaneous eruption echoed off the walls of the extravagant living room, but Rocky was enjoying the scene too much for the excessive noise to bother him. By now, he had been at the home at least a dozen times, but every time he visited, he was awed by the beauty of the split-level mansion.

The next wave of cheers threatened to break the sound barrier following the successful blowing out of the sixteen red candles that topped the cake. Then teenagers and adults alike began grabbing saucers and forks as they made ready to devour the sweet treat. Kyla was allowed to go first, but her friends crowded her, anxious for their turn to get a slice.

"Why are you sitting there like a stepchild?" Peter Jericho nudged Rocky's shoulder as he passed by. "Don't you see all these greedy kids? Man, you better come on and get it while the getting is good. You snooze, you lose."

Rocky laughed. Not that what Peter said was all that funny, but the irony of one of his words tickled him despite the bitter reality: "stepchild." It was all Rocky had ever been. He'd never had what he defined as a real family. It wasn't until he connected with the group of people he now sat observing that he had an inkling of what it was really like to have caring parents and fun siblings—even what it was like to have nieces and nephews to spoil. His eyes darted back to Kyla, Peter and Jan's daughter. The girl's face beamed, and Rocky could only imagine the joy she felt inside. Firsthand experience escaped him. At forty-one years old, he had not once had a birthday party thrown in his honor. Maybe it was because he'd never had any honor.

"Y'all hurry up so we can ride the horses before it starts to get dark!"

That was Malik, Hunter and Jade's son. When he said the words, his voice cracked a little, as all boys' voices tended to do when they are making the transition from puberty to manhood. Malik was a year or so younger than Kyla, and although they didn't officially call themselves boyfriend and girlfriend, everybody knew they had a special fondness for each other. Even the way Malik shadowed her right now sent a silent signal to all the other guys in the room that the birthday girl was taken.

Rocky still hadn't moved from his observation station. From where he sat, he could see them all. All the people whom God so graciously had placed in his unworthy life. Having spent so many of his years growing among thorns alongside other bad seeds, it had been an adjustment to establish a comfort level around his new Christian family. After four months, though, Rocky was starting to get the hang of it. His eyes continued to scan the room.

There was Hunter and Jade Greene, owners of Greene Pastures, the champion horse-breeding farm

that covered about ten acres of land outside their man-
or. It was their house in which the birthday party was
being held. Every time a special occasion arose in the
lives of any one of those in their inner circle, Hunter
and Jade's home was the expected venue to host it, and
the horses were the largest reason why. Whether it was
one of their birthdays, anniversaries, a holiday gathering, or whatever . . . Greene Pastures was automatically named party central, and riding the horses was
automatically a part of the celebration. The Greenes
were what Rocky defined as "filthy stinking rich," but
their humble attitudes didn't reflect it. Aside from
their lucrative horse farm, Hunter owned metropolitan Atlanta's hottest newspaper, the *Atlanta Weekly
Chronicles,* sometimes called the *AWC.* Jade was nothing to sneeze at either. Jade, or Dr. Jade Tides-Greene,
as the professional community knew her, owned and
operated her very own psychiatric business. Hunter
and Jade were one of those power couples, like Jay-Z
and Beyoncé . . . one of those beautiful couples, like Bo-
ris Kodjoe and Nicole Ari Parker. They had been married for more than three years now, but they still acted
like newlyweds. It was sickening and endearing at the
same time. They were the parents of Malik, who was
Hunter's biological son from a previous relationship,
and eighteen-month-old Leah, the gorgeous, auburn-
haired spitting image of Jade.

Then there was Peter and Jan Jericho. They weren't
nearly as lovey-dovey and touchy-feely as the Greenes,
but their fifteen-year marriage was as solid as a rock.
There weren't a lot of people in the world that Rocky
would admit to admiring, but Pete was one of them.
Just a few years ago, Pete had been one of five U.S.
Marines who became POWs, tortured and beaten in
Iraq while actively defending their country. Rocky was

incarcerated when it all unfolded, but he remembered being engrossed in the newspaper articles and the updates that he was able to catch on television. The day that Peter and the two other surviving soldiers were rescued, even the prisoners found reasons to rejoice. Peter retired from active duty after the ordeal, but he still wore the uniform and remained associated with the military. He now headed the Junior ROTC program at one of the local high schools. The master sergeant still had the mind of a soldier and the gait of a soldier. Every time Rocky looked at the battle scar that was still visible on the side of Peter's head—the scar that had been permanently etched there by the barrel of an Iraqi soldier's gun—his respect multiplied.

"Here. And don't make this no habit. You ain't got no servants around here, you know."

Rocky took the saucer, which was practically shoved in his face, and laughed out loud. The giver of it was Jerome Tides, the closest thing he'd ever had to a best friend. They'd met in prison, where they had shared a cell for a few months before Jerome was released after serving ten years. At the time, Jerome was a preacher's kid gone bad; but now, not only had he "found his way back to the Cross," as his father, Reverend Tides, put it, but Jerome was following in his dad's footsteps. He'd received his ministerial license about a year ago, and he was now serving in the capacity of assistant youth pastor. Talk about turning over a new leaf—Jerome had turned over a new tree.

As Jerome stood beside Rocky eating his cake, he was joined by his fiancée. Dark and oh, so sweet, Ingrid Battle reminded Rocky of the slice of chocolate cake he now held in his hand. He didn't know how a convicted felon could get so lucky as to net a woman as strong and supportive as Ingrid—not to mention one as curvaceous and feminine. In Rocky's eyes, she wasn't quite as pretty as Jan or Jade, but Ingrid Battle held her own, and every now and then, Rocky found himself feeling a little jealous of his friend's good fortune.

Rocky shoved a hunk of the cake in his mouth. "I wonder where Stuart is." He chewed and scanned the room like there was a chance he'd somehow over-looked the Lyons clan. "I can't see Tyler missing Kyla's birthday party."

"He'll be here." Jerome glanced at his watch. "He had to go pick up Candice from the airport. You know she had to fly to South Carolina to check on her dad, and she was returning to Atlanta today."

"I hope he's doing better," Ingrid said, slipping her arm around Jerome's waist at the same time.

The affectionate gesture must have triggered some type of emotion in Jerome, because he lowered his lips and planted a tender kiss on the top of her head before replying, "I hope so too, babe. Stu said they released the old man from the hospital on Wednesday, so that has to be a good sign. He probably just needs to take it easy for a few days. Chest pains ain't nothing to play with, especially at his age."

Ingrid nodded. "I know . . ."

They kept talking, but Rocky had tuned them out. It had been Rocky's question that started the conversation; yet his mind now wandered in the middle of it. It wasn't the presence of Stuart Lyons, the resident law enforcement officer, his son, Tyler, or Stuart's lady friend, Candice, that Rocky was missing; but he knew that if they walked through the door, so would the person whom he really wanted to see.

"Lord, I love this time of year. Seems like everybody got birthdays coming up. In a few weeks, we'll be cel-ebrating with Jade. Always a blessing to have a house filled with people. Milk, anybody?"

The voice of Mildred Tides invaded Rocky's thoughts. He unconsciously broke into a grin at the sight of her pudgy frame as she rounded the corner, balancing a rectangular-shaped wooden tray in her hands that had at least ten Styrofoam cups of milk standing on top. He didn't know what it was about the first lady of New Hope Church, but just the sight of her had a way of warming him. She could be a tad nosy at times, but Mildred was funny, affectionate, gentle, nurturing, and dutiful. As far as Rocky was concerned, she was the kind of woman whom everybody wished they had for a mom. She was another reason he was sometimes jealous of his best friend.

"I got that, Mother." Jerome separated himself from Ingrid and relieved his mom of the tray, just as she was preparing to protest.

"You're eating, son. I could have taken care of that." She reached out like she was going to reclaim her load.

"You're not the hostess of this party, Mother." It was the third time today that Jerome had to remind her of that.

"That's right," Peter said as he walked toward the voices he'd overheard. "Why don't you go and have a seat at the table with your husband, Mother Tides?" He took the tray from Jerome's hands, and then jerked his head in the direction of the dining room. "Go on and have a seat and enjoy your cake. Jan and I will make sure all the kids get their milk and whatever else is needed."

Rocky swiped a cup for himself. The cake was delicious, but if he didn't get something to wash it down, he wouldn't be able to finish it.

"Well, all right, if you say so." Mildred mumbled the words as Peter strode toward the teenagers who were sprawled all over the floor of the den enjoying their dessert. She shrugged her shoulders and added, "I was just passing them out. It's not like I was headed to some pasture to round up the cows and milk them."

Mildred had barely disappeared around the corner, which led to the formal dining area, before Rocky and Jerome burst into laughter. Ingrid tried to quiet them.

"She's gonna hear y'all," she warned.

Rocky shook his head and looked at Jerome. "I don't think your mama knows what to do with her hands if she ain't using them for work."

Jerome agreed. "She really doesn't. Did you see the look on her face just now? Mother looked like she was offended at the notion that we want her to relax."

"Speaking of relaxing," Ingrid said, looking at Rocky, "I'll bet you're glad to be moved into your house finally, huh?"

Still laughing, Rocky said, "Well, it ain't like I had all that much stuff to move in. It was more work to get the house than it was to move in it." He took a moment to sober himself, and then looked at Jerome. "Man, I don't know what I would've done without your parents speaking up for me. I would've been cool just to get a one-room studio joint somewhere in the city. I never dreamed I'd actually have a house. I couldn't believe they cosigned for me like that."

"That's Dad and Mother for you," Jerome said. "They offered to do that for me too."

Rocky shifted his weight on his stool. "Yeah, but you're their son; that's different."

"Man, please. As far as they're concerned, you're their son too."

Rocky found himself turning up his cup to his mouth to hide the threatening evidence that the words Jerome had spoken so coolly had stirred his emotions. He had known Reverend and Mrs. Tides personally for only a short while, but they already felt more like parents to him than his own ever had.

"Actually, you were your own worst enemy when it came to getting a house," Jerome added.

When Rocky used his napkin to wipe away his milk mustache, he also took that moment to quickly dab the corner of his left eye. He squared his shoulders. "My own worst enemy? What do you mean?"

"All your stupidity about the Shelton Heights legend—that's what I mean." Jerome kept talking as Ingrid snickered softly. "You could have been in one of the houses out there easily, but because of some silly superstition, you had to live elsewhere; and *elsewhere* was not as nice as Shelton Heights, but it was more expensive and required better credit than you could prove to have. In Shelton Heights, you could have gotten a two- or three-bedroom home for the same price as that little one-bedroom house you're in now."

It wasn't silly as far as Rocky was concerned. Even being locked behind prison walls didn't stop him from hearing about all of the strange happenings that seemed to take place in the Shelton Heights subdivision. The residents of that upscale, low-cost community had been served more than their share of hard-luck stories. He'd had enough misfortune in his life, and he wasn't about to volunteer to take on any more. The only way he could guarantee a good life was to live outside of that godforsaken sector.

"Yeah, well, it ain't like I didn't have reason to be nervous." Rocky tipped his cup in the air as if giving a toast, and then added, "It's better to be safe than sorry. I've had enough trouble in my life to last another lifetime."

"You and me both," Jerome said, laughing as the two of them slapped palms with one another, and then turned it into one of those creative handshakes that ended with them bumping shoulders.

The celebration would be short-lived. It ended when the front door of the home suddenly flung open with such force that it brought with it a hush that blanketed the entire house. In the open doorway stood a breathless Sgt. Stuart Lyons, looking distraught and borderline hysterical.

"Where's Rocky?" His words came between pants of breath. "Is he here?"

Rocky's heart dropped. He felt it beating in the bottom of his belly. He hadn't been out of prison nearly long enough to have forgotten what it felt like to be there. Every day, as a part of his morning prayer, he asked—no, *begged*—God not to let him do anything that would send him back. The look on Stuart's face was the reflection of a man who was ready to make an arrest. Friend or foe, if Rocky broke the law, then Stuart would be bound by duty to bring him in.

"What's wrong?" Reverend Tides asked as he walked from the dining room to an open space near the door. Concern washed over his face, and his finger made a slow migration in Rocky's direction, as though he feared that the gesture was turning him into some kind of unwilling snitch. "What's wrong, Stuart?" he repeated.

Stuart looked at Rocky, and for a moment, Rocky considered making a run for it. The crowd in the room was too thick, and his chances of escape were slim, but it might be worth a try. Anything not to see the inside of Phillips State Prison ever again. What had he done? Rocky's mind raced. *Oh God . . .*

What a satire this could turn out to be. Stuart's was the arrival for which he'd been impatiently waiting. He knew that when Stuart arrived, he'd be bringing others with him. One of those *others* was the person whom Rocky had been waiting all afternoon to see, but she was nowhere in sight. The only things accompanying Stuart were the deep worry lines that creased his forehead and the sunlight that beamed from behind him through the still-open door. The brightness of it seemed to make Stuart's extraordinarily dark skin glow. Stuart started toward Rocky, but a smaller version of the cop—his son, Tyler—ran through the open door and shot past his dad.

"Rocky!" Tyler's voice was elevated and full of fear. "It's your house!"

My house? What about it? Rocky's mind tried to process words that his paralyzed lips couldn't form.

"It's on fire!" the boy screamed. "Your house is on fire!"

Chapter Two

Ashes. Bricks and ashes. That's all that was left of what used to be Rocky's house. The flames had been doused days ago, but the smell lingered in the air. It had been his first home. The first thing of any real value that he'd ever owned. *Honestly owned,* that is. He also owned the black-and-orange two-year-old Harley-Davidson Low Rider that was parked in the driveway. However, he'd purchased the motorcycle for almost nothing, in a back alley, from a man who was wearing shades at midnight and an overcoat in the summertime. For the price he paid to get it, Rocky was almost sure that the seller had stolen it from somewhere. He sat on the edge of the property that surrounded his burned house and stared in disbelief at the debris. What had been destroyed on the inside wasn't worth much, but it represented just about everything he called his.

"Excuse me, mister."

Rocky didn't even bother to look up at the boy who stood near him. He didn't want to talk to anybody, and he didn't want anybody talking to him. But that didn't stop the nameless, faceless, and apparently clueless lad from dangling a sealed bottle of Dasani water in front of Rocky's face. A cold droplet of the sweat that had accumulated on the outside of the bottle fell onto Rocky's exposed arm.

"My mama told me to bring you this. She said it's ninety-three degrees out here, and you might want something to drink."

The icy moisture felt good against skin that had been battered mercilessly by the midday sun for the past two hours, but Rocky wasn't stupid. He may have turned in his "playa's card," but he still recognized game. Whoever the boy's mama was, he'd bet anything that it was her hunger—not his thirst—that drove her to pimp her son. The Dasani was just a lure, and "my mama" was just another term for *desperate housewife looking for fulfillment that her husband didn't provide* or *single mother looking for a daddy for her kid.* Either way, he wasn't the one. Especially, not today. Today, "my mama" could be that Asian beauty he was rooting for on *America's Next Top Model,* and he wouldn't care. Today, she could be his unspoken crush, the largely hated reality television star Omarosa, and she still wouldn't turn his head. Today, "my mama" could walk up to him looking like Halle Berry in that eye-popping Catwoman suit, and he wouldn't be impressed. Okay . . . maybe that was pushing it, but the point of the matter was he didn't want to deal with anybody right now, and one way or another, he had to drive that point home to this kid.

With his eyes still set straight ahead, Rocky's tone was as chilly as his stare when he said, "Go tell your mama that there ain't a darn thing water can do for me. Ask her if she's got anything stronger. If so, then maybe we can talk."

When he heard the boy's fading footsteps as the bottom of his tennis shoes crunched against the asphalt of the paved street, Rocky was tempted to call him back and offer an apology for his cynical response. No doubt the boy's mother would be ticked off by the message he'd just sent her way, and if she was anything like the women Rocky was used to, it might be to his advantage to reach for his helmet. At least his head would be protected. But as much as Rocky knew that he should take back his words, he wasn't feeling very apologetic or cordial right now. He didn't want to be bothered. Some of the old Rocky was beginning to resurface as he took in the enormity of the devastation in front of him. He was angry. He felt vengeful. Somebody had to pay for this.

One at a time, the knuckles on his right hand cracked under the pressure of his left. The cause of the fire hadn't yet been determined, but Rocky's mind was flooded by the laundry list of suspects who may have orchestrated the torching of his home: *Smoke, Killa K, Nose Face, Solo, Stank-Um, Popeye, Widow Maker, Blade* . . . All of them bore identifying names, and none of what they identified was good. At one time or another, Rocky had worked side by side in crime with each of them. Now, each one was in prison serving time, while he enjoyed freedom. Were they after him? He was sure they had people on the outside to whom they could assign his demise. Was the massive heap in front of him the result of an act of revenge? Rocky's mind was so preoccupied that he didn't even flinch when an approaching vehicle came within feet of running him over before it came to an abrupt stop. Only one man drove that crazy, and he didn't have to look up to know who it was.

"I thought I'd find you here." The truck door slammed shut, and a few moments later, Jerome found a space on the roadside next to his friend. Quiet ruled momentarily, but Jerome soon spoke again. "It's been a week, Rocky. How long do you plan to spend your afternoons out here staring at the ruins, man? Looking at it ain't gonna change nothing."

Sometimes saying nothing was the better choice, and Jerome wasn't making good choices right now. Rocky pressed his lips together as tightly as he could. If he allowed them to part, there was no telling what might come out. Impatient fingers drummed a rapid, unrhythmic beat against the shiny surface of the black helmet that sat on the grass between his knees.

"Look on the bright side." Clearly, Jerome was unaware that he was testing Rocky's tolerance. "God is good in spite of this. Just think. If this had happened to you before you moved back here and started living for Jesus, you would have been homeless."

Rocky's fingers stopped their tap dance. If he didn't need to use Jerome's spare bedroom as a temporary living quarters, he might have followed through with his urge to wallop him one good time. Even with the need, restraining himself wasn't easy. Rocky had to say or do something; holding it in was no longer a viable option. "The bright side?" He snapped his face to the right and looked at Jerome for the first time. Frustration edged his tone. "Man, there ain't no bright side to this. I ain't saying that God ain't good. Yeah, He's good. He's great. Super. Fabulous. All that. But do you think for one minute that I wouldn't have had any place to stay if this had happened to me in Calhoun? Please!" Particles of spit flew from his mouth as he huffed out that last word. He should have apologized when he saw Jerome grimace and use his hand to wipe away some of the evidence from his cheek, but once again, none was offered. "As a matter of fact, if this had happened there instead of here, I would have had my *choice* of beds to lie in. Believe that! So don't think you doing me no favors."

Jerome shifted his body so that he faced Rocky. "Man, what's wrong with you? Where is all this anger coming from?"

In one motion, Rocky was on his feet. He would have kicked away the helmet, but he didn't want to risk scratching it, so he maneuvered beside it, instead. His height—six feet five—would have towered Jerome's even if they were both standing. But with Jerome sitting, Rocky felt like a menacing giant as he hovered over him. "You don't think I have a reason to be ticked off? My whole freakin' house is gone, man! And you got the nerve to roll up on me talkin' some dumb smack about looking on the bright side?"

"I'm not being insensitive, Rocky."

"Really?" Rocky's laugh was clearly not an amused one. "You sure could've fooled me."

"No, man, listen. I'm not blind. I know this looks bad, but you've got to find the blessing in—"

"I don't want to hear nothing about blessings right now!" Rocky's voice bellowed, and his arms flailed. "That's all you been preachin' all week long, and I've about had it up to here!" He raised his hand to the level of his forehead, mirroring a military salute. "I don't see no blessing in this, and if it was your house and all your stuff that got burned up, you wouldn't see no blessing in it either." He pointed toward the rubble, but his eyes remained glued to Jerome. "This ain't no blessing. This is bull, and somebody's gonna pay."

"Rocky, calm down and—"

"Don't tell me what to do! I'm not in the mood for it. Not today, church boy!"

That last part brought Jerome to his feet too. He took a moment to brush off the seat of his shorts before standing to his full height. Rocky hadn't called him "church boy" in a year. Even before his release from prison, he'd respectfully dropped the nickname he had given Jerome while they both were serving time for their sins. They weren't exactly friends then, and the name was largely used to taunt Jerome and poke fun at the fact that he was the son of a preacher and still hadn't fared any better in life than the others who had come from despicable backgrounds.

There was about a half-foot difference in their heights and about a sixty-pound variation in their weights, but Jerome showed no signs of intimidation as he stood toe to toe with his foe-turned-friend-turned-foe again—at least momentarily.

"I'm right here, Rocky, and I ain't hard of hearing. You think you can bring it down just a notch?" It was in the form of a question, but it was really a statement, and there was no waver in Jerome's voice.

Rocky took one step back and used both of his hands to rub the sides of his shaggy face aggressively. For most of his adult life, he'd worn a full mustache and beard, which added years to his appearance. In Phillips State Prison, the untamed hair had been like a branding that marked him as the one *not* to mess with. By far, he wasn't the only inmate sporting a hairy face, but there was apparently something about Rocky's unkempt facial hair that made him look more daunting than others. He'd long ago come to the conclusion that the respect (or fear) he got in prison had a lot more to do with his brawn than his beard. Just to be on the safe side, though, he kept both.

"Listen, Rocky." Jerome's voice was more empathetic now. "You know I got your back, man. Eventually the house will be rebuilt, but until then, you've got a place to stay. I know it's not your own place, and I know that having your own place is important to you. But as long as I got a roof, you got a roof. You know that."

"I can't stay with you forever." Rocky lifted his shirt and used the bottom half to wipe his face. His rising irritation had coupled with the rising temperatures, and together they were making his entire head sweat. The heat made him wish he'd accepted that water, or at least borrowed one of Hunter's wife beaters instead of the stylish Tommy Hilfiger oversize shirt that he'd chosen to wear.

"You won't have to stay forever. Like I said, your house will be rebuilt. It's only a matter of time before the investigation ends and the insurance kicks in. But just for the record, if there was no insurance and rebuilding wasn't an option, then yes, you could stay with me forever."

Knowing Jerome meant every word of it made Rocky smile a little. He shoved his hands in the pockets of his blue jeans and quipped, "Thanks, but no thanks. I don't think I wanna be still laying up in your place after you and Ingrid get hitched. Y'all can't keep your hands off each other as it is. After the wedding, you're gonna need earthquake insurance on your crib."

Jerome's resulting laugher resonated down the relatively quiet street. Rocky would have laughed with him, but his mind was too preoccupied. This one wasn't the best neighborhood in DeKalb County, but it wasn't the worst either. Most of the families who lived on his street consisted of at least one working adult. It wasn't secluded and gated like Hunter's ranch, nor did it have hired lawn services that came by annually to plant blooming flowers and fresh trees at the entranceway, like Shelton Heights, but it was a nice middle-class community. Nobody rode down the streets of it blasting music, and there were no late-night street parties that disturbed the peace. It was six miles east of LA Fitness Center, where he went to work out three days a week, and six miles west of New Hope Church, where he went for monthly men's meetings and Sunday morning worship. It was perfect. But "was" was the operative word.

Rocky shook his head, and then looked back toward the charred heap. "I wish I knew who did this."

"What did I tell you last night, dude?" Jerome said. "You just insist on believing that this was a crime, but I don't necessarily buy that. The temperatures have gotten up to one hundred degrees in this unnaturally hot summer. We haven't had any measurable rain in almost a month. Heat plus dry grass is a fire waiting to happen—especially if somebody passed by and carelessly threw a lit cigarette on your property."

"Come on, Jerome."

"It could happen," Jerome insisted.

"If I lived in Shelton Heights, maybe," Rocky said. "That's the kind of freaky stuff that happens in Shelton Heights. I didn't move there on purpose so that I wouldn't chance that kind of stuff happening to me that normally has a one-in-a-million chance of happening." Rocky shook his head, with more purpose this time. "No, Jerome. This was intentional. One of those cats done found out where I am, and they're not happy that I'm out and they're in. I can't sit around thinking that out of all the houses on this street that could have caught fire, mine just happened to be the one. Naw, man. I know what these cats are capable of. I've got to keep one eye open every single minute of the day."

"That's no way to live, man."

A brief chuckle preceded Rocky's reply. "In my world, if you want to live, sometimes that's the only way. I've done it for most of my life. It won't be nothing new."

"Old things have passed away," Jerome said, sounding like his preaching father. "When you came to Christ, all things became new. You don't have to live like the old Rocky anymore, always watching your back and peeking around every corner. God has all-seeing eyes, man. He can see what you can't, and He'll take care of you."

Rocky couldn't believe how naïve Jerome sounded. "Man, you act like you didn't spend ten years in the joint. You were the son of one of the biggest preachers around, and you still knew not to ever close both your eyes. I ain't trying to underestimate God. I know He da man and all, but He gives us common sense." For emphasis, Rocky tapped the side of his head with his index finger. "If you know there's a chance you've got a target painted on your back, you'd better have a set of eyes back there to be sure there ain't nothing aiming at it. Smoke ain't scared of nobody, including God."

"Why are you thinking the worst, Rocky? Smoke or any of those other guys might not have a thing to do with this."

"But then again, they might."

"I don't think so."

"How much you wanna bet?"

"Listen to yourself, Rocky. You're gonna make yourself paranoid if you keep this up. You've already decided that there's some foul play, and the investigation ain't closed yet. Why don't you at least wait before you start worrying yourself to death. Why are you insisting on jumping to conclusions?"

"Because when you've lived the kind of life that I've lived, you have to stay one step ahead of the police, that's why. You think whoever did this is sitting around saying, 'Hey, let me just see if the cops can figure this out before I make my next move.' Of course not!" Rocky's arms were thrashing about in the air again. "And if I wait for the police to figure out what's what, I'll be a dead man waiting. I'm not gonna die doing nothing. If I'm gonna die—"

"You're not gonna die," Jerome cut in. "If you do, it's gonna be because you worried yourself into the grave, not 'cause nobody killed you. Now stop talking crazy. You're getting all worked up again. Let's just not talk about this anymore, okay? You skipped church last Sunday 'cause this had just happened. Why don't we switch gears and thought processes and focus on getting to K and G and buying you some clothes so that you'll have something to wear tomorrow? I'm positive that you'll feel better after Sunday morning worship."

Rocky shrugged his shoulders. "Maybe."

"Ain't no maybe about it."

Both men turned their heads at the sight of a young boy trotting in their direction with something cradled in his hand. He came to a stop at Rocky's side and craned his neck to look up into his face. Sweat glistened on the boy's forehead and the bridge of his nose.

"My mama said to bring you this." He held out his arm, revealing a 1.75-liter bottle of Orloff Light Vodka. "She said she's watching her figure right now, so it's diet, but this is the strongest thing she has that's cold. She told me to tell you that she don't mind running to the package store to get something else if you want it. She gotta run some errands, anyway."

Rocky dropped his head more from embarrassment than anything else. He actually hadn't expected the boy to return. He just assumed that "my mama" would be so outdone by the fact that he'd sent her son and her goodwill offering back that she wouldn't have cared less if his mouth got so dry that his tongue cleaved to the roof of it. This woman must have been bordering on desperate. Rocky could feel Jerome's eyes fixed on him. He knew that the thing to do was say "no, thank you" and shoo the boy away for a final time, but he'd already been mean to the kid once. Rocky slowly lifted his chin and looked in the boy's face. He was a handsome little fellow who couldn't have been older than ten. Reaching out, Rocky took the bottle from the boy's grasp. Jerome's disapproving eyes were now burning into his flesh.

"Tell her I said thanks," Rocky said. Then he reached into his pocket and pulled out a folded ten-dollar bill and pressed it into the boy's hand, hoping the bottle hadn't cost more. "Give that to her, and tell her I said thanks."

"Okay." The boy smiled before he began jogging back in the direction from which he'd come. The grin looked a bit mischievous, and Rocky wondered if his mother would ever see the money.

"What you plan to do with that?" The boy was barely out of listening range when Jerome's voice posed the challenge. "You asked for that liquor?"

"In a roundabout way, yes," Rocky admitted through a heavy sigh. When he placed the bottle in Jerome's demanding hand, he felt the need to defend himself. "I wasn't gonna drink it. I didn't even really mean for the boy to bring me anything. I was just trying to get rid of him when he came out earlier."

Jerome gave him a sideways glance, like he wasn't fully convinced. "I won't pour it out right here, because I'm sure that his mama is looking out a window somewhere up the street, and I don't want her to see us throw away her stash." Jerome pointed toward his pickup. "Let's load your motorcycle on the back of the truck and go home. I'll empty this poison down the drain when we stop by the house to drop off your bike." He looked at the bottle and shook his head. "Vodka." The word was followed by a pronounced tsk; then he added, "Lord, Sunday morning can't get here fast enough."

Chapter Three

Rocky plopped down on one end of the sofa and tossed his helmet on the other. The inside temperature cooled the sweat on his brow, which the outside temperature had ordered, but the air-conditioning did nothing to chill Rocky's hot frustration. "How many times do I have to say this? I wasn't gonna drink it." It felt to Rocky like he'd been defending himself to a jury of his peers for the past twenty-four hours. Quite frankly, it was starting to get old. From the moment Jerome, the blabbermouth, had gone and told everyone about the bottle of Orloff, he'd been on the witness stand. Ever since yesterday's church service, Rocky felt like everyone, including God, was examining, and then cross-examining him.

Stuart emerged from the den area of his home and rejoined Rocky, who was still making himself comfortable in the living room. Stuart had headed straight to the den when they walked into the house. Rocky knew that he was going in there to lock away his firearms. Stuart always did that whenever Rocky was around. It didn't hurt his feelings. As a convicted felon, Rocky couldn't be anywhere near a gun, and as a cop, Stuart knew that.

Stuart stopped in the open walkway, which led from the living room to the den, and began pulling the tail of his shirt out of his pants and loosening the buttons. "I didn't say you were going to drink it; I just said you shouldn't have accepted it."

Rocky removed his right knee pad, and then paused long enough to speak. "I was just trying to be polite, Stu. I had already sent the kid away once. I was just trying to be nice. When did being nice become a sin?" Rocky didn't understand it. Why was everyone making such a big ado out of the fact that he accepted the bottle from the kid? What was the big deal?

With his shirt fully open and exposing the white T-shirt he wore underneath, Stuart sat on the love seat opposite Rocky and groaned like he'd had a hard day of work at the station. "It's the principle of the matter, man," he said through a winded sigh. "You have to be concerned about what kind of message something like that sends. You with me? It may not be a sin, but the Bible does tell us to shun the very appearance of evil. You say you weren't going to drink it, and I believe you. Really, I do. But the fact that you accepted it gives the impression or the appearance to the boy and his mother that you, in fact, were going to drink it."

Rocky dropped the second knee pad on the floor beside the other one. He took a moment to gather himself, and then said, "Well, the way I see it, that's *their* problem. I ain't got no control over what stuff looks like to people. People are always gonna draw their own conclusions based on what they see. Ain't nothing I can do about that."

"Listen, Simon," Stuart said through a soft chuckle.

Missing the humor, Rocky snapped his face toward him. He felt heat crawling up the back of his neck. He didn't know what Stuart meant by that, but he'd give him about two seconds to explain. "What'd you call me?"

"Simon. That should have been your name, 'cause you're stubborn and hotheaded, just like Simon Peter in the Bible." Stuart shook his head. "Look at you. Over there looking like you're about ready to jump over here and swing on me just because I called you 'Simon.' Jeez, Rocky. At least it's a bona fide name. It wasn't like I called you 'idiot' or 'dunce' or something worse."

Rocky relaxed his back against the sofa and crossed his right foot over his left knee. "It might be a bona fide name, but it ain't *my* bona fide name. How would you like it if I called you 'Larry' or 'Keith' or 'Jacob' or something?"

Stuart laughed again, and then apparently choosing to change the subject, he asked, "How are things over at Jerome's? You settling in okay over there?"

As far as Rocky was concerned, Stuart had taken it from his second worst topic of conversation to his first. Talking about the results of his burned-out home was the only subject matter that was worse than the one about the liquor bottle. He rubbed his forehead before replying. "I don't know. I suppose."

His slow and hesitant answer raised Stuart's eyebrows. "You suppose? You and Jerome are boys."

Rocky didn't know how to express clearly his uneasiness with his new living arrangements. It was a twofold problem, but he was only willing to admit to one of those folds. "Sometimes—sometimes it feels too much like the past. You know, me staying in the same place as Jerome. Feels a little like déjà vu." Rocky tried to laugh it off, but there was really no humor in it, so his laugh was cut short.

Stuart nodded like he understood. "You mean because the two of you shared a cell back in the day?"

"Yeah." Rocky tugged at the hairs sprouting from his chin. "And it wasn't that long ago, so 'back in the day' is an overstatement." He uncrossed his legs and leaned forward in his seat. "Don't get me wrong, man. Staying with Jerome ain't nothing like being in prison. That's not what I'm saying. Me and Jerome . . . we're cool, but as good as I got it at his place, there ain't nothing worse than living with your cellmate."

"I imagine—"

The sound of keys unlocking the front door halted the conversation before Stuart could finish his thought. A smile begged to stretch Rocky's lips, but he refused to grant it permission. Instead, when the door opened, he fell back against the cushions of the sofa. In an exasperated tone, he mumbled, "Oops. Spoke too soon. There *is* actually something worse than living with your cellmate."

The deadly look in Kenyatta's eyes was solid proof that she had overheard him—not that he was hoping she wouldn't. She closed the door behind her and hung her keys on the rack posted on the front wall; then she set her signature big purse on the floor beside the coatrack before rendering her response. "What is *he* doing here?" She avoided eye contact with Rocky and chose to look at her brother, instead. "I've just come from a job where I have to fool with a bunch of delinquents. Can I come home without having to do the same?"

Kenyatta was a social worker, and Stuart had told Rocky horror stories of some of the cases she had to work. It was a shame the way kids were so often neglected and abused by their parents. Rocky could relate.

"Sorry, sis," Stuart said. "We crossed paths at the Panola Road intersection, and he followed me home."

"You're a policeman, Stu. Couldn't you have just pulled out your gun and killed him?"

"Oh, shut up," Rocky said over Stuart's laughter. "If he ain't riddled you with bullets in all the time he's had to put up with you, then I think I'm pretty safe."

Kenyatta stood next to the bar, which separated the living room from the kitchen, and placed her hand on her hip. "Negro, please. I'm an asset to society. If he kills me, it'll make headline news. If he guns you down, the other cops will say, 'Oh well, good riddance,' and help him dump the body in the woods."

That one stung a little. Not only because it was probably true, but because Kenyatta was the one to say it. Rocky swallowed the hurt and kept a straight face. "Yeah?" he challenged. "Well, at least every nail shop, hair salon, and—and—and Mary Kay consultant won't have to go out of business when I die." It was a weak retort, but it was the best he could come up with.

"Hey, hey, hey! Time-out!" Stuart said, just as Kenyatta was pointing a flawlessly manicured finger at Rocky in preparation of a comeback. Rocky was glad for the interruption because that last blow of hers had knocked the wind out of him. Stuart looked at Kenyatta. "You think you had a hard day at work? Try policing the streets of Atlanta for a day and see what you feel like. Now, I have a date with Candice tonight, and I would like to have a little downtime before preparing. Do the two of you mind putting it on hold for a day or two?"

"She's the one who started it," Rocky said.

"Oh, shut up and go out into the woods and wrestle some bears, Grizzly Adams," Kenyatta huffed.

His beard was always the main object of her insults, and Rocky normally had no comeback. But he was glad that she'd aimed at it today. He'd been doing some reading, and she had walked right into his trap. "If I want to wrestle bears, I don't have to go into the woods. How 'bout I just walk over there and wrestle you, Ling-Ling." He had just seen an article about the famous female bear two days ago and had filed the funny-sounding name in his brain so he could use it on her the next time she attacked him.

When her neck started rolling, Rocky knew he had her right where he wanted her. "Are you calling me a bear?"

"A giant panda, to be exact."

"Let me tell you something, fool. I will come over there and—"

"Okay, how about an hour or two?" Stuart yelled. "Can you just put it on hold for an hour or two?"

Rocky gave Kenyatta a look that said the decision was up to her, and then sighed with relief when she huffed and turned away before walking into the kitchen and opening the refrigerator.

How could all of their friends have gotten it so wrong? During Rocky's last few weeks at Phillips State Prison, while the courts were reviewing the new evidence and old transcripts from the testimonies of the trial that had sent him there to begin with, Jerome had filled his head with talk about this bombshell of a girl who would be perfect for him. All he'd heard was *Kenyatta this* and *Kenyatta that*. She was a divorcee who was ready to move forward with her life. Jerome kept telling him that he'd absolutely love her, but that she was a Christian girl, so it was important for him to first fall in love with Christ. After that, he could focus on the possibility of building a relationship with Kenyatta King. Was he kidding? Jerome had gotten the bombshell part right. No doubt about it. When the Commodores wrote "Brick House" back in the 1970s, they had to have had the Kenyatta type in mind. But that was where the fairy tale ended.

Jerome made Christianity the prerequisite, but what Christian man in his right mind could deal with *that* one? Kenyatta was the kind of woman only an alcoholic or, better yet, a straight-up thug could put up with. Whatever man she eventually got with was either going to have to be so drunk that he could tune her out, or he'd have to be the kind of brother who didn't mind going upside a woman's head every now and then. Even in his worst days, Rocky had never raised his hands to a woman. So why all his friends thought he and Kenyatta would hit it off, he didn't know. From day one, they had done nothing but clash.

"Y'all worse than kids," Stuart said, breaking Rocky from his thoughts. "Even when Tyler has his friends over and they get into a disagreement, they don't go at it like the two of you do."

Rocky was still irked by that unnecessary low blow that Kenyatta had delivered earlier, but he was satisfied that his newest counterpunch had evened the score. They could call this one a draw. Rocky leaned back in his chair and turned his attention toward Stuart. "So you had a hard day at work today?"

Stuart nonchalantly waved a hand. "No harder than normal, I guess. After all, this is metropolitan Atlanta, right? Law enforcement won't ever be an easy job in this city. You with me? If it ain't one thing, it's another. It's just that some days are more tolerable than others."

Sitting forward, Rocky posed the question he really wanted to ask. "Any leads on my house fire?"

"I'm not working that investigation, so I don't have a whole lot of inside information on it. But like I told you yesterday after church, it doesn't look like anything has changed. The early evaluations weren't showing any foul play, and I haven't heard them mention any new findings."

"I don't believe that." Rocky shook his head. "Somebody has it in for me, Stu, and I think if you guys find that person, you'll find the guilty party."

"The case isn't closed yet, and the source of the fire hasn't been pinpointed, as far as I know. Foul play isn't totally counted out yet, but—"

"Well, when is the case gonna be closed? How long am I gonna have to wait before I know something for sure?"

Stuart tugged at the bottom of his open shirt. "I don't know. I can tell that you're frustrated with the waiting, but let me give it to you straight, Rocky. You shouldn't look for any quick answers. There are a lot worse things going on in the city than your house fire. People are being mugged, raped, and killed every day, so your house fire probably isn't at the top of the priority list right now. You're going to have to be a little patient."

"See? Told ya." Rocky turned to see that Kenyatta had reclaimed her spot in the kitchen opening. This time, she was wearing a smirk on her face that said she was ready for a rematch. She had a glass of ice in one hand and a container of bottled water in the other. "The police couldn't care less about you and your stupid house. Now, if it were *my* house—"

"Kenyatta," Stuart warned.

"Hey, maybe y'all should investigate me, Stu," she said as she set the bottle on the counter beside her. "He just said that someone had it out for him, and that person probably had burned down the house. That makes me a prime candidate."

Rocky's jaws tightened. His squinted eyes scaled Kenyatta's full-figured, steep curves from head to toe. How could something so beautiful be so evil? As much as she ruffled his feathers, there was no denying her physical appeal. Kenyatta always looked like she'd stepped off the cover of *Vogue*. Her clothes fit like they were tailor-made for her body type, and her makeup gave her the look of a woman who'd stopped by the M•A•C counter just before walking through every door she approached. Rarely was there ever a hair out of place. Just as with most days, she wore it in a sculpted updo today, but Rocky had seen her once with it down. She was on her way to the beauty shop that day, and it hung straight, falling past her shoulders. Her updos were flawless, but Rocky liked it hanging better. He'd never tell her that, though. Kenyatta was built like a perfectly proportioned plus-size model. She had that Joanne Borgella thing going—that full-figured beauty that won the first season of *Mo'Nique's Fat Chance*.

"Kenyatta, cut it out," Stuart said, invading Rocky's thoughts for the second time.

"No, really," she continued. "I can't imagine that there's anybody who outranks me on the *can't stand Rocky* scale. So maybe I torched it." She made a motion with her hand as if she were striking a match, and then flung the imaginary flame toward the place where Rocky sat.

Rocky was trying to think of something belittling to say in return, but her beauty was messing up his ability to demean her. All of a sudden, he got an even better idea. He'd take this stupid attraction that he couldn't shake and use it to his advantage. "You want me, don't you?" He winked and lifted his chin in her direction.

"What?" Kenyatta looked horrified. Bingo! It was just the reaction Rocky had hoped to get.

Stuart dropped his head against the back of the sofa and stared up at the ceiling. "I give up."

Rocky knew he had just taken control of the rematch, and if he paced himself just right, this one could be a TKO, with him being named the winner. "Yeah." He turned to face her so that she could have a full, clear view of his facial expressions. Before he spoke again, he did his best LL Cool J impression, licking his lips in as sensual a manner as he could muster. All the hair around his mouth made it difficult. He watched Kenyatta cringe and recoil. "That's it, ain't it?" he taunted. "You want me."

"Ugh! I wouldn't want you if you were the last man on earth. You—you—you hairy beast!"

"Sure, you do," Rocky said. "You want me so bad that you burned down my house because it was too far away from you."

"For your information, I didn't burn down your house, you imbecile. I was just saying that."

"Yes, you did. You burned it down." Rocky was loving this exchange. "Out of all the guys I hang with, Jerome and Stuart are the two bachelors, and Stuart has the larger house. You burned my house down, hoping that I'd ask Stu if I could live here, didn't you? You wanted me to move in here so I'd be easy access for you."

"Shut up, you psycho moron. I did no such thing. And Stu might have the larger house, but we don't have any spare rooms. This is a three-bedroom house, and me, Stu, and Tyler take up all three rooms. In order for you to stay here, you'd have to share a room with one of us."

Rocky twitched his right eyebrow upward two quick times. "I know. And guess which one of you was the one you wanted me to share a room with."

"Ugh!" Kenyatta dug her hand in her glass and, one by one, hurled ice cubes across the room.

Rocky jumped from the sofa and began bobbing and weaving in an effort to dodge the homemade missiles. Even with all of his running and fancy footwork, he felt several cubes slam against his chest, arms, and back. The sting of them didn't stop the laughter that spilled from his lips.

"Hey! Hey! Cut that out," Stuart said, standing and waving his hands at Kenyatta like he was trying to flag down a taxicab on the streets of New York. "Stop throwing stuff, girl, before you break something in my house." He charged toward the kitchen where he snatched away the glass that had been emptied of most of its ammunition. Then he turned and faced the living room and pointed toward the front door. "Go home, Rocky!"

Still laughing, Rocky replied, "I don't have a home, remember? Your sister burned it down."

"Well, go *somewhere!* I have to get ready for my date, and ain't no way in the world I'd leave the two of you in this house together after I'm gone. My house will be on the news with yellow crime tape draped around it."

Kenyatta agreed. "It sure will, 'cause if you leave that ex-con in this house with me, I'm going for my purse, and when I stick my hand in it, I'm not going to be reaching for ice cubes."

Rocky gathered his belongings and headed for the door. The fight had been called, and he had already been named the victor, as far as he was concerned, but Rocky couldn't resist one final jab. He turned to look at Kenyatta and scratched his beard. "And listen, babe. When the house is rebuilt, don't go setting it on fire again. Just let me know when you're missing me, and I'll come by. You know I don't mind coming to see my 'Ke-Ke.'"

"'Ke-Ke'? What?" Kenyatta vacated her spot and began charging toward her prey. Rocky quickened his steps and reached the door as Stuart grabbed his sister around the waist. It appeared to take all of his strength to hold her back.

"Get out, Rocky!" he yelled. "Go!"

Rocky did as he was told. He wasn't certain how much longer Stuart would be able to restrain his sister, so he ran the distance from the front door to his waiting Harley-Davidson, strapping on his protective gear in the process. He had done little other than sulk for the past week. The bellyaching laughter that he continued to release even as he pulled out of the driveway felt better than good.

Chapter Four

"Whoa, boy. Whoa. Good boy." Hunter held on to the reins and looked over his shoulder. Running a close second was his wife of three years. He grinned. Jade was getting good at this horse-racing thing. She joined him in the sport shortly after the birth of their daughter and credited the regular riding with helping her lose the baby fat Leah had left behind.

"Whoa, Spirit!" Jade patted her horse's head as she slowed to a trot, and then came to a stop beside the place where Hunter waited. She beamed with pride. "Pretty good, huh?"

"Yeah, but still not as good as me." Hunter was gloating.

"Just give us a few more weeks. This one is gonna make you eat those words." She looked down at her horse and said, "Aren't you, girl? You're going to show everybody who the princess of Greene Pastures is."

Hunter laughed. "You're giving that crown to a horse? I thought you were the princess of the pasture."

"Are you kidding? I don't play second fiddle to anybody. I'm the *queen*."

Hunter laughed louder, then lowered his head in a bow. "Please forgive me, Your Highness. I don't know what on earth I was thinking."

Jade straightened her back and stuck out her neck. Hunter guessed it was her best attempt at mimicking the way royalty must act. "Your apology is rejected, peasant. Be gone!"

Hunter cowered in mock fear. The reins in his hand shook as he trembled. Since she was taking her monarch role seriously, he might as well do the same. "No, Queen Jade, please. Please don't banish me from your empire."

It didn't take much coaxing. "Very well. It's your first blunder, so perhaps the queen will have mercy on you *this time*. You won't be banished, but make no mistake about it, you *will* be duly punished."

With his mouth curling into an overtly mannish grin, Hunter replied, "And when should I expect this . . . punishment?"

Jade kept her expression and voice stern. "Be in my chambers promptly at midnight. I will pass sentence at that time."

"Yes, Your Majesty." He ducked his head once more. "And I'll wear the leopard print loincloth. You know, the one I was wearing when you . . . *punished* me on Tuesday night. And Wednesday night. And Saturday night. *Twice*."

Jade burst into a giggle and covered her face. "Shut up."

Hunter loved that blush of hers. He loved it even more that he could still redden her face like that after three years of marriage. He laughed with her, and then reached over and brushed her horse's mane with his gloved hand. The black-and-white filly was a beauty. He understood why she was his wife's favorite. Ever since the horse was born, she'd been Jade's choice. "Spirit is getting to be a fast one; I'll definitely give her that. But I hope you're not getting too attached, babe, because this one probably won't be here much longer." He looked sideways at Jade. "You saw the way that breeder was checking her out last week when he was reviewing the stock. I know that look. He wants her. I expect him to make an offer any day now."

Jade climbed from Spirit and pressed her cheek against the side of the horse's face. If Hunter had a camera, he would have captured the moment. It was fleeting, but frame worthy. "I remember when she was born. It was six months or so before Leah's birth. That means Spirit is practically still a baby herself. I think you should keep her around a little longer and let her enjoy the pasture some more before selling her to some man who only wants to turn her into some baby maker."

In a single motion, Hunter swung his leg over the back of his horse and came to a stop with both feet planted firmly on the ground. Jade almost looked like she was ready to cry. Apparently, she was more attached than he had thought. "She's two, babe, and a horse's two is not the same as a human's two. A two-year-old horse is old enough to foal."

"But she's not even finished growing yet."

Hunter sighed. He should have seen this coming. In all the years that he had run the farm alone, he'd been careful not to become emotionally attached to any one of his stock. Well, that wasn't exactly true. There was Slew, the picturesque stallion so flawless that it looked like he was handmade special by God. From the time he was just a colt, he loved to run around the pasture whether he had a rider or not. Sometimes Hunter would look out his bay window and see Slew galloping at full speed for no reason at all. That was how he got his name. He'd named him after gold medal sprinter, Carl Lewis. Originally, Slew's name was C. Lewis, but Slew was easier to say and sounded more horselike, so Hunter changed it. Slew's black coat was so shiny Hunter could almost see his reflection. The horse stood proud and tall, and every time Hunter would come to the pasture, Slew would look at him in a way that made

Hunter feel that he was calling his name. Rarely did Hunter ever leave the pasture without at least stroking and nuzzling his favorite stallion. He had Slew for four years and refused every offer that was made for his purchase.

But then the unimaginable happened. Hunter came to the pasture one day to find Slew lying on the ground; the horse was unable to stand. At some point during the day, maybe during one of his runs, he had somehow broken his leg. The vet said there was nothing that could be done, so Hunter had no choice but to hire the vet to put Slew to sleep by euthanasia. The horse's death was more painful than Hunter had ever admitted. It was during that experience that he promised not to ever attach himself to any of the animals again. He'd give them the best care that his money could afford, but he'd never get emotionally involved. Jade was doing it, though, and the memories of his own heartbreak made him want to protect the same from happening to his wife. How ironic was it that Spirit was Slew's biological granddaughter?

Hunter walked around and placed his arms around Jade. He was normally several inches taller than she was, but she was wearing her thick, naturally wavy hair in an Afro-puff, which was pulled up to the top of her head, and added height. The hairs tickled Hunter's nose as they embraced. "Okay, I see that I'm going to have to ban you from the pasture for a while. This is a horse-breeding farm, babe. I breed them, break them in, and then sell them. That's the nature of the business. You know that."

"I know." She pulled away and brushed her hand across his chest before adding, "You put the horses away. I'm going to go in to get cleaned up and finish dinner. Malik and his friends had a long afternoon out here riding the horses, so I'm sure he's bushed. I hope he didn't fall asleep while he was supposed to be watching Leah. I told him I'd only be out here about an hour, and my time is up."

Malik was responsible beyond his years. Hunter knew he wouldn't fall asleep when he was supposed to be watching his little sister, and he knew that Jade knew it too. She just didn't want to talk any longer about giving up Spirit. He reached out and grabbed her by the arm. "Babe—"

"It's getting late, sweetheart." Jade looked up at the sky, acting as if she hadn't noticed before that very moment that the sun was beginning its descent. "I'm sure the chicken cacciatore is almost done by now." She stepped closer and planted a brief kiss on Hunter's lips. "Everything will be ready by the time you put the horses away and get your shower."

"Okay, babe." Hunter gave in. This wasn't a battle worth pursuing. If she didn't want to talk about it, he shouldn't press her. "I'll be there in just a little while."

"Okay." She smiled before turning to walk away, but Hunter doubted the genuineness of it.

For a moment, he enjoyed watching the way her jeans hugged her nice curves as she embarked on her journey back to their house. Then he released a breath and turned to face Spirit. "I should've known you'd be trouble." The horse looked at him with inquisitive eyes as if to say, "Who? Me?" He couldn't help but laugh. She had her grandfather's eyes. Hunter took her reins and those of the nameless horse he'd been riding and led them both to the stall. Keeping the horses unnamed helped Hunter remain unattached. Ever since Slew's death, he decided that it was best to let the person who would be their permanent owner be the one to give them a permanent identification. Greene Pastures currently consisted of twenty-two thoroughbreds, all of which were identified by the common noun "boy" or "girl." All, that is, except Spirit; that, of course, was Jade's doing.

The skies were clear this evening, and there was no rain in the forecast. Sometimes when the weather was this perfect, Hunter would allow the horses to roam freely throughout the night on the fenced-in property. Normally, they liked that. His property was secure, and there was never a fear that anyone would tamper with any of his livestock; but with this summer's uncommonly hot weather, the horses preferred the temperature-controlled stall. Even during the day hours when he allowed them freedom, they preferred to be inside. Hunter would have to shut the doors so that they didn't have options. Reverend Tides accused his son-in-law of spoiling his herd. He said that the horses probably cried for days after being purchased by someone else. Reverend Tides said that there was no way that the animals got the same amenities elsewhere. Hunter hoped he was right. Not about the horses crying, but about the notion that the treatment he provided was unmatched.

With the herd safely tucked away, Hunter began his own trek back to the house. One half acre separated the entranceway of Greene Pastures from the front door of "Greene Manor," as Rocky called it. Hunter chuckled at the thought of it. He recalled the first time Rocky visited his home after being released from prison. For minutes, he stood inside their doorway with his eyes roaming around the massive, well-kept space, like he was afraid to walk any farther. They'd literally had to coax him into the den to sit down. It wasn't a reaction that Hunter wasn't accustomed to. Almost everyone did so the first time there. Heck . . . if Hunter was honest about it, he'd have to admit that there were times when he was still overwhelmed by it all. He had come a long way from his childhood days of sharing a government-subsidized two-bedroom apartment with his mother and four brothers. And there wasn't a day that he didn't thank God for it.

"Hey, Daddy." When he finally walked through the front door of his home, Hunter heard Malik's voice before he saw him in the dining room. The aromas from the kitchen soaked into his nostrils and made his stomach rumble.

"Hey, sport." He knew that at some point he'd have to stop referring to his son by the nickname he'd given him as a toddler, but until Malik complained, Hunter figured he'd keep doing it. He removed his riding boots at the door and set them against the wall. His gloves fell to the floor beside them. Hunter made a mental note to properly put them away later. Looking back toward the dining room, he asked, "You helping set the table?"

The answer was obvious, since the boy was placing glasses at each table setting, but Malik answered, anyway. "Yes, sir. We're having baked chicken."

"So I heard. Smells good."

"Tastes even better." Malik grinned like he had one up on his father. Then he lowered his voice level. "I snuck a taste before Mama came in the house."

"It's chicken cacciatore, not baked chicken," Jade corrected as she rounded the corner from the master bedroom. She was dressed in a pajama set made up of a spaghetti-strapped shirt and cotton pants.

"She's got ears like a bat." Hunter was talking to Malik, but he couldn't take his eyes off Jade. The new rumble in his stomach had very little to do with his desire for food. He took long strides to get to her before she walked into their son's view. He slipped his arms around her waist and placed his lips near her right ear. "You're dressed for bed kinda early, aren't you?"

Her voice matched the low volume of his. "That's nothing new. You know I like to lounge in my pj's when I'm not planning on going back out. Just thought I'd get comfortable."

Hunter nibbled the side of her neck and enjoyed the sound of her soft moan. "You smell more delicious than dinner," he remarked.

Jade giggled. "That's because I'm dessert."

"Oh yes." Her neck muffled Hunter's words. "Can't wait till midnight. I don't think I've ever been punished by a dessert before. If you're still smelling like a peach when I get to your royal chambers, it could be a very long night."

Jade pushed him away. "Yeah? Well, speaking of long nights, if you still smell like a horse when you get there, your punishment will be that you'll be sleeping on the floor. Alone."

Hunter laughed and took an additional step back, but not before giving her neck one last peck. "Yes, Your Highness." He took a final bow.

"Now go on and get ready. I'm going to set the food on the table and get Leah situated in her high chair. I know how you like to take long showers, but we're going to wait for you, so don't let the food get cold."

"I won't, babe. Give me five minutes." Hunter tapped her on the behind as he walked around her on his way to the bedroom.

"Oh." Jade's one word made him stop and turn to face her again. She walked closer and whispered, "When we get settled at the table, ask Malik about the new project that he and Tyler are working on. And then act really fascinated when he tells you. He's excited about it."

Curiosity made Hunter's eyebrows rise. He wanted to ask Jade to give him a hint, but she turned and walked away as soon as she finished speaking. Besides, he knew she wouldn't tell him any more than she already had. He'd get the rest from Malik later.

Chapter Five

Hope for Men was the name that had been assigned to the specialized fellowship meetings that were held at New Hope Church once a month. Shortly after giving his life to Christ, Jerome had brought the gender-specific ministry idea to his father's attention. The church already had a ministry called Women of Hope, and Jerome argued that if the organization had a women's support group, it should also have one for the brothers. After spending ten years in prison, Jerome had come to the conclusion that if more men had a safe place where they could come together and not only discuss scriptures, but also hash out the concerns of life, less of them would resort to crime as a means of dealing with problems.

Sometimes Rocky felt that he enjoyed Hope for Men a little too much, and when he really allowed himself to dwell on the reality of it, he would get a little depressed. The truth of the matter was, he looked forward to the meetings with so much anticipation because he didn't have much of a life. All of his friends were either married or in committed relationships. Most of them also had children. Rocky had neither. Since his home was reduced to ashes, he didn't even have a job to keep him occupied. The neighborhood where he lived had no rules and regulations that hindered him from repairing cars in his backyard. As long as he didn't let junk cars pile up, there was no problem. Jerome's subdivision had written rules in place that would hinder him from moving the business there. Besides, there wasn't enough yard space to do it, even if it were allowed. Their homes were built so close together that sometimes Rocky could hear music coming from the home of the couple who lived on their right, and the woman on the left of them with the unruly kids could be heard scolding them late into the night. The occasional racket didn't seem to bother Jerome, and it probably wouldn't bother Rocky either, if he had a stream of income.

When his friends weren't at church, they were at work, with family, or on dates. When Rocky wasn't at church, his options were to sit in the house of one of his friends who happened to be off that day, or to sit in his room. He was starting to go stir-crazy. Rocky valued his new Christian walk and couldn't think of anything he'd trade it for. However, it was becoming increasingly clear to him that in the natural sense, his prior life—sinful, though it was—had seemed much more exciting. Not the twenty-two years of it that he had spent behind bars, of course, but the six months of freedom that he'd lived before moving to Stone Mountain.

After two hours of discussion, laughter, and prayer, the August session of Hope for Men came to a close. As was customary, Rocky, Jerome, Hunter, Stuart, and Peter became a five-vehicle convoy as they headed to one of the area restaurants to get something to eat. Rocky led the pack tonight. He had been told that a seafood joint called Crabby D's had been their after-meeting place initially. After the one that was conveniently located to them closed its doors, the men began meeting at an eatery near the Mall at Stonecrest. Arizona's was an African American-owned restaurant that sold everything, from burgers to steaks to seafood. After using most of his meager savings to buy clothes to replace those he had lost in the fire, Rocky's pockets were slim; but he wasn't about to go home and sit there alone while his friends enjoyed winding down over a good meal.

The evening air was refreshing as it pounded against his body en route to Arizona's. It allowed Rocky to forget his problems temporarily. In reality, the summer's night temperatures were only slightly more bearable than those of the day, but traveling at seventy miles per hour on an open motorcycle, it felt good. Rocky whipped his bike in an open space in front of the restaurant, and then he dismounted. He was the first to reach Arizona's entrance doors, but he waited for the others to catch up.

"Let's eat, soldiers." Peter brushed past him and pushed open the door.

Ever since linking up with this unofficial brotherhood, Rocky had been trying to get a feel for the rank of command among the men. Hunter seemed to take the lead most of the time. He seemed to be the voice of reason, and the one that the other men went to when they needed sound advice. Rocky wondered if it was because Hunter was married to a therapist. Maybe that made the others feel he was most qualified by reason of association. Although that was the direction that others leaned toward, Rocky's radar told him differently. If ever there came a time when everything was placed on the line, Peter's hands would be the ones in which Rocky would place his life. He fell in line right behind the retired master sergeant turned ROTC instructor as they walked inside.

Arizona's was a popular spot, but with only ninety minutes left before closing, there was no wait time. The hostess greeted them as they entered the doors, and upon getting a head count, she escorted them to a semicircular booth. Rocky found himself positioned in the middle, with Peter and Stuart sitting to his left and Jerome and Hunter to his right. Once they were all seated, the hostess distributed menus, and a male waiter immediately replaced her when she walked away. Rocky didn't even open his menu. He knew what he was ordering. His taste buds begged for a rib eye steak, but his wallet recommended the chicken tenders platter. Rocky took the advice of his wallet.

"Great meeting tonight, huh?" Stuart broke the silence, which had been lingering after the waiter walked away with their orders. Sounds of agreement ran around the table.

"Almost everybody had some kind of testimony," Hunter observed. "Victorious testimonies too. That hardly ever happens."

"I liked yours, Rocky," Peter said, nodding in his direction. "I'm sure it was a load off your shoulders when you got the call."

Rocky straightened his back. He didn't know why he felt like his posture had to be just right when he spoke to the military hero. "Thanks, man." He cleared his throat. "Yeah. Yeah, I'm glad the ball is rolling."

Rocky had gotten the word on Tuesday that the insurance company had approved his claim. It was good news, indeed, but the part he didn't like was that the investigation had been closed and the fire was determined to be accidental. The final report said that there was possibly some faulty wiring behind the walls of the structure that ignited the blaze. Even with the official word, Rocky wasn't convinced.

"I was pleasantly surprised," Stuart said. "They finished the investigation much quicker than I thought they would. God gave you some real favor, man. I was sure it would take longer."

Rocky faked a smile and nodded. "Yeah." He didn't know what else to say. He kind of wanted to change the subject, and when the delivery of their beverages paused the chatter, he thought his wish would be granted.

"So, do you have any idea how long it's gonna take to get the house rebuilt?" Hunter immediately dashed all hopes of a new topic of conversation.

Rocky shook his head from side to side. "No. Not yet."

"You'll probably want to stay in contact with your insurance company," Peter advised. "Unfortunately, if you don't hound them, sometimes they drag their feet."

"Right." Unconsciously, Rocky squirmed in his seat and sat taller. He was addressing Peter again. "I have a number to call. I'll get on that right away. It's been cool staying with this one"—he jerked his head in Jerome's direction—"but I need to get the house rebuilt before I lose all my customers. As long as the property is full of debris or has construction workers swarming around it, I don't have enough clear yard space out there to work safely on cars. I need to rebuild fast so I can get back to business. I don't want to be a freeloader."

"Man, you know you ain't got to worry about that," Jerome assured him. "I got your back until whenever."

Rocky nodded. "I know, but a man don't feel right living off another man. I gotta get my own."

"I definitely respect your attitude," Stuart said.

"How about coming to work for me at the paper?" Hunter's unexpected words drew Rocky's eyes to him. Hunter looked like a lightbulb had turned on in his brain. "It's the perfect answer, even if it's only temporary. Kwame moved to DC in May. He was my right hand, and I hated to see him go, but he reconnected with his high-school sweetheart, and they wanted to make a go of it. Neither of them wanted a long-distance relationship. Since she has a teenage son who is in his last two years of high school, and she's in the middle of finishing up her Ph.D., Kwame said it made more sense for him to uproot than for her."

Peter let out a low whistle. "Love will make you do some things, won't it?"

"Yep," Hunter said. All the other men agreed too. Rocky remained quiet. He wouldn't know anything about that subject matter. "Anyway, I'm training Jerome for Kwame's position now, so Jerome's position is open. I had been planning to put an ad in the paper, but if you want it. . ."

"Are you serious?" Rocky didn't even know what skills the position would call for, but he needed a job like yesterday, and this could be an answer to a prayer. At least, until he could start fixing cars again.

"Very," Hunter said. "Pray about it. I'll hold it open for another week before making it public. If you're interested, come by the office next week and let's talk some more."

Rocky wanted to tell him that he'd take it, that he didn't need to pray about it. However, he knew if he dared to say such a thing, they'd be all over him. Plus, he didn't want to show the level of his desperation. "Thanks, man. I 'preshate that." Rocky reached for Hunter's hand and they shook on it.

"Good," Hunter replied, "but first things first. You need to take care of any red tape with your insurance so the construction can get started on your house."

"If you really want to expedite the process, you should start being really nice to my sister," Stuart said before sipping from his glass.

Rocky looked at him and grimaced. "Kenyatta? What does she have to do with anything?"

"She could get that insurance paperwork filled out for you in no time flat."

"Oh yeah." Jerome snapped his finger. "She used to work in that line of business for a while when she lived in Florida, didn't she?"

"Uh-huh." Stuart placed his glass on the table. "She worked in the claims department."

Rocky couldn't even believe his ears. *He* should ask Kenyatta for a favor? Not hardly. He gave Stuart a sideways look. "Why would I ask your sister for any help? So she can sabotage me?"

"Come on, man," Hunter said. "You know Kenyatta wouldn't do that. Granted, the two of you do have your differences, but she wouldn't intentionally botch your paperwork."

Rocky leaned his head back against the seat and had a hearty laugh. When he finished, he sat up straight again. "Are we talking about the same Kenyatta? Stu's sister? Kenyatta King? Are you kidding me? Of course, she would intentionally jack things up for me."

"No, she wouldn't, Rocky." Stuart sounded defensive. "You know Kenyatta is all bark and no bite."

Quickly disagreeing, Rocky said, "Maybe *you* know that, but I don't. This is the same girl that threatened to shoot me just a few days ago."

"Big deal." Jerome shrugged his shoulders. "She's threatened to shoot all of us at one time or another."

"Even me," Stuart added.

Rocky looked at him. "And you don't find that disturbing?"

"Man, please," Stuart said. "Kenyatta ain't got no gun."

"Have you ever checked that big, clunky purse of hers?" Rocky was more than a little doubtful that Kenyatta wasn't armed and dangerous. "That mess is so big, she may also have a machete and a few grenades in it."

Peter laughed. "Dang, Rocky. You're making her sound like one of the enemy soldiers that I came face-to-face with in the war zone."

"She's probably worse." Rocky shook his head. "I think she's capable of extreme violence, and I ain't asking her to help me do nothing. This is the same girl who claimed responsibility for burning my house down, in the first place."

"What?" Peter, Hunter, and Jerome said in unison.

"Come on, Rocky!" Stuart looked offended by the remark. "That's not even fair, man. She didn't say she burned down your house. She said she *might* have. And she only said that because you were taunting her, and you know it. You're always ticking her off. She was just retaliating when she said that. She wasn't serious."

"Whatever," Rocky repeated.

An uneasy hush rested over them for a moment, and then Hunter chuckled. "I'm just wondering which emotion is gonna win out in this love/hate relationship that you and Kenyatta have."

Rocky craned his neck to look past Jerome. "Excuse me?"

"Don't act like I'm talking Chinese." Hunter placed his elbows on the table and leaned forward. "The way you and Kenyatta act is classic behavior for two people who really love each other despite what their actions show. My bride and I were discussing this not long ago."

Jerome released a heavy breath with an accompanying groan before looking at his brother-in-law. "It's been three years, man. You can stop calling her *that* any doggone time you get ready, okay?"

Not responding to Jerome directly, Hunter kept his eyes on Rocky and started again. "My *bride* and I were discussing this not long ago. There's actually a psychological term for it." When a contagious snicker ran around the table, Hunter talked louder, totally disregarding his friends, who always got amused when he turned into an instant psychotherapist. "'Frenemies' is the term tagged on people who are friends and enemies at the same time. They love each other one minute and hate each other the next."

"Well, since there's never been a time when Kenyatta and I have ever loved each other—not even for one minute—that brings this little bubblegum therapy session to a close, don't it?" Rocky sucked water through his straw, hoping to cool his heated insides. He felt hot and flushed.

"That sounds like the relationship between Kenyatta and Ingrid," Jerome stated.

"It is." Hunter used his napkin to wipe water from the table that had pooled under his glass of lemonade. "They were the ones that Jade and I were talking about when we had this discussion. The love portion of the love/hate relationship between frenemies doesn't have to be romantic love." He looked back at Rocky and added, "But it *can* be."

"Can we just change the stupid subject?" Rocky could feel himself getting angry, and the frenemy conversation about Kenyatta and Ingrid was actually upsetting him more than the one about Kenyatta and him.

"I'm with Rocky," Stuart said. "Let's leave the counseling and analyzing to Jade. Besides, I have just the subject we can change it to."

"Wedding plans for you and Candice, maybe?" Jerome asked.

Stuart laughed. "Man, it took six months of wooing to get her to agree to go out on a real date with me again after that fiasco with Tasha. I think I'd better wait awhile before going ring shopping. Candice is gonna make me work to earn her hand, like Jacob worked for Rachel's hand in the Bible."

"Let's hope it doesn't take you seven extra years, like it took Jacob." Peter shook his head. When their food arrived, the men took a moment to say grace, and then Peter turned toward Stuart. "So what's this new subject you want to discuss?"

"Shelton Heights." With those two words, Stuart had the men's full attention.

Rocky shifted in his seat. Something about the mention of that neighborhood made him uncomfortable. Some of the tales that he'd heard and read about over the years were spine-chilling. As upscale as the Shelton Heights subdivision was, Rocky always found himself looking over his shoulders whenever he entered the gated community to visit his pastor or Stuart. He always felt like somebody was following him, or at least watching his every move.

"Are you talking about Shelton Heights, the man, or the property?" Jerome asked.

"Both." Hunter's chiming in indicated that Stuart had already clued him in on the topic. He pointed a finger from himself to Stuart, and then back to himself again. "Our sons are working together on a report for school."

"That place gives me the heebie-jeebies." Rocky hadn't meant to say it out loud, but the chicken finger that he'd stuffed in his mouth couldn't stop the words from spilling out.

"Man, don't start that," Jerome said. "All the talk of Shelton Heights being cursed is just a bunch of hogwash. How many times do I have to tell you that?"

"Oh yeah?" Rocky swallowed his meat. He was ready to challenge all of them if he had to. He knew all the stories, and a few of his friends had played leading roles in some of them. "What about your dad being abducted by that psycho?"

Jerome shrugged his shoulders. "What about it? Somebody in some part of the city of Atlanta gets abducted every other day. It ain't got nothing to do with Shelton Heights."

"Okay. Then why didn't you grab one of the available houses when you were released from prison? The houses are nice and relatively cheap, right? So why didn't you move in one? Your dad helped me get a house. I know he would have helped you."

"Yes, he would have, but I had been enough of a burden to Dad and Mother. I didn't want to get out and continue the trend. Besides, Jackson owned a two-bedroom house that nobody was living in, and I'd rather rent from my brother than from a stranger," Jerome said. "I got a job with Hunter right away, but I was still trying to get on my feet. I didn't need to worry about what would happen if I had a couple of bad months and couldn't come up with rent."

"He's right," Stuart said. "It really is all a myth."

"Is that so?" Rocky eyed Stuart. "And what about your crazy ex-wife who ran around breaking in your house and sending you threatening letters and stuff?"

Mirroring Jerome's tone, Stuart said, "Every other day, somewhere in Atlanta, there's a crazy woman or man who's stalking their ex too. Stalking isn't any more a Shelton Heights thing than abduction is a Shelton Heights thing."

"We've all been where you are, Rocky," Peter said. "I believe there was a time when each of us had our suspicions about that place, but after a while, common sense kicks in, and we realize that all of that stuff is just buried in folklore."

Rocky sat back in his chair and relaxed a bit. He couldn't sound accusing when he called Peter to the carpet. He was a war vet. It just wouldn't be right. "So when you retired and decided to settle in Atlanta, why didn't you choose Shelton Heights? You can't tell me that every other day, somewhere in Atlanta, a person is taken as prisoner of war and tortured by Iraqi soldiers."

Peter laughed. "No. But I can honestly tell you that my choice not to live there had nothing to do with me thinking the ghost of a dead man named Shelton Heights played a part in my abduction. My decision not to settle out there had nothing to do with a crazy myth. It had everything to do with a crazy mother-in-law. Leona Grimes lives in Shelton Heights, and there was no way I was going to live anywhere near her. They couldn't sell houses cheap enough to lure me. They could have been giving them away, and I'd still choose to live somewhere else."

Even Rocky had to laugh at that one. He'd met Peter's mother-in-law. All of his life, he'd heard the term "crazy church folks" used when people talked about saved people, but he had never met one before meeting Leona. She really was a sanctified nutcase.

"What kind of report are Tyler and Malik doing?" Jerome asked.

"They're playing Sherlock Holmes." There was pride in Stuart's voice.

"Literally," Hunter said.

Stuart spoke again. "For the next few weeks, they'll be spending a lot of time on the Internet and at the library, trying to find any information they can on the late Mr. Shelton Heights."

Hunter added, "They want to find the origin of his warlock label. Nobody can ever answer the question of why he was thought to be a male witch. Plus, the police never caught Mr. Heights's murderer."

"Now, that's gonna be quite an embarrassment to me and every other man and woman in blue," Stuart said with a chuckle. "If a couple of fifteen-year-old kids find out who killed that man, all of us at our precinct will have to change our names and move to another part of the country."

"Well, I think it's commendable." Peter picked up his glass and lifted it in a toast. "Listen, guys. Malik and Tyler are embarking on something positive. As members of the men's ministry, which also involves mentoring our church's teen boys, I think we should encourage and assist them in any way needed."

"I'm in," Hunter said.

Stuart lifted his glass. "Me too."

"I'll be glad to help them." Jerome raised his beverage to the height of the others. Then he looked at Rocky. "You in, man?"

The voice in Rocky's head screamed, *Have all of you lost your ever-lovin' minds?* But in slow motion, he reached for his water and lifted it in silent agreement.

"Great." Hunter grinned. "In whatever way we can, we'll help the boys."

"And may heaven help us all." Rocky's mumble was covered by the sounds of their clinking glasses.

Chapter Six

Rocky's life was still a long way from being back to normal, but the progress that he was finally starting to see eased some of his anxieties. After two weeks of being employed by Hunter, he was beginning to wonder if he'd ever go back to his shade tree job. Never in his life had he envisioned himself as a suit-and-tie—or in this case, a dress-shirt-and-slacks—guy.

During his job interview with Hunter, when Rocky first heard the changes he would have to make in order to get the job, he was more than a little skeptical. Hunter had referred to them as minor adjustments, but for Rocky, they were major. T-shirts and jeans, which he was accustomed to wearing, were out. As one who would be in a supervisory position, he had to dress business casual every day. Because of the tattoos on his arms, his dress shirts had to be long-sleeved. Then there was the matter of his bearded face. Hunter said he'd either have to shave it way down and keep it neatly trimmed, or shave it off altogether. Corporate America came with too many rules and regulations, and Rocky didn't know if he would be able to do it. Not if it meant shaving his beard. He'd had it for so long, it had become a part of his persona. If it hadn't been for Reverend and Mrs. Tides talking to him and urging him at least to give it a try, he probably would have turned down the job offer. What they said made sense.

If it turned out that he didn't like the job, he could always quit and let the beard grow back.

Each morning when Rocky prepared for work and looked at his reflection in the mirror, he was glad he'd taken on the challenge. Early graying was in his family genes, so his silver-sprinkled beard had added years to his face that shaving had subtracted. In some odd way, Rocky felt that he'd gone through a rebirthing process. It was comparable to how he felt when he first accepted Christ as his personal Savior. On that Sunday, it almost seemed as though he was being given a blood transfusion. Like all of the old stuff was flushing out of him, and new stuff was being pumped in. With this new job, it was as if his outside now matched his inside. His clean-shaven face and neatly pressed clothes made him feel like a new man, a *successful* man. It hadn't been an easy process, though. On his first day of work, he arrived in wrinkled, sweaty clothes. Hunter reprimanded him, and as a man not accustomed to anybody telling him what to do, Rocky didn't like it. His disdain didn't budge Hunter's stance. "Take it or leave it," Hunter had said. "And when I say *leave it,* I mean the job. There are a lot of unemployed men and women in the city of Atlanta. If you left today, your position could be filled tomorrow."

Had a man stepped to Rocky like that when he was in prison, that man would have earned himself a trip to the infirmary. Rocky needed this job—at least, until he could work on cars again. At the end of the day, he knew that Hunter meant well. He had to get used to the fact that every weekday during business hours, Hunter was his boss and not his friend. It was an oversize pill to swallow, but Rocky did it; and ever since day two, he had been riding in with Jerome in his air-conditioned pickup.

The pros of his new job were piling so high that they were making the cons bearable. Two of his favorite pros were the guaranteed pay and the corporate job title. He'd made decent money as a mechanic, but he felt bad that his job had him praying on a regular basis that people's vehicles would break down so he'd earn enough money to make ends meet. At the *Atlanta Weekly Chronicles,* his salary was a given. He'd have an assured amount of money in his hands every two weeks, and it was more than enough to meet his needs.

Jerome had to work his way up to his former position of press foreman, but his newest promotion, along with God's favor, had handed the title to Rocky on a silver platter. He was sure that the other three guys who worked in the press area under Jerome's supervision weren't all that pleased with Hunter's decision to bring in an outsider, instead of offering the vacancy to one of them. Rocky supposed they figured it was best that they not make a big deal out of it after one look at their new supervisor's towering stature and the ripped biceps that even his long-sleeved dress shirt couldn't hide. The men, two white and one black, accepted him as the man in charge without giving him any problems.

Rocky considered working at the *Atlanta Weekly Chronicles* as similar to being a part of a prison work-release program, but ten times better. It wasn't the job experience itself that made him draw the comparison; it was the employee roster. Jerome told him that almost all of the men who worked there were former inmates. Even Kwame had served time in the big house. It was apparent that Hunter considered his business to be ministry. It afforded people that society saw as incompetent the chance to build confidence and become assets to the world around them. They had mandatory corporate prayer every morning before starting work, and although all of the *AWC* employees didn't claim to have personal relationships with Christ, many of them did. In particular, one who alleged so was Hunter's administrative assistant, Lorna Adkins. While Rocky didn't want to be judgmental, he wasn't at all convinced. She didn't act anything like Jade, Ingrid, or Jan. Lorna wasn't even as convincing as Kenyatta.

If Lorna stood in a lineup with four or five other women, Rocky would never pick her out as the one serving God or serving as Hunter's secretary, for that matter. Pretty, she was. Classy, she wasn't. Not by Rocky's definition, anyway. Lorna had a nice figure, and it was clear by the way she dressed that she knew it. As the boss's secretary, her dress code was business casual too, but all of her suits came with short skirts or tight pants, and plunging necklines. Her fingernails were so long that they looked like deadly weapons. It was a wonder she could type a letter or even send a text message. If that wasn't enough to make her stand out like a sore thumb, her hair changed colors and lengths every two or three days. She had to be wearing wigs, or at least weaves, but oddly enough, regardless of how outrageous the colors or styles were, they actually became her. Lorna had Rocky tagged from day one, and he knew it. Her eyes followed his every move whenever he was in her presence, and, quite frankly, he'd caught himself watching her a time or two as well.

"Hi, Rocky."

Speak of the devil.

Rocky turned from the watercooler, where he'd just filled his cup. "Hi, Lorna." She was dressed uncharacteristically decent in a pair of white Capri pants and an asymmetric silk top that contained what looked like all the colors in the rainbow. The strappy, metallic, spike-heeled sandals she wore, however, looked like they were purchased from a store called Hookers "R" Us.

"How are you enjoying the job so far?" She bounced toward him taking those one-leg-cross-over-the-other pony-like steps that runway models made famous. Barefoot, she was probably around five feet seven inches, but the shoes she wore gave the illusion of a woman of six feet.

"Still good" was Rocky's reply. She'd asked him that same question yesterday . . . and the day before. He took a few sips of water to ease the parchedness that was spreading in his throat. On any other day, a consistent flow of employees would file through the break room to get water, napkins, a bag of chips from the vending machine, a handful of Skittles from the gumball machine . . . something. Today, of all days, everybody was apparently in work mode. Lorna wasn't exactly Rocky's type, but he had gone without female companionship for more than four months. It felt like she was dangling red velvet cake in his face today and offering him a slice, And red velvet cake was his favorite.

"I think you're really gonna love it here." Her right breast brushed against his arm when she reached beyond the tower of cups that was only inches from her to take one from the stack that was closest to Rocky. "The job is good, but the *benefits* are even better."

It was possible that his ears were taking her words out of context, but with the way Lorna stressed the word "benefits," Rocky was almost certain that she wasn't talking about the vacation time and dental insurance.

He took another gulp of water, and then tried to shrug his shoulders in a happy-go-lucky manner. "I'm taking it one day at a time. We'll see what happens." He took a few steps backward and hoped that by glancing out the nearby window, he was masking the real reason for putting more space between them. "I'm more used to fixing machines than running them or managing the people who do. Fixing cars is what I really do. I got a lot of training with that when I was . . ." Rocky caught himself. Lorna probably already knew where he'd spent the last two-plus decades of his life, but it still wasn't something he wanted to broadcast aloud. "That was what I did before moving to this end of the city." There. That sounded better.

When Lorna joined him at the window, the first thing Rocky noticed was that she still hadn't gotten any water. As a matter of fact, even the cup that she literally went out of her way to get was no longer in her hand. It made him wonder if she really had come into the room for water.

"We all have a past, Rocky." Her voice was soothing, but when she ran a gentle hand down the length of his arm, Rocky tensed. He hoped she hadn't felt the hardening of his muscles. It didn't seem she had, as she allowed both her hands to rest at her sides. "I know I'm not proud of everything I've done, but I'm not ashamed of them either. Good or bad, they made me who I am, and I like me."

Rocky smiled a little, but he found himself thinking hard. Could he truthfully declare the same? Did he like himself? It was a good question that he'd never before pondered. "What's done is done," he opted to say. "Can't change the past, so the object is just to make the best present and future, right?"

"Right." She smiled back, and even as Rocky made his way back to the cooler for a refill, he could feel her eyes on him. "We should do lunch one day."

Rocky flinched; water splattered. For a woman wearing stilettos, Lorna walked with the skill of a cat burglar. Rocky hadn't heard her approach, and the sudden nearness of her voice startled him. Embarrassed by his blunder, he pulled a few sheets of paper towels from the roll, which sat on the counter, and began soaking up the spill from the floor. "Sorry." He didn't know why he was apologizing. It wasn't like the water had splattered on her.

"Do I make you nervous?"

"No. Not at all." Rocky's lie was quick, but it fell short of being convincing. He avoided eye contact with Lorna as he stood back to his full height. He took longer than necessary to crumple the soiled paper and toss it in the trash can. Women had never unnerved him before. In the past, he was the one who controlled the atmosphere. What was happening here? Rocky was starting to feel like he had lost some of his edge, like less of a man, even. No way could he let that happen. He drained the water from his cup in three big swallows, and then dropped it in the can on top of the paper towel he'd just disposed of. Then with renewed confidence, he turned to face Lorna and said, "So you say we should do lunch?" He was looking her straight in the eyes now. "Why should we do that?"

As though they were the prongs of a wide-tooth comb, Lorna used her long polished nails to rake hairs away from her face. She was wearing her do today in a layered, short style, with jet black being the predominate color. But the very front was Kool-Aid red, and those were the hairs that fell in her face in a swooplike bang that almost covered her left eye completely. "Why shouldn't we?" She smiled at him, never once breaking eye contact. "I've been working here for a while now. I can fill you in on who's cool and who's not. And maybe you can fill me in on some things too."

"Like?"

"Nothing major. Just simple stuff, like your name, for instance."

Rocky cocked his head to the side. "You know my name."

"I mean your *real* name."

"You know my real name."

Lorna giggled like a silly schoolgirl. "'Rocky' has to be a nickname or something. I don't believe for a minute that it's the name your mama gave you."

Rocky pulled a sheet of paper towel off the roll and used it to dry nonexistent water from his hands. "My mama didn't give me a lot of things. Some things in life ain't given to you. You have to earn them."

"So you *earned* your name?"

When a voice behind them interrupted with "Lorna," it became her turn to flinch. They both turned to find Hunter standing in the doorway of the break room.

"Oh . . . Hunter . . . hey. You—you need me?" Lorna looked a bit flustered.

Hunter's eyes went from Lorna to Rocky, and then back to Lorna. They narrowed when they fixed on her. "Do I *need* you? Lorna, I asked you fifteen minutes ago to bring me some paperwork from the storage files. I still don't have it. Did you forget?"

"Oh—oh . . . I got sidetracked. Sorry." She giggled a little, but it was plain to see that Hunter didn't share the humor. "I'll go get it right now." Her pony walk had disappeared as she scurried toward the door. The cat-burglar thing was gone too. Rocky could even hear every step of her heels clicking against the flooring tiles when she made her complete exit.

Hunter remained in the doorway for a moment before fully entering the space where Rocky still stood. "Did I just interrupt something?"

"No. Yeah. Well, no," Rocky said. "Not what you think, anyway."

"What do you think it is that I think?" There was a challenging tone in Hunter's voice, and Rocky wasn't particularly fond of it. It was one thing for him to tell him how he could wear his clothes and his facial hair on the job, but he'd be dog if he would stand for Hunter telling him whom he could talk to. Just because Hunter was the owner of the place didn't give him a right to run everybody's life who worked there.

"I don't know what you were thinking, Hunter, but Lorna and I were just shooting the breeze. Is that another thing that ain't permitted around here?" Rocky knew he sounded flippant, but at the moment, he didn't care.

Hunter took a second to close the door to the break room, and when he turned back to face Rocky, Rocky knew the undertone of his remark hadn't escaped his boss's ears. "Look, Rocky, I don't care who you *shoot the breeze* with around here, as long as you're not shooting it when you should be working."

"Then why don't you talk to your secretary? Why you just automatically think I'm to blame? I came in here to get some water." Rocky wished he were still holding his cup. If he had that to use as Exhibit A, maybe he wouldn't be deemed guilty, and maybe he wouldn't feel like he was wasting his breath trying to defend himself. "She's the one who came in and started talking to me. I was minding my own business. I didn't even know that she was—"

"Make no mistake, Rocky. I will talk to Lorna." Hunter cut into his rant. "Nobody is accusing you of being the initiator of the conversation that led to overtime in the break room. I'm simply telling you not to make it a habit. Actually, all I was really doing was asking if there was something going on between you and Lorna that I didn't know about. And to tell the truth, I was kinda half-joking when I was hinting at that. Why you felt the need to fly off the handle and get defensive, I don't know."

Rocky sucked in his jaws and said nothing. He didn't know why he always felt the need to defend himself either.

"Listen, who you hit on . . . or who you allow to hit on you, for that matter, is your business. Granted, I would *strongly* not recommend Lorna, but once again, that's your business. However, *this,* Rocky"—he spread his arms out and allowed his eyes to roam the room—"is *my* business. And in my business, I demand a certain level of professionalism that, admittedly, everybody can't handle. But at the end of the day, the choices are simple." Hunter put up his index finger. "If you want to work at the *AWC,* you'll meet that level." His middle finger followed. "If you think my expectations are too high, there's always the door." Shoving both of his hands in the pockets of his slacks, Hunter concluded by saying, "I love you like a brother, man. But around here, you don't run things; I do."

The roll of thunder that sounded off at that moment almost seemed timed, like God had some sort of amen corner up in heaven that had just rallied their support of what Hunter had said. Rocky remained quiet. At Phillips State Prison, that kind of mouthing off would have earned Hunter four lost teeth and at least one broken rib, maybe two. But as bitter as the reprimand was to ingest, Rocky knew that Hunter wasn't being unreasonable, nor was he the one who needed an attitude adjustment. Rocky was the problem, and he knew it, but it was still best that he didn't reply. At least, not right now. So his lips remained sealed while he watched Hunter open the door to the break room and make his exit. Rocky took in a deep breath, and then released it. Maybe he wasn't cut out for this corporate thing, after all.

Chapter Seven

Friday was Kenyatta's favorite *and* least favorite day of the week. It meant for the next two days she wouldn't have to talk to deadbeat dads or the clueless women who loved them in spite of their deadbeat-ness. It also meant that the day would be a long and frustrating one that largely consisted of talking to deadbeat dads and the clueless women who loved them in spite of their deadbeat-ness.

Working as a social worker was far more stressful than what most people realized. It was more than riding around the city and checking on the well-being of the children in her caseload. Kenyatta's job involved actually working directly with those who were accused of neglecting and even abusing innocent children. She had to look them in their faces and not give away the fact that she literally wanted to tie them to rusted metal chairs in the middle of a flooded floor and lay live wires at their feet. Her duties were far-reaching, involving everything from making sure children were safe to making sure they were financially supported.

At the end of every workweek, Kenyatta scampered to find the positive. She searched for at least one encouraging thing that had come out of the week that she could identify as her reason to kneel before God in thanksgiving. She called it her "BOW moment," the reason for her to bow before His presence. BOW was her acronym for "blessing of the week." Finding the blessing among the frustration kept her sane, but the longer she worked with the Department of Family and Children's Services, the harder it became to find her BOW moment. After the travesty of clients that she'd dealt with over the past five days, Kenyatta concluded that this week, there was no blessing to name. When she prayed her special prayer tonight, it would be one wherein she'd just thank God for having steady employment. She complained about her job religiously, but in a recessed economy like this one, it alone qualified as a BOW moment.

Why were men so stupid, and why were women so tolerant of their behavior? For the life of her, Kenyatta couldn't wrap her brain around the mind-set of women who were attracted to the likes of Troy Baker, the thirty-eight-year-old supreme loser to whom she'd just spoken ten minutes ago. Every now and then, she'd give a pass to the seventeen- and eighteen-year-olds with whom she occasionally dealt. Those boys barely had enough sense to bathe and put on deodorant. They were still kids themselves. Most of them probably couldn't even spell "sex," but they were recklessly having it on a regular basis, and leaving behind the evidence in the form of babies whom they could barely contribute a monthly dollar to support. At least they were still basically children themselves, and on the broad scale of things, Kenyatta didn't expect much from a child—not even one who had fathered a child of his own. An almost forty-year-old, however, got no empathy or sympathy from her.

Troy called himself "T-Baby." Even the women whom he'd loved and left called him T-Baby. He had four children with three mothers, and his file showed documentation of him being notorious for quitting jobs just so he wouldn't have to pay child support to his children's mothers. He'd work a job here and there for as long as it took child services to find out. As soon as he was busted, he'd find a reason to quit or get fired. He didn't see it as child abuse or neglect. He actually said those words to Kenyatta. Troy defined himself as a "smart businessman" who did what it took to survive. It was sickening. Maddening, actually. Deadbeat men—*black* men in particular—were possibly Kenyatta's greatest pet peeve. To read all the statistics on black men who were on drugs, in jail, or just plain no-good was one thing, but to work in an environment that proved it to be true was another.

Were there *really* any good ones left? All of her sister-friends insisted that good men not only existed, but that there was a harvest of them out there just waiting to find the right woman. The thought of it made Kenyatta shake her head. That was easy for them to say. Every one of them had a good man. Experience told Kenyatta that if there was truly a harvest of good, available men out there, she had been plucking from the wrong fields for her entire life. All the good ones she knew were taken. Even if they weren't taken when Kenyatta met them, they eventually became taken, and she was never the lucky girl to be named the taker. Like Jerome Tides, for instance. She had been in the picture before Ingrid, but in the end, all Kenyatta had been good for were fun dates and fine dinners. When Jerome was ready to settle down with one woman, he chose Ingrid, and within six months of his decision, they were engaged.

That was only one example. Her string of losses didn't start with her pastor's handsome son. Kenyatta had been batting zero since she began dating as a sixteen-year-old high-school sophomore. She didn't understand it. She had always been popular among her peers—the ones who weren't jealous of her, that is. Kenyatta was smart, a definite fashion diva, and attractive. Those adjectives described her then, and they still held true now. These days, the words "saved" and "successful" could be added to the list, which raised her net worth even higher. It didn't make sense for a woman with all that going for her to be single, with no prospects. Even the one man who, she thought, was her shining knight turned out to be her shameful nightmare.

Joseph King was the worst of the worst. She should have listened to Stuart from the beginning. Her brother had never liked Joe and had tried to talk Kenyatta out of marrying him, but she wouldn't listen. Since she ignored the signs, she was still wearing the last name of a certified fool. It took her ten years to get rid of that maniac, and even then, she had to escape during the night like Harriet Tubman or something. Joe was a wolf in sheep's clothing. So even when she thought she'd won, she'd lost, and the streak continued.

"Maybe that's why so many women go for these stupid men," she muttered while shoving a file in her drawer. "They don't have any other choice. All that's left are stupid men."

She'd surmised a long time ago that she had been too good for Jerome, and probably too good for most of the others too. Kenyatta was convinced that the average man really did have a problem with educated women who could take care of themselves. She was smarter and prettier than Ingrid, and she doubted that anyone, including Jerome, would challenge her on that. Both of them were good women who were very much into Jerome. Both of them were saved women who were very much into the Lord. The biggest difference, as far as Kenyatta could tell, was that she had a college degree, and Ingrid didn't. As good and good-looking as Jerome was, when it came down to it, he was still a convicted felon, who had gotten his GED in prison. It made all the sense in the world that he would be less intimidated by, and more attracted to, somebody like Ingrid. Birds of a feather . . .

Kenyatta tried to shake the thoughts from her head, but they continued.

A man would have to be exceptional to be able to appreciate her. He had to have his own so that he wouldn't be threatened by the fact that she had hers. Her Boaz needed to be strong, educated, and not so easily threatened by a woman who wasn't a "yes man." Kenyatta reached across her desk and placed the pen she'd been using back in the holder with the rest of her writing instruments; then she sat up straight.

"Yep. That's the problem," she spoke into the air. "I've been surrounded by losers for too long. I'm more on the level of Jade and Jan, so I need a man like Hunter or Peter, but, of course, they're already taken too. All that's left now are ex-cons like Jerome, and that scruffy-faced hoodlum, Rocky." She stopped and scowled. Just saying his name made her want to gag. The best part about Rocky getting that new job at the *AWC* was that he didn't have the free time on his hands to lounge around her brother's house all afternoon making her life miserable. Between Kenyatta's vacation and Rocky's job, she'd been blessed by not having to cross paths with him for two weeks.

And there it was! Kenyatta clapped her hands at the realization of it. That was her BOW moment. She hadn't seen Rocky in two weeks.

Kenyatta smiled as she stood from her desk and smoothed out her shirt. The clock on the wall said that she was three minutes away from two days of freedom,

and that was about how much time she needed to gather her things. This had been her first week back to work
since taking a seven-day vacation. She really shouldn't
be this burned out already. Maybe that was the problem. Maybe she'd taken too much time off. That Sunday to Sunday "me time" that she spent living in time-
share housing on the beach in Daytona had spoiled her.
Walking barefoot on the white sands, sleeping in late,
reading books by her favorite authors, spending hours
in the spa . . . Kenyatta had hated the thought of returning to Atlanta, let alone returning to work.

She didn't realize how much she missed Florida until last week's getaway. She and Stuart had been born
and raised in Jacksonville, and if her crazy ex-husband
didn't still live there, Kenyatta was sure that she would
have moved back home a long time ago. The only thing
she really loved about living in Atlanta was New Hope
Church. None of the churches in Jacksonville that
she'd attended ever came close to the worship experience that New Hope offered. The two Sunday morning
services that she'd missed while on vacation were her
only regrets.

"You mean you're actually leaving?"

Kenyatta looked at her coworker Carter Tomlinson
and wondered why she would ask her such a thing. It
wasn't like her leaving was abnormal. She hightailed
it out of the office every day at five o'clock on the dot.
Pretty much everybody did. Even now, it seemed that
everyone except Carter had beaten her to the punch.
"Yes, I'm leaving. Aren't you?"

"I thought I'd wait until the rain slowed. I wasn't so
surprised when the others ran to their cars in the rain,
but I'm shocked that you're going out in it." Carter
laughed and swiveled her neck so that the fat curls of
her long red hair tossed over her shoulder.

Kenyatta stopped in her tracks. She hadn't realized it was raining, but now that she'd been told, the sounds of it pounding on the roof of the building seemed to amplify. "Oh man, it's raining?"

"Cats and dogs, hun," Carter replied. Kenyatta hated it when Carter called her that. "The sky opened up about ten minutes ago. You must have really been absorbed in work not to have heard it."

"I guess I was." Kenyatta knew that it wasn't all work that had been on her mind for the last ten minutes.

"I'll bet you're not in a hurry to leave anymore, are you?" For about as long as Kenyatta had worked there, the office joke was that she'd die before she allowed her precious hair to get wet. They accused her of always taking tub baths and even sleeping in an upright position so as not to disturb her hairdo. Carter sat in a nearby chair and, with confidence, patted the empty one beside her. "We can kill time by swapping ridiculous case updates. I have some, and I'm sure you do too."

Kenyatta definitely had her share of stories to tell, but using them as entertainment was far from appetizing. She had a standard Saturday hair appointment, so it really didn't matter if she got wet today. "Sorry, Carter. I'm out. We'll have to swap stories another day. I've got places to go and people to see. I'll be visiting the beautician tomorrow, anyway, so I'm good."

"Places to go and people to see?" Carter almost sang the words. That heavy Southern drawl of hers, which could be endearing in small doses, got more and more annoying the longer she talked. She sounded like that woman who used to play Dr. Harry Weston's office nurse on *Empty Nest*. "Does that mean you've got a date this weekend, hun?"

Having a date would have added a nice touch to the weekend, but even if she had one, Kenyatta didn't know if she'd tell her coworker. Carter was nice and all, but they weren't friends; they were just business associates. Kenyatta didn't want to exchange work stories with Carter, and she didn't want to exchange personal stories with her either. Carter was a few years Kenyatta's junior. She was born in 1977; on the day that Jimmy Carter took office. Kenyatta had heard the story time and time again. Apparently, Carter was very proud to be named after the thirty-ninth president of the United States. Kenyatta liked Jimmy Carter too, but good grief! If she had to hear the story of how Mrs. Tomlinson's water broke at the moment the president was being sworn in, she would scream. It never failed. The conversation could be about something totally different, but Carter would find some way to navigate it to how she'd gotten her name. *Who cared?*

"It's been a long week—that's all," Kenyatta decided to say. "The only place I want to see right now is my house, and the only people I want to see are the ones who will creep up in my dreams. I plan to eat dinner by seven, be asleep by nine, and not get out of bed until my eyelids open on their own accord tomorrow—whatever time that might be. My hair appointment isn't until two, so I can sleep in late if I want. And I do."

Carter seemed disappointed that she'd be left alone. "Okay. Well, drive safe, hun. Rush hour on a Friday in Atlanta is bad enough on a clear day. Add rain to that and you've got triple trouble. My mama found that out when she came up for a visit last year. She kept saying, 'Carter, I can't believe you let me get out and drive in that madness.'"

"I live thirty minutes away. Believe me, I'll be fine." Kenyatta rushed toward the door. She knew the onset of a story involving how Carter got her name, when she heard it. It always started with the introduction of some other story that involved Carter and her mother.

The rain was coming down in buckets. She had used her remote to unlock the door before making the mad dash into the parking lot, but Kenyatta was still amply wet by the time she got inside her car. The napkins that she had shoved in her glove compartment after a lunch visit to Zaxby's earlier in the week served as poor substitutes for a towel, but she patted away as much water as she could from her hair, face, arms, and hands before starting the engine and heading home. Her normal half-hour drive took nearly an hour today in the bumper-to-bumper traffic, but Kenyatta was still glad she hadn't waited. She'd take being stuck in traffic any day over being stuck in the office with Carter.

"Oh great. Today of all days!" she grunted. Several presses to the portable garage door opener, which she kept in her car, indicated that her battery had died. The warning light had been illuminating for days, but she'd failed to change the battery. Now she'd have to pay for it with another run in the rain. Unless . . .

Kenyatta retrieved her cell phone, dialed the number, and prayed that this was one of those Fridays when Stuart had beaten her home from work. She knew his voice mail was set to pick up on the fifth ring. Kenyatta was just about to hang up when she heard the fourth, but her brother's voice stopped her.

"Hey, sis. What's up?"

He sounded relaxed. Kenyatta hoped that meant he wasn't still at work. "Are you at home? Please tell me you're at home, Stu."

His voice tone changed. "Yeah, I am. What's wrong? Where are you? What do you need?"

Kenyatta couldn't help but smile. If only all men were like the two her parents had raised. "Nothing. Nothing's wrong. The battery in my garage door opener is dead. I'm sitting out front. Can you open the door for me?"

"Girl, don't scare me like that." She could hear noises on the other end of the line that sounded like Stuart might have been closing kitchen cabinet doors or something. "Give me one second."

While Kenyatta waited for the garage door to open, she shoved her cell back in her purse, then she increased the volume on her car radio. She loved listening to Praise 102.5 on her way home from work. The gospel mixes that were played during that time of day always helped get her through the woes of rush-hour traffic. It made rainy Fridays and ruined hairdos more bearable. Kenyatta bounced in her seat while singing the tune of "They That Wait," along with Fred Hammond and his choir, but she stopped midbounce when the garage door lifted and a familiar muscular figure wearing a helmet backed his motorcycle out so that she could pull her car in.

With two closed fists, Kenyatta banged her steering wheel one hard time. Her deep-throated groan took the place of the ungodly words that she really wanted to spit out. The last thing she needed after the day she'd had today was to deal with Rocky. Once she pulled her car in and climbed out, she pushed the button on the wall that closed the door. She prayed inwardly that since Rocky was wearing his safety gear, he was headed out and wouldn't come back inside.

"Please tell me that that bothersome lumberjack out there is leaving" were the first words she blurted out upon entering the house.

"Nope. He just got here a little before you did. I told him he could come by so that I could help him with one of his online courses." Stuart bit into an apple that was in his grasp, and after maneuvering the treat to the side of his mouth, he added, "He's just as wet as you are, but at least he was riding an open bike. Go put on some dry clothes, girl. And don't you and Rocky get started today, okay? I really don't feel like dealing with y'all."

"Don't worry." Kenyatta stomped down the hall, but kept talking. "I won't be in here to look in his stupid face, and if you want to eat anytime soon, you'll make this study session a quick one. I'm not coming out to cook a single thing until he's gone." She closed her bedroom door behind her entrance and locked it for reassurance. What a nuisance! That must have been why Rocky was still dressed in his riding gear. Not because he was leaving, but because he was just arriving. Why couldn't he just go home after work? Why couldn't he get his housemate to help him with his studies? Kenyatta kicked off her shoes. "Jerome has his GED, so whatever that idiot needs to know, wouldn't his best friend be the perfect person to ask? Why does he have to come to our house? Stu ain't no doggone school-teacher." Kenyatta muttered the words as she peeled off her wet clothes and flung them, piece by piece, on the floor.

Now she halfway wished that she'd stayed at the office with Carter. By leaving, she'd escaped the pot, just to get thrown in the frying pan! As annoying as her coworker could be, Kenyatta could deal with her much easier than Rocky. Carter got on her nerves. Rocky got under her skin. There was a big difference.

Kenyatta walked into her bathroom and turned on the shower. While the water warmed, she pulled out the hairpins, which had helped to hold her style in place since last weekend. It was a good thing that the rain hadn't come any sooner. She stepped into her shower stall, and for the next several minutes, she lathered her body and her hair. When she was all done, she dried herself, and then wrapped her hair in a towel while she moisturized her body and put on fresh clothes. She had purchased the floor-length, strapless melon-colored sundress while she was vacationing in Daytona Beach. Next came the task of blow-drying her hair. She and both her sisters were blessed with their mother's thick, coarse hair. Kenyatta's perm masked the coarseness, but the volume of her hair still made drying it a chore. Twenty minutes later, she was done.

"I wonder if he's gone," she thought aloud. It had been nearly an hour since she retreated to her room. Kenyatta hoped that had been enough time for her brother to help Rocky with his work and then send him on his way. "I don't see his bike." While she peeked through her blinds at the outside world, Kenyatta talked as though someone was in the room to hear her. The rain had stopped. That bettered the chances that Rocky had gone. She walked to her room's door and pressed her ear to it. No noises were heard on the other side. Easing it open, she stepped into the hall.

"Hey, Auntie Kenyatta." Tyler was in his bedroom with the door open. He was lying across his bed with his head buried in a book.

"Hey." Kenyatta stopped at his door and leaned on the frame. She loved her nephew. Her brother had done such a good job of raising him. The last year had been especially hard for Tyler—ever since his mom had gotten locked up for stalking Stuart. "How was school?"

Tyler sat up Indian style on the bed and placed the book in his lap. "It was cool. Football practice was canceled due to the rain, though."

"I imagine so." Kenyatta brushed her hands over her straight hair. "How's the Shelton Heights project coming?"

"It's coming." Tyler tapped the book. "That's what I'm working on right now. Did you know he was a rich dude?"

"I heard that he was. I can't say that I fully believe it."

"It's true. Both Malik and I are working on the project this weekend. I just asked Rocky if he would take me out to the cemetery to take some pictures of 'Old Man' Heights's grave this weekend." Tyler grinned. "I really just want to ride his motorcycle."

Kenyatta froze. "You *just* asked him?" She dropped her voice to a whisper. "Is he still here?"

To her dismay, Tyler nodded. "He's in The Lyons Den with Dad."

She sucked her teeth in disappointment. Rocky hadn't left. She should have known it was too good to be true. "The Lyons Den" was the name that Stuart had given his den. He loved that room. "Well, I'm gonna let you get back to work," she told Tyler. "If you want someone to read over your report before you turn it in, let me know."

"Okay. Thanks, Auntie."

Kenyatta glanced at the nearby closed den door, and then tiptoed up the hallway toward the kitchen. She was hungry, and it looked like this thing with Rocky might take a while. She could grab something to take in her room to munch on, and that would tide her over until she had the chance to prepare dinner. Kenyatta had taken a pound and a half of ground turkey out of the freezer last night, and would use it to make a quick meal of spaghetti and meatballs. Trying to put together the quickest snack possible, she grabbed two slices of bread from the loaf that sat on the dining-room table, and a slice of sandwich meat from the refrigerator. Condiments weren't necessary. It only took her a few more moments to fill a cup with cranberry juice.

"Hey. What's up?"

It was little consolation that she'd used a cup instead of a glass when she turned around to face her quiet intruder. The cup slipped from her hand and crashed to the floor, splattering red juice everywhere, including on her new dress. If the voice wasn't so familiar, Kenyatta wouldn't have readily recognized the face.

"My bad." A clean-cut Rocky bent down and picked up the cup that had rolled toward him and came to a stop at the big toe of his bare right foot. "Didn't mean to scare you."

Kenyatta reached to accept the empty cup, which he handed her, but she couldn't take her eyes off his face. Rocky's strong jawline, his smooth cheeks, his subtle, Jude Law–like cleft chin; it had all been hidden by the hairs that had once littered his face. The beauty mark, which was perfectly placed near the side of his nose, couldn't have been covered by the beard, but Kenyatta had never noticed it until now. She could tell by the way he returned her gaze he was enjoying her eyes' thorough critique of his new appearance.

With a grin pulling at one side of his lips, the tall, dark, handsome stranger extended his now empty hand toward her again. "Hi," he said. "My name's Rocky."

Chapter Eight

First Sundays at New Hope were like the other Sundays of the month, multiplied by ten. It was the only Sunday that Reverend Tides was guaranteed to speak; it was the Sunday on which the congregation partook of Holy Communion together; it was the one Sunday that the mass choir took the stand, clad in robes that bore the church's emblem; and without fail, it was the Sunday where attendees danced and worshipped more than any other. As a result, all those things added together to make first-Sunday services longer than any other, but despite that, it was the Sunday that drew the largest crowd. Morning worship began promptly at eleven-thirty. It was five minutes before starting time, and not only were the regular seats already filled, but the announcement had just been made that the overflow rooms were at capacity too.

Because he always carpooled with Jerome and Ingrid on first Sundays, Rocky never worried that he wouldn't get prime seating. Other Sundays, he sometimes rode his Harley-Davidson in because dressing up wasn't the norm for him. During almost any given service, Rocky could be found sitting in the pew wearing blue jeans, a Phat Farm T-shirt, and steel-toe boots. On first Sundays he chose to dress up, usually opting to wear slacks, a button-down shirt, and a tie to complement the ensemble. Jerome was on the ministerial staff and always arrived early to get in on the corporate prayer that the staff had in one of the back offices before service began. So riding in with them on the busiest Sunday of the month served a dual purpose. It guaranteed Rocky a good seat, and without the sweat and wrinkles he chanced getting on the motorcycle, it guaranteed that he'd look good sitting there.

Another thing about first Sundays that Rocky had made note of was that it was the only Sunday that Kenyatta actively served as one of the attending ushers. He knew which door she manned, and when he and Ingrid walked in early this morning, Rocky led the way to ensure they'd walk through Kenyatta's door. She wore the same black A-line dress, with white trim around the collar and sleeves, that all of the other ushers wore, but by Rocky's evaluation, Kenyatta's dress fit better than all the others.

"Good morning," he'd said to her while she dutifully handed offering envelopes to both of them. Kenyatta wasn't as close to Ingrid as she was to Jade, Candice, and Jan, but her smile appeared genuine when she greeted Ingrid and handed her an envelope. On the contrary, although she returned Rocky's greeting with a weak "Good morning" of her own, Kenyatta didn't smile at him, and she totally avoided eye contact. Rocky noticed it, and he liked it.

Ever since Friday evening, Ms. Kenyatta King had been on his mind. Rocky couldn't get *that look* out of his head. He had always had a secret attraction to her, but ever since she looked at him like that, things were different. Rocky saw something in Kenyatta's eyes on Friday that he'd not noticed before. He'd always enjoyed knowing he had the power to rile her and make her mad, but until Friday, he had never known his ability to unravel her and make her nervous. Rocky enjoyed that one even better. A big part of him wanted to seize an opportunity; take advantage of that rare, weak, guard-down moment of Kenyatta's and put her in a lip-lock that she'd never forget. Even now as he thought back on it, Rocky was sure she wouldn't have forbade him. She might have hauled off and slapped him afterward, but he believed that he could have kissed her at that moment, and she wouldn't have stopped him. She *couldn't* have stopped him. Rocky had spent half the night kicking himself in the rear for not taking his chances. He was going to have to kiss somebody soon, or he was going to combust spontaneously.

Before the evening was over on Friday, things were back to normal. He and Kenyatta were at each other's throats, and she had threatened yet again to put a bullet through his head, but that didn't cancel their earlier moment. As short-lived as it may have been, it had lasted long enough to raise a question in Rocky's mind that he'd never even deliberated before. *Could it be? Was it possible that beneath all the contempt and disdain, there was a layer of attraction that she had for him?*

Rocky's thoughts were broken when he saw Elder Jackson Tides, Reverend Tides's eldest son, enter from the side door and join the other ministers on the platform. Jackson rarely hung out with Rocky and the rest of the guys. He was a bit older than all of them and had his own set of friends, which consisted mostly of members of the ministry staff. Rocky involuntarily rubbed his chin while he watched Jackson approach the speaker's stand, but his mind floated back to Kenyatta. He had been a bit upset with Hunter for making him shave hairs that had served as a brand for most of his life, but after Kenyatta's reaction upon first sight of him, he wondered if he should stop by Walgreens on the way home and buy his new boss a thank-you card.

"Let us stand, and give our Lord and Savior a hand clap of praise."

Jackson's words brought Rocky to his feet, and his focus to the pulpit, but it didn't completely erase Kenyatta from his thoughts. He turned and looked toward the rear of the church. The crowd was too thick for him to see her, and with him sitting so near the front, and Kenyatta stationed at the very back, the chance that he could have seen her was slim to none, anyway. The mental snapshots of her standing in front of him in the kitchen in that pretty dress, which had been ruined by cranberry juice, finally started to fade as the worship service got into full swing.

Even before Rocky made the decision to live for Christ, he enjoyed the Sundays that he visited New Hope. It was like nothing he had ever experienced. He had never heard a choir sing like the choir at New Hope, never heard a preacher preach like the pastor of New Hope, never saw people explode into unrehearsed, unrestrained worship like the people of New Hope. It was all a little intimidating at first, but now that he knew God for himself, Rocky understood the praise. He didn't have the voice to sing like the choir members; he didn't have the coordination to dance like many of those around him; and he certainly didn't have the ability to preach like the men and women who ministered from the podium, from week to week. But Rocky knew what the move of the Holy Spirit felt like, and by the time the praise team was on their second song, the hand of God was already beginning to sweep through New Hope. Before praise and worship was over, Rocky had to step into the aisle twice to let Ingrid out so that she would have more space to get in her dance.

By the time Reverend Tides got up to preach, they had already been in church for ninety minutes, but nobody seemed to mind. As was customary, the congregation stood when the pastor took the stand and remained standing until after he had read the passage of scripture from which today's message would be drawn. It took a few minutes for Reverend Tides to read all of the verses that made up Matthew 7:13–29, but immediately when he was done, he announced his topic.

"'The Two Foundations,'" Reverend Tides said. The murmurs of praise that ran around the sanctuary let Rocky know that some of the crowd already knew where the pastor was going with this one.

Most of the scriptures and the breakdown of them that had been shared at church over the course of the past five months had been brand-new to Rocky. Before the men's ministry began coming to Phillips State Prison, Rocky had never read any portion of the Bible. In fact, if he'd ever even picked up a Bible prior to that time, he couldn't recall it. Every time he heard a message from Reverend Tides or any of his staff ministers, it was a fresh Word to Rocky's ears. In the past months, he had injected Bible reading in his evening as a part of what he did before going to bed. That was how he'd learned The Lord's Prayer, a scripture so common that most children could rattle it off with no hesitation. Rocky had just fully committed it to memory two weeks ago.

He sat forward in his seat and listened intently while Reverend Tides talked about everything from wide gates versus narrow ones, to good trees versus corrupt ones, to authentic Christians versus bogus ones. He expounded on the likeness and differences, and warned how easily it was for a person to be fooled and misled if they didn't look with their spiritual eyes instead of their natural ones. Then he began honing in on his primary comparison—the difference between rocks and sand. Foolish men built their houses on sand, he said. Wise ones built theirs on rocks. Foundations made of sand couldn't withstand the harsh elements that the world brought its way. But houses built on rocks didn't easily fall when harsh winds, floods, and other torrential elements presented themselves.

Rocky couldn't help but think about the destruction of his house several weeks ago. Could God be trying to tell him something through this message? Maybe he should have a talk with the people at the company who had been contracted to rebuild. Yesterday, Rocky had ridden his motorcycle to his old neighborhood and sat at the edge of the property watching them at work. They were still early in the process, but things were looking good. The old rubble had been removed, and the reconstruction process was already under way. Maybe Jerome, Stuart, and the rest of the guys had been right all along. The gangsters with whom Rocky used to run the streets might have had nothing to do with his house ending up in a burned heap. Maybe the foundation was jacked up from the beginning, and the house just wasn't sturdy. Maybe the whole thing had simply collapsed because it was built on sand, and as it was falling in, electrical wires snapped that caused the whole thing to ignite into flames. Maybe . . .

"I'm not speaking of common dirt or concrete that we can see with our eyes or touch with our hands; I'm speaking of the foundation of our inner man. Our spiritual foundations, our very souls." Reverend Tides's words jerked Rocky away from his thoughts. "If we aren't watchful and tuned in to the voice of God, we'll be fooled into building our house on a flimsy foundation that won't withstand the test. But when we build it upon a rock; when we build it upon *the* Rock; the Rock of ages . . . the Rock in a weary land . . . the Rock of our salvation . . . Jesus!" he bellowed. "Jesus, the solid Rock!"

Those who had been sitting around Rocky were on their feet now, clapping and shouting out "Hallelujah" and "Amen" behind their pastor's declaration. Rocky stood too; mostly so he wouldn't lose his view of Reverend Tides as the preacher walked the length of the platform, with the keyboardist striking chords that egged him on.

"If we build our house upon the Rock, the Word of God tells us that winds will blow and rain will fall, but our house will be steadfast!"

"Glory to God!" Ingrid yelled.

Rocky shifted a little to the side. He knew it was only a matter of time before he'd have to let her out again.

"Not only won't the rain and wind be able to take you out, but neither will the unexpected," Reverend Tides continued. "See, the rain and the wind are things we expect. It's natural for them to come every now and then, but when your foundation is Jesus—when your foundation is the Rock—even the devil himself can't consume you. As Jesus says, in around about the sixteenth chapter of this same book of Matthew: 'Upon this rock I will build my church; and the gates of hell shall not prevail against it.' God has all power, and when we allow Him to be our foundation, we can know that we can stand strong because our feet are planted on the Rock!"

Rocky's prediction was right. He cleared the way just in time to allow Ingrid to run past him. After she cleared the row, she kept right on running. He lost sight of her after she rounded the front pew, but he didn't miss the grin that beamed from Jerome's face as he watched from his place on the platform. Rocky and Jerome had just had a conversation two nights ago, and one of the things Jerome expressed was how much enjoyment he got out of seeing Ingrid go forth in praise. According to Jerome, his fiancée had come a long way from where she once was. He loved her metamorphosis. He appreciated the fact that it didn't happen overnight; he actually had been able to see the stages. Most of the changes had happed before they officially became an exclusive couple, but Jerome still had been around to see it. Something about seeing it made him value it more—made him value her more. Rocky wondered if he'd ever be so lucky, or as Jerome would define it: *blessed.*

By the time Holy Communion had taken place, and the benediction had been given, it was nearing three o'clock. Rocky shook a few hands when people began dispersing, but instead of heading for the door, like most did, he made himself comfortable in the pew. Ever since Jerome had become youth pastor, he was like a rock star with the members under the age of twenty-five. Rocky knew it would be a minute before they would be leaving.

"Hey, Rocky. How's it going?"

Rocky bounced to his feet and stood as straight as he could. "I'm good, Pete. How are you?" He accepted Peter's firm handshake. "Hi, Jan," he added, and placed a kiss on her cheek.

"Hi, Rocky." Jan grinned. "I'm still getting used to this new look of yours. You look like new money, boy."

"That's because I pay him well," Hunter said as he approached Rocky from behind and patted him on the shoulder before reaching around him to shake the hands of both Peter and Jan.

"Yeah, that must be it," Rocky said. He and Hunter hadn't talked much since their exchange at work last week. Conversation between the two of them had been kept to a bare minimum, with them only discussing work-related issues.

"How are things going for you at the newspaper?" Peter asked the question like he had been reading Rocky's thoughts. The inquiry caught Rocky off guard.

"Uh . . . okay, I guess. I'm still working on getting used to everything." He really didn't know how to answer the question in Hunter's presence. There was no telling what Hunter thought of his work ethics right now. They'd already clashed, and Rocky wasn't even out of his ninety-day probation period yet.

"He's doing great," Hunter said. Rocky was sure that everyone could see the surprise in his eyes at Hunter's declaration, but Hunter continued speaking. "Any man who can make the transformation from doing his own thing fixing cars to working in an environment as structured as the *AWC,* and manage to keep on task, is exceptional." Hunter gave Rocky's shoulder a squeeze, which Rocky found oddly encouraging.

"Thanks, man," he said. He looked down at his hands when he said it. Rocky didn't quite feel deserving of the generous compliment.

"Mama told me to tell y'all that she cooked dinner today and there's enough for everyone." All eyes migrated to Jan at the same time.

"You're kidding," Hunter said just as Jade joined them.

She leaned over and kissed Rocky's cheek. "Hi, Rocky." Then without skipping a beat, she looked at her husband. "Kidding about what?"

Rocky felt chills run down his spine. Jade was so pretty that it was ridiculous. He'd thought that from the moment he met her, but most days her natural striking beauty didn't affect him like today. It wasn't the first time she'd kissed his cheek either, and normally those didn't do to him what today's had done either. He was having a weak moment. He'd been having an increasing number of them lately. Rocky took a deep breath. *God, I need a woman.*

"Ms. Leona invited us over for dinner," Hunter answered.

"Oh." Jade looked away like something in the distance had suddenly become interesting.

"Come on, guys," Jan pleaded. She tapped Jade's arm. "I'd come to your mom's house for dinner if they extended an invitation."

"Not a good comparison, bay," Peter said. "Mother Tides can cook, *and* she's sane."

Jan slapped her husband's arm. "I can't even believe you said that. My mother can cook, thank you very much."

Rocky laughed, but when the others didn't join in, he wondered if they had missed the fact that Jan hadn't defended her mother's sanity, only her ability to cook.

"Come on, guys." She made her second bid. "Mama really likes you-all."

Rocky shook his head in protest. "She might like the two of them," he pointed to Jade, and then to Hunter, "but she don't like me. Every time she sees me, she starts quoting scriptures about how I'm going to hell if I don't get my tattoos removed."

"She quotes scriptures to everybody about everything," Jan defended. "That doesn't mean she doesn't like you."

"No," Peter said. "It just means she's crazy."

That got his arm slapped again by his wife. "Stop saying that."

Rocky noticed that Jan still didn't deny the accusation. "Thanks, but no thanks," he said. "I'm sorry, Jan, but I can't deal with your mother."

Jan released a heavy sigh, and then looked at Hunter. "Stuart said that he, Candice, and Tyler are going out to dinner, and Jerome and Ingrid, well . . ." She looked toward the platform. "We'll be finished eating by the time they're ready to leave the church. And Kenyatta can't stand Mama, so she wouldn't come, even if I paid her." Jan looked to be on the verge of desperation. "If I don't get somebody to join us, I'll never hear the end of it from Mom. Come on, Hunter. Will the two of you come?"

"Come on, man," Peter said. "You don't have to stay all afternoon, just eat with us."

"What?" Hunter challenged. "Aren't you the one who just called Ms. Leona crazy?"

"Yeah, but I don't have a choice but to go, and I need some backup. Jan and Kyla ain't no help. If I can get the two of you and Malik to come, then that'll help ease the pain." When his arm got hit for the third time, he turned to Jan and said, "I hope all of this spanking is leading to something."

Jan giggled. "Stop being bad. We're still in church."

Rocky bit the inside of his bottom lip. He needed to get away from all the married folks. Where was Jerome? Wasn't he ready to go yet?

"Well, let's round up the kids," Hunter said. "If we're gonna eat at Ms. Leona's, we may as well go ahead and get this party started."

"Thanks!" Jan embraced Jade as if she were the one who had accepted the invitation. "You sure you don't want to come, Rocky?"

"I ain't never been surer of nothing in my life." Rocky sat down on the pew to show his decision was final.

"Well, I'll see you at the office tomorrow," Hunter said.

"Yeah. Sure. I'll be there." Rocky watched the four-some maneuver around those who were still lingering. Service had been nearly three and a half hours long, and some of the people acted like they still hadn't gotten enough. Unfortunately, Jerome was one of those people. Rocky watched the youth pastor talk and laugh with a group of teens. Ingrid was by his side. She was definitely going to make a good first lady one day if Jerome ever took on the role of senior pastor.

Rocky crossed his right ankle over his left knee and sank deeper in his seat. *Jerome has his; Hunter has his; Pete has his. Where's mine?*

"Hi." When he looked in the face of the pretty lady who'd just spoken to him, Rocky had to blink twice to be sure it wasn't his imagination. The timing of her appearance was almost uncanny. "I wanted to speak to you before I left, but for a while there, you had a crowd around you."

"Hey, Lorna." Rocky finally found his voice and his manners. "What are you doing here?"

She laughed. "The same thing you're doing here, silly. I came for the service. It was good, huh?" She sat in the empty space beside him. The navy blue pantsuit that Lorna had on was the most conservative outfit that Rocky had ever seen her wear. Admittedly, the huge silver hoop earrings and the dozen or so thin silver bracelets that decorated her wrist cheapened it a little, but overall, it was a good look for her. Even her hair was quiet in comparison. It was very long today, but it was all one color, and she wore it pulled back into a clip. It reminded Rocky of the tails on Hunter's horses.

"Do you go to church here?" Rocky had never seen her at New Hope before, but he supposed with a congregation the size of theirs, it was possible to have overlooked her.

"I've been here before, but it's been a while. I was overdue for a visit, so I thought I'd do it today."

"Oh. Well, I'm glad you enjoyed it." Rocky fidgeted in his seat. She was sitting so close that their legs touched. He was already sitting against the edge of the pew, and there was nowhere to go.

"So why are you sitting here? Are you waiting to speak to the pastor?"

"No, I rode in with Jerome. I'm waiting on him and Ingrid."

Lorna stood. "I'll take you home if you like."

"Uh, no. I don't mind waiting. I don't want to put you out."

"I don't mind, Rocky, really. It doesn't make sense for you to sit here waiting when you have options."

Rocky looked toward the front of the church. He really was ready to go, and there were at least eight people still talking to Jerome and Ingrid. He took a quick look around and saw Tyler standing at the back door talking to other children his age. Rocky figured that he could have Tyler tell Jerome that he'd caught a ride. "Okay." He stood. "Thanks. I appreciate it."

"Don't thank me," Lorna said as they walked in the direction of the exit doors. "I'll enjoy the company."

Chapter Nine

"Kenyatta, you've been picking at your food ever since I put the plate in front of you. You don't like my tilapia?"

Kenyatta looked up from her plate. "Oh no, Candice. It's fine."

"Then why aren't you eating it? Did I go overboard on the lemon pepper? My mom says I always go overboard on the seasoning."

"Your mama doesn't know what she's talking about," Stuart said while taking in another mouthful. "This fish is off the hook, sweetness."

"You're just saying that."

"Oh . . . really?" Stuart used his fork to point at the empty space on his plate that two servings of tilapia once occupied.

"It really is good, Ms. Candice," Tyler said. His entire plate was almost clean.

Candice's smile was a satisfied one, but her eyes still carried a hint of concern when she looked at Kenyatta again. "There's some spaghetti in the refrigerator from yesterday. If you don't mind leftovers, I can reheat some of that for you."

It had taken Kenyatta a while to warm up to Candice Powell. She came into Stuart's life very shortly before he began being stalked by an unidentified person. After suspect after suspect was cleared, all arrows started pointing in Candice's direction, and for a while, many people, including Stuart, became more than a little suspicious of the woman he had met through a Christian online dating service. When Candice was finally cleared, she put Stuart through the wringer. He had fallen hard for the middle-school math teacher, but his distrust of her had placed him in a doghouse that was apparently located in somebody else's backyard. Candice wasn't hearing his barking or his begging. Kenyatta hadn't liked the cold treatment Candice gave her brother, but in the end, she had to put herself in Candice's shoes. When she did, Kenyatta realized that regardless of how apologetic Stuart had been, not only would he not have been able to talk to her then, but he wouldn't be able to talk to her now either—let alone sit at her table sharing a meal.

"You want the spaghetti?" Candice pressed. "I promise, it won't hurt my feelings if you toss this and choose to eat the pasta, instead."

Kenyatta shook her head from side to side. "No, Candice, the fish is good, really." She picked up some with her fork and placed it in her mouth to prove her point. "It's not the food. I just have a lot on my mind—that's all. Besides, we had spaghetti Friday and ate leftovers from that yesterday. Thanks for the offer, though."

Kenyatta hoped they could drop the subject, and when Stuart asked Candice something about how she was adjusting to the new school year, Kenyatta got her wish. Candice was always asking Stuart about the goings-on at the police station, and he was constantly becoming engrossed in her classroom tales. Candice was an educator to the core. It was very evident in her conversations that she really cared about enriching and cultivating children, and she thought very little else was more important. Kenyatta had heard her say more than once that if children got the education that they needed, then many of the world's problems would be nonexistent. She faulted ill-equipped schools and ill-prepared teachers for much of the shortcomings of today's youth. It was a stance that Kenyatta had known very few teachers to take.

Candice took it as a personal failure when she heard that a student she'd taught in middle school had given up and dropped out before finishing high school. She did the same when she read newspaper stories or heard news features that another teenager had been arrested for theft, rape, or murder. She felt as though teachers, along with parents, were the primary people who had been assigned by God to cut them off at the pass. Stuart had bragged once that Candice lived, breathed, and bled education. He thought her dedication was estimable. Kenyatta thought it was excessive.

Even her apartment looked like a schoolteacher's dwelling. Serving as the centerpiece of her coffee table was one of those big wooden apples that were normally found on teachers' desks. Her wall clock was in the shape of a school building, and just in case one would be confused about the nature of her livelihood after seeing those hints, there was a frame that sat on the entertainment shelf beside her flat-screen television that showcased the words "Teachers Do It Write," with a big yellow pencil serving as an underline for the word "write."

As extreme as Kenyatta thought it was, she couldn't help but also think it must be nice to be that passionate about a profession. It definitely wasn't her testimony.

"You gotta stop bringing work home with you, sis," Stuart said. Sometimes his timing was creepy. Apparently, he and Candice were done talking about education, and now the spotlight was being placed back on Kenyatta. Stuart pointed at her from across the table.

"You've been in a funk ever since you got home on Friday."

"Yeah, I know." Kenyatta agreed with him, but she knew full well that her job wasn't the real culprit. It was true that she was no fan of social work, and she had been unusually moody for the entire weekend, but the woes of her occupation paled in comparison to what she was dealing with. She wished she could explain it to her present company, but that would be impossible. Especially when she didn't quite understand it herself. Just a few days ago, she couldn't stand to think about Rocky. Now she couldn't stop thinking about him. He seemed so different the last time she saw him. It was more than the shaved beard. The clean-cut Rocky was definitely a more attractive Rocky, but there was more. Kenyatta just couldn't quite put her finger on it.

Whatever the defined difference, Kenyatta saw it again when he walked in church today. She'd seen Rocky dressed up before. He did it at least once a month on Sunday mornings. But today, the copper shirt and the mahogany pants set against his brown skin made Rocky look like three shades of chocolate. So much so that she'd actually licked her lips as she watched him and Ingrid head to their seats. Whereas Kenyatta had seen Rocky in dress attire before, she'd never noticed his swagger. There was a confidence and a command about his presence now. There was an air of sexiness to him that wasn't there before. Or maybe it was, and the beard had hidden it. When they had been standing in the kitchen together, there had been a moment when she wanted him to make a bold move. A kiss would have been nice. When he had that scruffy hair on his face, she would have gagged at the thought of it, but now . . .

"Do you want more, Tyler?" Candice's offer brought Kenyatta's mind back to the table, where her body sat.

"No, ma'am. I'm full."

"Does that mean you don't want dessert? It's brownies and ice cream."

"Yes, I want some."

"He ain't that full," Stuart added with a laugh. "You want me to help?" He made a move to stand when Candice began collecting empty plates from the table.

"No, you sit here. I'll bring dessert for both of you." Kenyatta felt the pressure of Candice's eyes when they settled on her. "What about you, Kenyatta? You want some brownies and ice cream?"

Brownies were her favorite. Any other day, she would have been craving them, but her stomach just wasn't being very cooperative today. She didn't want to hurt Candice's feelings, though. "Maybe just a little ice cream, but no brownie." Kenyatta noted the way both Stuart and Tyler looked at her. They knew her favorite dessert, and hearing her turn it down had shocked them. "One scoop of ice cream is fine," she added as Candice walked away.

"Tyler, why don't you go and help Ms. Candice," Stuart said.

"But she said she didn't need no help."

One look from his father must have been enough to let Tyler know that what originally sounded like a suggestion was actually an order. Without saying another word, Tyler stood and made his way to the kitchen.

"What's going on, sis?" Stuart wasted no time. "Something's up with you, and I get the feeling it has to do with more than work. So what's up? What's going on?"

Kenyatta wasn't surprised by the inquisition. She knew Stuart wasn't getting rid of Tyler just for kicks.

She and her brother had always been close. There were very few things in life that she didn't feel comfortable talking to him about. "Nothing, Stu. I'm fine." But this issue with Rocky was one of them. Kenyatta wasn't quite ready to face the truth about whatever it was she was feeling.

"No, you're not," Stuart charged. He was never one to give up easily, especially where Kenyatta was concerned. He was the one who finally pulled out of her the truth about Joe and the daily hell that his unfounded jealousy was putting her through. "I know you, Kenyatta. Remember that."

How could she forget? He reminded her every time they had one of these chats. She laid her fork on the napkin beside her plate. There was no need to continue the illusion of eating. Candice wasn't there to see it, anyway. "It's personal, Stuart, okay? I have something personal that I'm working through. If you don't mind, I'd like to work through it alone—at least for now."

Stuart sat back in his chair and held both hands up in surrender. Before either of them could say anything more, Candice and Tyler were returning with plates decorated in brown and white. All except Kenyatta's— hers had only the white.

"The brownies are still warm, so the ice cream is going to melt fast," Candice said.

Stuart cut into the moist cake with his fork and moaned when he put it in his mouth. "Sis, later on this evening, when we're back home and you've had some time to unwind, you're gonna want to kick your own self in the butt for not having any of this."

Kenyatta placed a spoonful of her ice cream in her mouth and forced a smile. She seriously doubted it. She'd be too busy trying to find the shoe she used when she stuck her foot up the butt of *that girl.* Who was she? And where were she and Rocky going when he got in the car with her after church today?

Chapter Ten

In the auto mechanic business, Rocky wasn't affected by the proverbial hill that was known by most as "hump day." When he worked on cars in his backyard, nothing stood out about Wednesday. As a matter of fact, if there was a hill to climb, it was on Fridays. That was the day when every vehicle that every person brought in *today* needed to be repaired by *yesterday* so that they could have a way to get around *tomorrow,* which was apparently the day when everything good happened.

At the *Atlanta Weekly Chronicles,* however, hump day happened on a weekly basis, and what a hump it was. Mondays, Tuesdays, Thursdays, and Fridays came with typical nine-to-five schedules. On those days, most of what had to be done lay in the laps of the staff writers, reporters, photographers, and those who did the actual layout of the paper. Wednesdays, Rocky had the option of catching a few more hours of sleep, because his official hump day work schedule was noon until eight. But, of course, he didn't sleep in late because Jerome had to be at work by nine, and if Rocky was going to arrive in clothes that passed Hunter's scrutiny, he had to catch a ride with Jerome. Well, he really didn't *have* to. There was another option, and it was called Metropolitan Atlanta Rapid Transit Authority, better known as MARTA. It was Atlanta's public transportation service, and almost half a million people used it every day.

The bus service had a stop that was conveniently located one block from Rocky's temporary housing and another stop directly across the street from the *AWC*. It would practically be a doorstep-to-doorstep commute, but as suitable as the service was for his needs, Rocky wasn't a fan of MARTA. Not that there was a problem with the transit system itself. It just so happened that Rocky was on one of those buses the day it was suddenly surrounded by black-and-white cars with flashing blue lights on top. Gun-toting policemen stormed the bus, and when all the heart-pounding, fit-for-the-six-o'clock-news mayhem was over, they carted off a handcuffed teenager who was suspected of playing a vital role in a murder that had taken place two nights earlier. That teenager was Rocky, and the subsequent twenty-two years he'd spent behind bars had resulted in a MARTA phobia that he just couldn't shake. He'd rather pass on the extra sleep and arrive at work three hours early than relive the memory.

The print run for the *Atlanta Weekly Chronicles* was only about a third of that of the *Atlanta Journal-Constitution,* the largest (and only) major daily newspaper in Atlanta. But last year, one of the news stations reported that the *AJC* overall had somewhere in the neighborhood of 2.2 million weekly readers, while the *AWC* had a staggering 2.6 million. That number included readers all over the world who either received the paper from the newsstand, on their doorstep, in their mailbox, or by means of modern technology. The database of online subscribers made up the largest portion of the *AWC* readership.

The popularity of Hunter's paper began skyrocketing about five years ago when he became the only paper providing continuing coverage on what was thought at the time to be the accidental death of New Hope's pastor, Rev. B. T. Tides. Hunter's paper had helped indirectly to solve the mystery of what turned out to be the popular pastor's kidnapping. His determination to make sure the full story was told not only credited him with saving the pastor's life, but it also netted him the heart of the pastor's daughter. Since that time, he'd had to add more square footage to the *AWC* building so that he could have the warehouse space needed to accommodate the workers who prepared the paper for its weekly distribution. It just seemed like heaven was never going to stop showering favor on the guy who had put everything on the line to save the man of God.

But all that favor came with a price, and it was called hard work. That was where Rocky and the others came into play. The paper had to be in print by seven on Wednesday evenings, so that the warehouse workers could have them prepared for pickup by two on Thursday afternoons, so that stands would have them on display by start of business on Friday mornings, and subscribers could have them in the mail by whatever time their postal carrier delivered on Saturdays. Everything had to work like a finely oiled piece of machinery, or everything would be thrown off schedule.

When Rocky first took the job, he thought it would be easy money. He could give orders to the three patsies that worked immediately under him, and they'd have to do all the work while he sat in his office, with his feet propped on the desk, and watched from the open door. Not so. Indeed, he was the in-charge person and gave the orders, but if anything went wrong, it was he, not them, that was under fire. And while he made more money than the pressmen, Rocky earned every penny—make no mistake about it. Whereas he had been sitting on his high horse during that first week relishing the thought that Myron, Brad, and Smitty were green with envy that Hunter had given him the job instead of offering it to one of them, Rocky now wondered to which local bar the threesome had gone to celebrate the dodging of the bullet.

Oddly enough, though, Rocky was starting to like it. *All* of it. Even the part that held him accountable for the success of his department. Something about knowing if his guys messed up, he'd get chewed out, made him feel good. Maybe it was the fact that Rocky also knew if they did well, his back was the one that got patted; and the latter had happened far more than the former over the past month. Rocky made sure it did. Every week he challenged the pressroom to a higher standard, which meant he had to hold himself to one too. To show his workers that he wasn't trying to abuse his power, Rocky began bringing a change of clothing to work every Wednesday. If he felt that any of the guys were running out of steam on hump day, he changed into clothes that allowed him to climb the hill with them. This week, the printed matter didn't just meet the 7:00 P.M. Wednesday deadline, it beat it by half an hour. The job wasn't just done fast; it was done right. When he walked into the building on Thursday morning, everybody was patting him on the back.

"Are you gunning for a pay raise?" Hunter joked after inviting both Rocky and Jerome into his office. "You don't qualify for one of those at any time before your probation is over, you know."

Rocky didn't care for the term "probation" just because of what it meant in the legal sense, but he had gotten used to hearing it used at work. He took the liberty of sitting in the leather chair beside where Jerome stood, looking through a folder that he'd picked up from Lorna's desk on the way in. "Well, by that time, maybe my house will be finished. If so, a raise would be nice 'cause it would come just in time for me to buy additional stuff for the house that I didn't have before. That insurance money is only gonna replace the stuff that I lost."

Jerome looked up from his paperwork. "He ain't trying to get no raise, Hunter. He's just trying to make me look bad. I worked as a press operator before I was press foreman, and it still took me how long to get the hang of the job?"

"Yeah, it did take you a minute." Hunter looked thoughtful. "As a matter of fact, it even took you the longest to get the hang of the press operator duties." He shook his head. "I don't think I ever told you this, man, but if I hadn't been trying to impress your sister, I would've fired you."

Rocky laughed out loud. What Hunter said was funny enough, but the expression of total shock and injury that was displayed on Jerome's face was even funnier.

Jerome slapped the back of Rocky's head with the folder. "I'm glad we were able to give you your comedy break early this morning. Ain't you got work to do?"

"Good morning, everybody." A knock to the door frame accompanied Lorna's chipper salutation. All of the men looked in her direction, but only two of them returned the greeting. Rocky hadn't meant not to speak, but the words just wouldn't come. "Here's your coffee, Hunter, and here are a few standout letters from readers that you might want to consider for print in next week's paper." She placed the steaming cup in the center of her boss's desk, then handed him the opened envelopes.

"Thanks, Lorna." Hunter accepted the small stack. "By the way, I may be getting a call from the West Street Nursing Home in Macon, Georgia, this morning. If I do, please put it through to me."

"Will do, boss," she said as she turned to leave. "Hope your luck is better than mine when it comes to *expected calls.*"

The air in the office was thick for several moments after Lorna left. Rocky stared at the surface of Hunter's desk and rolled his tongue around the inside of his mouth, trying to keep it from drying out completely. He couldn't quite bring himself to look up. He wanted to believe that the guys were quiet because they couldn't make sense of what Lorna had just said, but his gut feeling was that they were quiet because they at least had some idea of what she was insinuating.

"Pull that door shut, Jerome."

That alone meant trouble. Hunter had an open-door policy. His office door was rarely closed, unless he was in a business meeting, on a private phone call, or unless somebody was in trouble. The last time the door was closed with Rocky inside was the last day he drove his motorcycle to work. Back then, he was in trouble for arriving in wrinkled, sweaty clothes. Now he had a whole new set of problems. Jerome barely had carried out the order, when Hunter started in.

"What have you done?"

Rocky still hadn't looked up, but he knew the question was for him. He rubbed his chin and took a breath. "I haven't done anything."

"Don't lie to me, Rocky. Is there something going on with you and Lorna that we don't know about?"

"Man, what is your problem!" Rocky sprang to his feet in indignation. "Is there something going on with *you* and Lorna that we don't know about?"

"Who? Huh? What?" Jerome turned his head so fast that Rocky was surprised he didn't give himself whiplash. His eyes were wide, and they were aimed directly at his brother-in-law, but Hunter's sights were set on Rocky.

"Have you totally lost your mind?" The words poured out of Hunter's mouth at the speed of molasses, and the volume of his voice was lowered, but his fury wasn't lost in any of it.

"I might not be the smartest kid on the block, but I ain't stupid, and I ain't blind," Rocky replied. "Every time you see any kind of interaction going on between me and her, you got something to say. Like when we were talking in the break room that day, and you rolled up in there talkin' . . . *smack*." Deliverance from profanity hadn't happened overnight for Rocky, but that was the closest he'd come to slipping up in quite some time. "I know when I see a man marking his territory."

"What the . . . " Jerome dropped the file he'd been holding on top of the desk. Then looking at Hunter, he said, "Okay, dude, you betta start talkin', and you betta start talkin' fast."

Rocky looked at Jerome. That was a pretty close call too. From the sound of it, his mouth wasn't the only one that God was still working on.

Hunter glared at Jerome like a rabid pit bull. Rocky had never seen him so angry. Hunter literally looked like he was about to detonate at any moment. His normal brown skin was two shades short of being beet red, and he was visibly shaking. "Man, sit yo' . . . " He clenched his teeth and his fists. "Sit down!"

He wasn't even talking to Rocky, but he sat too. Maybe all three of them needed to get special prayer this coming Sunday. When enough anger got in the mix, tongue taming, he saw, didn't come easy. Not even to seasoned Christians like Hunter. Before he spoke again, Hunter walked up and down the length of the floor space behind his desk. It was obvious that he was trying to get his emotions in check. After a few paces, he turned and locked eyes with Rocky.

"Marking my territory? Are you kidding me?" Rocky squirmed in his chair. "My territory?" Hunter repeated the words, and then coughed out a bitter laugh. "Lorna's not my territory; she's everybody's territory." He turned his eyes toward Jerome. "And you should know that better than anybody. I'm about the only man in this whole company that she *hasn't* been with."

Rocky's face slowly turned toward his best friend. If he hadn't already made up his mind not to pursue a relationship with her, that tidbit of information would have sealed it for sure. "You dated Lorna?"

"No," Jerome said. "I didn't date her. I just . . . *did* her. It was one time. One stupid mistake I made when I first started working here." He looked at Hunter. "And I never would've told you if I thought you'd have the audacity even to think about telling somebody else."

"Yeah, well, I never would have told anybody else if you hadn't had the audacity to think I would cheat on Jade."

"How come you didn't tell me you messed with Lorna?" Rocky still couldn't believe it.

Jerome shrugged his shoulders. "I don't know. I didn't see no reason, I guess. I mean, I would've told you if I'd known you were messing with her, but you didn't tell me that. So how was I supposed to know?"

Rocky settled back in his seat. Jerome was right. He hadn't made his interest in Lorna known to anyone. He had no one to blame.

Hunter sank in his chair and placed both elbows on the top of his desk. "Lorna's a man-eater, Rocky. She's the love-'em-and-leave-'em type. I wasn't trying to protect her when I interrupted that little meeting you both were having in the break room. I was trying to protect *you*." He sighed heavily, almost like it was burdensome to say his next words. "How far has it gone?"

Rocky looked from Hunter to Jerome. Suddenly it felt as though they were at Arizona's following one of their Hope for Men meetings, talking about the stuff they didn't necessarily want to divulge in front of the entire body of church brothers. Only there was no good food to enjoy while they conversed. "What do you mean?" Rocky knew full well what Hunter meant; it just seemed like the right question to ask.

"Did you sleep with her?"

"No."

"Rocky—"

"I didn't." Rocky was glad that he could say it in truth. "She wanted to, but it didn't happen."

"How do you know she wanted to? What gave you that idea?" Hunter was slipping into psychotherapist mode.

"She told me." Rocky saw Jerome's face snap in his direction. That was probably the same way it played out with him.

Hunter spoke again. "So she wanted to, but you knew it was wrong, so you said no and left?"

Rocky released a soft chuckle. "If I ever write the book, that's the way I'm gonna write it, but no, that's not the way it happened." A part of him was ashamed to admit the details, especially now that he knew the man who had once prided himself on being the playa had almost gotten played. But a larger part of Rocky was glad to release the guilt he'd been carrying for the past few days. "She wanted to, and I wanted to. We started messing around a little bit . . . Okay, a lot, but we didn't have sex."

"How far did it get, Rocky?" Hunter pressed. "It doesn't have to be intercourse to be sex, you know. Just because you didn't drive all the way to Florida doesn't mean you didn't drive."

Rocky shook his head. "We didn't drive at all. We got in the car, started the engine, maybe even shifted into gear, but we didn't ever press the gas. There was no driving."

"Man, what y'all talkin' 'bout?" Jerome asked.

Hunter sank back in his chair. "He's a mechanic. He knows cars. I had to put it in a way that he would find relatable."

"He's also a grown man," Jerome said. "You couldn't just ask him straight up?"

"Shut up," Hunter said. "I'm still peeved at you."

Jerome turned to Rocky. "Did all of this happen when she gave you a ride home from church last Sunday?" Jerome asked.

Hunter sat up straight again. "Last Sunday? Lorna was at church Sunday?"

Rocky nodded. "Yeah, but that's not when it happened. We did go out and grab a bite to eat Sunday, but she took me home after that. I went by her house on Tuesday evening. That's when this happened."

Jerome looked at him. "I thought you went to Stuart's to get more help with your class assignment on Tuesday."

"I did, but she called me while I was there and asked me to come by. So when I left Stuart's, I went to see her."

"And what time was that?" Hunter asked.

"I don't know, a little after ten, I think. It was close to eleven when I got to her place."

Hunter tapped his desk. "And it didn't dawn on you that an invitation that time of night couldn't have good intentions?"

Rocky could lie, but why start now? "I knew what kind of call it was. As a matter of fact, that's the kind of call I was hoping it was." He stood and shoved his hands in his pockets. "Man, it's been five months, and I'm starting to feel like a drug addict who needs a fix. And please don't give me the God-ain't-pleased speech. I know He's not, but that don't change the facts. This living-saved thing . . . Well, it ain't easy."

Hunter stood too. "Of course not, Rocky. If it was easy, everybody would do it. It's not easy for any of us."

"Amen," Jerome interjected.

"I was once a single man too," Hunter added. "You think I didn't have wants and needs? I did, and I wish I could say I made all the right choices all the time, but I can't. But one thing I know for sure is that whereas living saved ain't easy, it's the right thing to do. It's worth the wait, man. Take it from me. It's worth the wait. And whether you know it or not, God *is* pleased with you." Hunter rounded his desk and stood beside Rocky. "We know where you've come from, Rocky. You've told us the stories. You were the equivalent of a sex addict before you came to Christ. So while giving it up cold turkey might be no great sacrifice for some, it was astronomical for you, and it's a testimony of your dedication to Christ and your desire to do His will. You may have bent when it came to Lorna, but you didn't break. You did the right thing in the end, and God is *very* pleased with that."

Rocky nodded slowly, but traces of guilt still remained. "Yeah, but now I gotta look in her face every day. Man, I saw parts of that woman that I ain't had no business seeing. My hands touched places on her that they ain't had no business touching." He looked at his open hands, and then balled them into fists like he was trying to squeeze away the memories of what his hands had felt.

"Helloooo!" Jerome sang out. "I went all the way, and you're worried about *you* having to look in her face?"

He stood too. "Rocky, we have all sinned and fallen short of God's glory. You can't wallow in it, and you can't let guilt beat you down. The only face we have to worry about looking into is Jesus'. What you need to do is make sure you get it straight with Him. Bump Lorna. Believe me when I tell you that she's resilient. Give her a few days, and she'll move on to her next prey."

Rocky turned to Hunter. "I don't understand it. You run this tight ship, but you've got a secretary who's throwing herself at the whole crew. Why do you keep somebody like that working for you?"

"All I require of anyone here is that you do your job, and you do it well. Lorna might be loose outside of this office, but inside these four walls, she's the best secretary I've ever had. She does an exceptional job, and I'm not going to fire her because all of you can't resist her charm. Besides . . . Lorna's got a soul just like everybody else. I believe she's going to be brought to Christ before it's over, but that's not gonna happen if I throw her out. In order for her to be brought to the Cross, she has to stay here, and she's got to see living examples, and she has to see that she's good for more than a romp. She needs to see men like me . . . like *us* who see her as more than a piece, so that she'll know she's more than a piece. I believe if more of us live a Christian life before her, she'll start to see the God in us. And if we don't show her Christ, that's not her fault—not even if she walks to your front door butt naked at midnight.

"We're all grown men, and we're responsible for our own actions. When she first started working here, she was hitting on me. I set the boundaries, and she hasn't crossed them since. You both are going to have to learn to draw some lines too, in *ink*. Because you know what? You won't be able to fire or avoid every woman who wants to get with you." He looked at Jerome then.

"Even after you're married, they will still be around. Salvation doesn't kill the desires of your flesh, but God gives us the power not to fall prey. You need to identify your weaknesses, and let the Holy Spirit guide you on how to handle them."

Rocky sighed. "In that case, tell Jade that the Holy Spirit said for her not to kiss me on my cheek after service on Sundays."

Chapter Eleven

Unlike the Hope for Men ministry, which met once each month, its counterpart, Women of Hope, met every Thursday night. The specialized women's ministry was three or four times the size of the men's; largely because, as was the case with most churches, the female population at New Hope far outnumbered the male. Even with the prison ministry that a section of the men's ministry headed, Women of Hope was a more active entity of the church. They fed the homeless during holidays, collected school supplies for less fortunate children, and volunteered at nursing homes around the city. Their activity called for them to meet more often than the men.

Kenyatta yawned as she sat in the church parking lot with her seat in a reclined position. In ten minutes, the clock on her console would strike seven. The forty-five-minute power nap she'd gotten had done her body good. Instead of going home first, as she normally did before coming to the meetings, she'd left work and headed straight to the church. Traffic reporters warned of a three-car accident on I-285 that had afternoon commuters sitting in traffic that crept on that portion of the highway. Even the surface streets were cluttered as people tried to detour around the mess. Kenyatta expected a nightmare when she hit the pinpointed area, so to ensure that she wouldn't be late arriving at the women's meeting, she decided not to go home first.

By the time she reached the reported trouble spot, the accident had been cleared and traffic was flowing again. As a result, she'd arrived early.

Kenyatta had a gym membership she used so seldomly, it was a waste of money on her part. Well, really not on her part. The membership was through Stuart's job. The gym gave deep discounts to men and women in uniform, as long as the uniform was that of a policeman, fireman, doctor, nurse, or military servant. She kept gym clothes in her trunk just in case she had a rare craving to exercise. A stop at the gym was also an option she could have used in order to kill time before the ministry meeting. A nap sounded far more appealing, though, so that was the alternative she chose.

A few vehicles were already in the lot when Kenyatta arrived. Most of them she didn't recognize, but she identified Hunter's SUV and Jade's car right away. They were parked in neighboring spaces close to the entrance of the church. Hunter was such the model husband. Kenyatta admired his and Jade's relationship, but some days, she envied it too. What did women like Jade have that she didn't? Was it physical, or was it spiritual? Maybe it was both . . . or maybe it was neither. After all, Jade's dad was one of the most admired preachers in the United States. That alone probably made her more appealing to a man like Hunter—the praying, successful, romantic type. For a moment, the thought that having a nationally known preacher for a father had given Jade the leg up gave relief to Kenyatta. There was no way she could compete with that, so there was no shortcoming on her part; Jade had just been lucky. The moment of reprieve was fleeting. What about Jan? Her dad wasn't prominent, and her mother was a certified dingbat. So what was it about her that drew the strong, attentive, heroic type like

Peter? And what was it, then, about Candice that had Stuart—the smart, protective, creative type—hooked by the nostrils?

Even *her*. What was it about *her* that had Rocky sitting in the church pew last Sunday talking to and laughing with *her,* and then climbing into the front seat of *her* car shortly thereafter? For a while, Kenyatta had put Rocky in the same wastebasket as Jerome. As far as she was concerned, neither of them deserved her, but something was different now and it was a good kind of different. What was it about that woman that had Rocky—the sexy, adventurous, athletic type—all but ignoring Kenyatta when he came over Tuesday evening? Now that Rocky had improved on Kenyatta's scale, she wasn't even worth his arguing with anymore. Stuart helped Rocky write his paper, and then he was gone. No nagging, no teasing, no taunting, nothing. Kenyatta's intuition told her that the woman in the navy blue suit had a lot to do with that. Was he going to see *her* when he left their house?

"Well, are you going to join us or what?"

The muffled voice and the knock on Kenyatta's closed window nearly scared her to death. When she looked toward her driver's window, she spotted Candice having a good laugh at her expense. She must have noticed the way Kenyatta flinched when the knocking first startled her. Kenyatta turned off the engine of her car, grabbed her Coach bag and Bible, and opened her door.

"Did I scare you?" Candice was still laughing.

"You wouldn't think it was so funny if I had pulled out my gun and shot you in the face," Kenyatta said as she pressed the remote that activated the security on her car. "When people sneak up on me, I'm inclined to shoot now and ask questions later."

Candice slipped her arm through Kenyatta's. "You wouldn't do that. Your brother and nephew would never recover."

"Whatever," Kenyatta mumbled, but she knew Candice was right. Stuart had it bad for this one, and Tyler, poor thing, was just about as in love with Candice as his dad was. If they weren't father and son, and Tyler was about twenty-five years older, he'd probably be his dad's greatest rival.

Once inside the church, they spoke to the short woman who manned the welcome desk as they signed in, then headed toward the classroom. Kenyatta never did care much for that woman. She couldn't have been more than five feet tall, but she was always holding her head down and looking over the rims of her eyeglasses at people like she was some nosy schoolteacher. Don't let it be that one of them dared to show up in the middle of the week and ask to speak to Reverend Tides without first having made an appointment. She'd look at them over those glasses of hers like if they didn't have the title of pope, prime minister, or president, they had a better chance of getting a sit-down meeting with Jesus Christ than with Reverend Tides.

"Hi, ladies." Jade welcomed them with a smile, as always, but the smile didn't reach beyond her lips tonight. The glee that Kenyatta was accustomed to seeing in her eyes was absent. Hunter was standing beside her when they entered. He looked a bit concerned too. Was there trouble in paradise?

"I guess I'm out," he said, and then planted a kiss on his wife's lips. She was receptive, but Kenyatta could still tell that something was wrong. Hunter looked at her and Candice. "You ladies be good, and don't trash us too bad, okay?"

"What makes you think we'd spend our time trashing y'all?" Candice asked. "Is that what you-all do to us in your meetings?"

"Of course not." Hunter immediately pasted an exaggerated smile on his face after saying it. Then he turned his attention to Jade and sobered. He reached out and tweaked her chin. "Perk up, babe. It's gonna be okay. I promise."

"I know. I'm fine. I'll see you later on. You're going over to Stuart's, right?"

That got Kenyatta's full attention. She didn't know her brother had anything special going on.

"Yeah," Hunter said. "We're helping the boys with some of the research for their Shelton Heights project, but it's a school night, so we won't be out too late. I'm sure you and your girls will be going out to eat or something after the meeting is over. So by the time you get home, Malik and I will probably be back. Don't worry about Leah. I'll pick her up from your parents' house on my way home. You just take care of you."

"Thanks, sweetheart."

"No problem, babe." He leaned in and kissed her again. "Call me if you need anything."

Kenyatta waited until Hunter closed the door behind his exit; then she said, "I think I just got two cavities watching that whole exchange."

Jade laughed. "You are just too stupid."

Their touches and kisses were still as sugary as ever, but there was still something wrong. Kenyatta wanted to dig deeper, but the arrival of more women wouldn't allow it. When the women had problems, Jade was always the one toward whom they naturally gravitated. Now Jade had a difficulty of her own, and Kenyatta's curiosity was piqued. She didn't *want* for there to be discord between Hunter and Jade, but she couldn't deny that knowing there was intrigued her. Kenyatta followed Candice to the chairs to grab a good seat before it got too crowded. She supposed she'd just have to wait until after the meeting to find out what flaw had stripped Hunter of his unofficial title of Mr. Perfect.

A horse? Kenyatta couldn't believe she'd waited two whole hours for this.

"Well, don't you like any of the others?" Jan's voice was very sympathetic. "I mean, there has to be at least twenty other horses in the pasture, Jade. Surely, this one isn't the only one you liked."

Jade grabbed a chip from the basket in the middle of the table and twirled it in Applebee's specialized salsa. "No, Spirit isn't the only horse I like, but she's the only one I love." After all that twirling, Jade dropped the chip on her plate and left it there. "I can't believe Hunter sold her."

"I can't believe you're making all this fuss over a horse," Ingrid blurted out.

Kenyatta looked at her. Of all of them, Ingrid was closest to Jade. If any of them could feel Jade's pain, Kenyatta expected it to be Ingrid. Instead, Ingrid's reaction was more like one that Kenyatta would have expected from herself. It was like Ingrid had reached into Kenyatta's head and became a mouthpiece for her thoughts. That was frightening, seeing that she and Ingrid weren't really what one would call friends. The only real reason that they spent any time together at all was because their friends were friends, thereby forcing them to hang in the same circles.

"I don't expect you to understand, Ingrid," Jade said, "but can you at least pretend you care?"

"I do care, Jade, but it's a *horse*," Ingrid stressed. "You're moping around like the man sold one of your kids."

"Oh yeah?" Jade plopped her elbow on the surface of the table so hard that the whole thing shook. "Remember Anastasia?"

Ingrid's bottom lip dropped like she couldn't believe Jade would take it there. "That's not a fair comparison. She didn't get sold. She got run over."

Ingrid looked like she was about to cry, and as Kenyatta reached for her glass, she actually felt sorry for her. Ingrid was right. That wasn't nearly the same thing. Kenyatta couldn't believe an expert psychologist like Jade would actually compare the pain that came with the death of a beloved pet to what came after the sale of livestock.

"What was Anastasia, a cat?" Candice asked.

"A doll," Jade spat out. "A stupid Raggedy Ann doll!"

Kenyatta grabbed her napkin and covered her mouth just in time. Had it not been for her quick reflexes, sweet tea would have showered the table and ruined everybody's meal and probably their appetites as well. The other women laughed too; at least, Candice and Jan did. Jade still looked frustrated, and Ingrid still looked near tears.

"Sorry," Kenyatta said as she composed herself. "Just wasn't expecting that."

"It's still not the same thing," Ingrid said. "Anastasia was a family heirloom. And she wasn't a Raggedy Ann. She was a handmade original. I watched with my own eyes as my grandmother sewed that doll."

"And I watched with my own eyes as Spirit's mother give birth to her," Jade shot back. "You cried for two straight weeks after that crazy ex-boyfriend of yours took Anastasia out in your backyard and used your own lawn mower to make pillow stuffing out of her. Can't I get just two days to mourn for Spirit?"

"Can we please change the subject?" Kenyatta dabbed at the water that had accumulated in the corners of her eyes during her laugh.

"Please do," Candice said.

"Fine by me" was Jade's reply. She picked up the same chip that she'd dipped in the salsa earlier and shoved it in her mouth. For a while, the table was quiet.

"Let's talk about this project that the kids are working on," Candice suggested.

"Well, I don't know much about it," Jan said, "but it must be pretty exciting. It started out being a project that just Malik and Tyler were working on, but a couple of nights ago, Kyla was on the telephone telling Malik about some information that she'd found."

The change of subject seemed to brighten Jade a bit. "It's not just the kids who are getting into it. Malik told Hunter that Old Man Heights had a living uncle, a man who was almost one hundred years old, who was in a nursing home somewhere. Hunter checked it out and found it to be true. A couple of days ago, he was trying to get an interview or something with the man that he could print in the paper."

Kenyatta didn't see the big deal. "Is that really print-worthy news?"

"Yeah," Jade said. "When Mr. Heights died, they said he had no living relatives to leave his fortune to. He had a will, and in his will, he left everything to his son. Well, nobody ever knew of any son, and no one ever stepped forth to claim the status of his son."

Jan flipped her wrist. "From everything I've heard, the man was senile. He had a lot of money, so if he actually had a son, believe you me, even if he'd never been in Shelton Heights's life before, he would have risen to the occasion then."

"I never heard that he was crazy," Kenyatta said, "what I heard was that he was a witch, or a warlock . . . or whatever they're called nowadays. They say he lived in that big old house all by himself. All that money he had, and he chose to live in an old house while other people lived in brand-new housing in a community that he paid to have built."

"That alone says he was senile," Jan pointed out. "What person in his right mind would do something like that?"

Ingrid snickered. "If they look under the floorboards of his house, they just might find his son . . . or, at least, what's left of him."

"*Ewww*. Can we change the subject again?" Candice asked.

Jade took a French fry off Ingrid's plate, dipped it in ketchup, and then placed it in her mouth. Just like that, they were friends again. "They tore that house down a long time ago, anyway."

"So what happened to the money?" Kenyatta asked. "And since the old man is dead, who's getting the money that we pay in mortgage every month?"

Ingrid tapped the table with her fingernail. "If a person dies and doesn't have living relatives, the money goes to the state, right?"

"Maybe it would if they didn't have a will," Jade said. "Mr. Heights had a will."

"But the person he left everything to doesn't exist," Jan said. "And doesn't that make it null and void?"

"Under normal circumstances, maybe," Candice said. "And this is why I don't necessarily think Shelton Heights was senile. According to what Tyler and Malik say, he didn't just leave everything to his son. He left it to his son and his son's offspring, and he gave them twenty years to claim it."

"What?" That was about the most ridiculous thing Kenyatta had ever heard.

Jade nodded to indicate that Candice was telling the truth. "He sure did. And because it's a legally binding will, it has to be honored. He named the bank as the responsible party, so not only is all of the money he had when he died sitting in some bank vault somewhere, but all the money that has been paid in mortgage to the bank for Mr. Heights's property is being placed in the vault too."

Jan let out a low whistle. "Can you imagine how much money is in there by now? I wish Pete were his son."

Ingrid shook her head. "Well, the state is gonna be in for a nice bundle when this nonexistent heir of his never shows up."

"I think some of that money should be dumped into children's services." Kenyatta knew her thoughts were selfish, but they really could use the funding.

"Or to raise our pitiful pay as public-school teachers," Candice said, looking out for her profession as well. After a thoughtful pause, she added, "I'm sure they've already earmarked it for whatever they're gonna use it for. According to the pictures that Tyler took of Mr. Heights's headstone the other day when Rocky took him out there to get more visuals for their display board, that twenty-year grace period will be up in just a few months."

Kenyatta chewed on the inside of her bottom lip and robotically stared down at her near-empty plate. The mention of Rocky's name sent her mind drifting elsewhere.

"Can you imagine dying and leaving that kind of loot behind?" Jan laughed. "I wonder if Rocky felt like he was walking on greener grass when they stepped near Old Man Heights's headstone."

"I wonder if he took his shoes off." In an exaggerated Southern accent, Jade added, "Rich folks don't take kindly to you tramping dirt in their carpet."

"I wonder if something's going on between him and that lady he got in the car with after church on Sunday." When the laughter at the table came to an abrupt hush, Kenyatta held her breath. That was just a thought in her head, right? She hadn't said that out loud, had she? In slow motion, she raised her head and looked around the table. Every eye was on her. *Oh my God . . . I did.*

Chapter Twelve

With a tired moan, Rocky sat up in bed. It was Saturday morning, and he shouldn't have been so lethargic. It was the one day of the week that he could sleep in as long as he wanted. No work and no church. Nothing to force him up one minute sooner than he desired, but sleep hadn't been his friend last night. In fact, Rocky hadn't had a night like last night since he first moved into Jerome's house. Then it was the anger and disbelief of his burned house that had kept him awake. This time, sleep escaped him for a different reason.

By far, yesterday evening wasn't the first time he'd ended a relationship with a woman. As a matter of fact, Rocky was a pro at it, but something about last night's experience was different. Probably because it was the first time he'd felt bad about it. Rocky wasn't even sure why he felt so worthless. If he were going to have to wake up in the morning feeling this guilty, he might as well have done something last night to justify it. His conscience might have felt bad, but at least his flesh would be satisfied. There was no sense in both his mind and body being jacked up.

Hunter called her a man-eater, and Jerome had assured Rocky that she'd be fine and would move on with ease. The way Lorna went off on him last night, Rocky wondered if they were both wrong. She wasn't fitting Rocky's definition of the love-'em-and-leave-'em type. They had only spent a couple of evenings together—once for dinner and the other for what almost turned out to be dessert—but Lorna acted as though Rocky had led her on. Like he'd made her believe they had a future, and then dropped her once he got what he wanted from her. Rocky hadn't even come close to getting what he wanted. The calendar on the wall told him that it had been months since he'd gotten what he wanted.

He was starting to wonder if people were interpreting the scriptures right. He was a grown man in his forties, for Pete's sake. God couldn't really expect a grown man in his forties to go without. Rocky was starting to have his doubts about other things too, like Jerome and Stuart, for starters. Were they *really* keeping it zipped, as they professed? They actually had women, *pretty* women with whom they spent "alone time" on a weekly basis. They took these women to dark movie theaters and candlelight dinners . . . There were even times when they just hung out at their ladies' homes. It was just the two of them, together—no one else around, by themselves—in a whole house that had a perfectly good bedroom, with a perfectly good bed sitting in the middle of it. How could they be dating women who looked like Ingrid and Candice, and were as sweet and attentive to them as Ingrid and Candice, and not be getting any? Something just wasn't adding up. Last night, Lorna was looking like a madwoman while she cussed him out. However, even in the middle of her attempt to emasculate him verbally, Rocky was asking himself why he wouldn't just go for it.

He swung his feet over the side of the mattress and planted them firmly on the floor. There was no use in trying to go to sleep now. Maybe getting out and doing something would help. He hadn't gone to check on his house in two days. During the week, it was hard to find the time now that he had the job at the *AWC*. Between his online classes and work, Rocky was both mentally and physically tired at the end of the day. Stuart had been a lifesaver. Writing had never been a strong point for Rocky, but the course was made much more bearable because of Stuart, who just happened to have a knack for creative writing. Last night, Rocky was able to kill two birds with one stone. Candice was visiting, and as a math teacher, she was able to give some insight on the next subject he would be required to tackle. Stuart told him that Kenyatta had gone to take Tyler to Hunter's house, where he'd be spending the night, so there was no one there for Rocky to fight with. It was just as well. Lorna made up for it quite capably.

Rocky's feet felt heavy as he made his way down the hall toward the bathroom. A lukewarm shower would do him good. Jerome was either asleep or gone. Rocky didn't bother to check to see which, but he'd place his money on the latter. Rarely did Jerome sleep in on Saturdays. Mrs. Tides always got up early on Saturdays and cooked a big breakfast that she not only invited, but expected her children to share in. Must be nice to have that kind of love within a family. Rocky knew that the door was open for him to join them. Both Reverend and Mrs. Tides had made that very clear. He'd taken them up on it two or three times, but not since moving in with Jerome. He was grateful that the Tideses extended every opportunity for him to feel like a part of the family, but sometimes gatherings like those had a conflicting effect on Rocky. They just reminded him of what he'd never had . . . and never would have.

By the time he stepped out of the shower, Rocky had mentally penciled in two things on his day's agenda. He'd go to the gym to get in a good workout, and then he'd go and check on the progression of his house. The decision to go to the gym had made the decision to take a shower seem senseless. He was going to have to do it all back over again after his run, but the shower he'd just taken wasn't a total waste of time. It had washed away a little of the tiredness. Rocky would make up for the lost sleep tonight. There was a chance of a thunderstorm passing through the area this evening. Some people feared the combination of lightning, thunder, and rain, but Rocky got some of his best sleep during unfavorable weather conditions.

On his way to the kitchen, he used his knuckles to rap on Jerome's door. After getting no answer, he peeked inside. Just as he knew it would be, the bed was made and the room was empty. Rocky closed the door, then finished his mission of grabbing a banana from the kitchen counter and filling his twenty-ounce pop-cap drinking cup with water. It was his favorite cup. It was black and red with the Atlanta Falcons logo on one side and an image of Michael Vick, the team's former lead quarterback, on the other. Rocky didn't care what anybody said. He still liked the man.

It only took Rocky a few minutes to put on his Nike workout gear. He shoved a change of clothing in his gym bag and securely strapped the bag to the back of his motorcycle walking out of the house, into the garage and locking the door behind him. The ride to the gym took about twenty minutes. The company had two facilities that were closer to Jerome's house than the one Rocky decided to go to, but this one was the state of the art and had the latest cardio equipment and a larger weight room.

Rocky placed his bag in a locker in the men's room, and then headed for the only treadmill that wasn't in use. Saturday was probably the busiest day at the gym, and machines that were normally vacant weren't. With his water bottle in its slot, Rocky strapped his MP3 player on his arm and set the speed that would pace him at a full jog. It had been a while since he ran. Normally, whether he worked out at home or at the gym, the weight room was his choice. Today, the more he ran, the more he wanted to run. It felt good. Forty minutes in, Rocky was sweating so heavily that his shirt clung to his skin. In the middle of the twelfth track that played on his MP3, the treadmill automatically began slowing down. That meant that he had been running for a solid hour. Although Rocky felt like he'd had a good workout, he wasn't overly winded or tired. In fact, he felt less tired now than he did when he first woke up.

Satisfied with what he had accomplished, and anxious to get to the construction site, Rocky chose not to enter the weight room. Instead, once the belt on the treadmill came to a complete stop, he picked up his water bottle and prepared to head to the showers. In his haste, he blindly backed into the person who was apparently trying to grab the treadmill he was vacating.

"Oops . . . sorry."

"No, I'm . . ."

At the sight of his crash victim, Rocky grinned and used his hand towel to wipe away sweat from his face. She looked rather cute in no makeup, and her hair pulled back into a ponytail. "Well, well, well. Hey, Kenyatta."

"Rocky."

His name had never sounded so cold. He noticed that she was in athletic shoes rather than the heels that he was accustomed to seeing her wear, and the ten-inch difference in their height was more evident than ever. "What are you doing here?" he asked.

"Exercising, just like you."

Rocky chuckled. "Somehow I never figured you to be the exercising type." He saw the offense when it blanketed her face, but she didn't give him time to defend what he'd said.

"What's that supposed to mean? Is that some kind of crack at my weight?"

"That's not what I meant at all," he replied. "Ain't nothing wrong with your weight. I just meant that working out causes most of us to sweat, and I never figured you to be the sweating type. You know . . . with the perfect hair and all. But I see you took it down." In the back of his mind, Rocky wondered if it was a growin or a sew-in. If it were weave, her beautician deserved an award.

"I have an appointment later to get it done, so you can stop picking. It'll be together again by the end of the day."

Rocky looked at her and shook his head. He'd always been told that he had a chip on his shoulder, but Kenyatta had him beat by a mile. "I wasn't picking at you. I actually like your hair down. You should wear it down more."

Her body relaxed a little, and Rocky could see that his back-to-back compliments about her weight and hair had caught her off guard, as well it should have. He'd never complimented anything about her before. Kenyatta immediately tensed again, though, when another woman stepped onto the treadmill that she had been intending to nab.

"Darn it! You made me lose my turn."

"I made you do that?" Rocky laughed at her accusation.

"Yes. If you hadn't been running off at the mouth, I would have been on it before now." She smacked her lips, gave the woman on the machine *the eye,* and then stomped off in the direction of the stationary bicycles. The bikes weren't popular among gym attendees. There was always plenty of availability there.

Rocky watched her for a moment, and then decided to follow. When Kenyatta made her choice, he sat on the one beside her and began scanning the settings to find the course he wanted to take.

"What are you doing?" she asked.

"'Exercising, just like you.'" Rocky mimicked the same tone and words she had used with him when he inquired about her presence earlier.

Kenyatta started pedaling. "Didn't you just finish exercising?"

"On the treadmill, yes." Rocky saw her when she rolled her eyes, but he kept talking as he began using his legs to rotate the pedals too. "Any law says a person can only get on one machine each visit? Membership is too high not to get your money's worth."

"Don't you have something or some*one* to do?"

Rocky looked in her direction. "What?"

"Nothing," she said. "If you're gonna workout, then fine. Just do it quietly. Don't talk to me."

"What's your problem? Did you miss your morning coffee?" Kenyatta didn't verbally respond, but although she kept her face toward the television screen that hung from the ceiling in front of her, Rocky saw her roll her eyes again.

Women! Rocky was starting to wonder why on earth he'd been pining for one lately. If he had the sense he was born with, he would be praising God that he was a free man. Come to think of it, he was rare gold: employed, had his own vehicle, on the verge of moving into a brand-new crib, never been married, no children, no baby mama drama. Any poll would agree with him that these were rare for a man of his age—especially those last three. So what if he'd just gotten the job a few weeks ago? So what if he *did* spend the last twenty-two years of his life in prison, which was probably why he had never been married, had no children, and had no baby mama drama. So what if the reason he was about to move into a new house was because he'd lived such a sordid life that drug dealers and murderers were trying to send him a message by burning his old house down? So what? The pollsters didn't have to know all that. The point was that he was a blessed man, and the last thing he should be doing was waste his time aching for some woman who wasn't going to do anything other than come in and mess it all up with her mood swings. He was doing fine by himself, and sometimes, as he'd heard Mother Tides say, it's best to just leave well enough alone.

The drama that came along with women wasn't even worth it. He'd had one screaming vulgarities at him last night, and this one looked like she was doing the same thing now, only in her head. He pedaled for a while, halfway hoping that Kenyatta would say something to break the silence, even if what she said was something mean. She never did, so with no interest in the CNN news feature that was playing on the television, he removed his soaked shirt, turned on his MP3 again, stuck his earphones in his ears, and leaned against the backrest. When he ran the treadmill, he listened to upbeat music. The bike called for something mellower.

Rocky was pretty absorbed in the jazzy beats of "Brotha" when he opened his eyes to find Kenyatta looking at him. Not his face, but his body. It dawned on him that she'd never seen him shirtless before. Kenyatta was about as lost in the rippling muscles of his torso as he had been in the lyrics of Angie Stone's song. It wasn't until he slowed his pace that she realized that he was watching her watching him. "What?" he asked while unplugging his ears and turning off the music.

"What?" she echoed. Her eyes broke their fixation for a moment, but only for a moment.

Rocky didn't quite know what to make of the fascination that Kenyatta was making no effort to hide. He didn't know whether to feel flattered or foolish—largely because he wasn't exactly sure whether her staring was a good sign or a bad one. His body was well developed, but it was also well decorated. Was she staring because she was impressed by his muscles, or was it because she was disgusted by his tattoos? Lately, with Kenyatta, it was hard to tell. Not many days ago, the answer would have been a given. There was nothing that he did that didn't appall her, but Rocky had been getting mixed signals lately. She'd be checking him out one minute, and just plain checking him the next. One minute, he was sure it was longing that he saw in her eyes, and the next, it was unquestionable loathing.

"What's that?"

Rocky looked down at his chest, the direction to which she pointed. It was the first tattoo he'd ever gotten. He was fifteen at the time, and still remembered the two-hundred-pound man who drew back a fist and punched him square in the center of the still-red, swollen, and sore spot when he came home with it. Rocky thought he would die from resulting pain. If he had known that his mom wasn't home alone, he never would have walked into the house shirtless. When his mother ran and knelt beside him as he lay on the floor, writhing, her concern earned her a kick in the face from the same man—her husband, Rocky's stepfather.

That was over twenty-five years ago—before the crime, before the prison, before the twenty-year daily schedule that included pumping iron. Rocky's chest had expanded by leaps and bounds since then, and the bird that had been drawn directly on his left pectoralis major had grown right along with him.

"It's the face of an eagle," he explained. "I was a kid when I got it. It was the emblem of the gang I was a part of."

"You were a part of a gang?" Her already arched brows lifted even higher.

"Got a bullet wound on my thigh to prove it." Rocky took his towel and dried his face and chest of new perspiration, which the cycling had brought on. "You can't be surprised," he added.

"No. Not at all. The only thing I'm surprised about is that you don't have a stab wound to match it."

Actually, he had two, but he wasn't about to tell Kenyatta that, especially when her tone clearly said that she was being flippant. Rocky considered making a smart comment of his own, but any response on his part was canceled when she suddenly pulled away the black scrunchie that had held her hair prisoner. He watched the thick mass fall past her shoulders. She climbed off her bicycle and stepped closer. Rocky's heart rate was beginning to rise, and exercise had nothing to do with it. The look in Kenyatta's eyes wasn't one of admiration, necessarily, but just knowing she was mesmerized turned Rocky on.

"How many of these things do you have?" she asked.

Rocky dismounted his bicycle so she could have full view. "It's not that many different tattoos. It just looks that way 'cause they're so large. I have six, and the eagle is the smallest one." He stretched out his right arm. "This is a black dragon. Just one dragon, but as you can see, it covers just about the whole arm." He pointed at his left shoulder. "This is a motorcycle, and this"—he pointed at the artwork that encircled his left bicep—"is just a chain link."

"They look painful."

Rocky shrugged. "Not really. This one hurt more than all the others." He turned around so that she could see the cross that had been inked in the center of his back between his shoulder blades.

"Probably because it's bigger than all the others."

Laughing, Rocky said, "No. It's because I wasn't as drunk when I got that one as I was when I got the others." He saw the numbers as they began computing in Kenyatta's head. He knew what her next question was going to be, so he beat her to the punch. "The sixth one is my name," he said. "It's in bold script, but if you want to see that one, you'll have to follow me to the showers."

As soon as the words left Rocky's mouth, he knew he'd made a colossal error. If he could have snatched them back, he would have, but it was way too late for that. Just like that, the most civilized conversation that he and Kenyatta had ever had was over. With her lips twisting in perceptible anger, she made some strange sort of *sucking-clicking-smacking* sounds that were probably Morse code for: *You bleepin', bleepin', bleepin' jerk.* Then she snatched her towel from the handlebars of the bike she'd been on and turned away.

Rocky reached out to stop her. "Kenyatta, wait. I was just joking."

"Take your filthy hands off me." She snatched her arm from his grasp. "You weren't joking. You're only saying you were joking because I didn't go for it." Rocky could see tears in her eyes. He knew what he'd said was inappropriate, but was it really that bad? Was is bad enough to make her cry? He wanted to apologize, but Kenyatta wouldn't let him get a word in edgewise. "You're all the same. Just a bunch of dogs. You make me sick. If I had been game for your offer, right about now, I would be looking at whatever nasty area of your body it is that you have your name tattooed in 'bold script.'"

There was absolutely no truth to that! Regulations didn't allow women in the men's locker room, so there was no way they could have showered together. Common sense told Rocky that was a thought that had better not leave the confines of his mind. A better stand to voice would be to dispute outright her claim that if she had gone for it, he would have gone for it too, but Rocky honestly didn't know that he wouldn't have. If they had been alone in a private setting instead of in a public place like this one, when he had thrown that same "joke" out there,— and Kenyatta had given consent—Rocky couldn't say what he would've done. "That's why you climbed in the car with her on Sunday, isn't it?"

"What? Her who?" Rocky's mind was racing to play catch-up.

"Oh, don't play dumb with me. You know who *her* is! You didn't get into but one car on Sunday."

Rocky's eyes widened. So that was it. That was the reason that Kenyatta's behavior had been so erratic all week. *She's jealous!* If she were jealous, that meant that she actually did like him. Hunter had been right, after all. It really was a love/hate relationship. Rocky didn't even know how to react. He felt happy and sad at the same time. Happy, because he now knew that despite the name-calling and shouting matches, Kenyatta had been feeling him just as much as he'd been feeling her. Sad, because he couldn't think of a way to explain what had or *hadn't* happened between Lorna and him that wouldn't prove him to be the dog she'd just called him.

"Yeah, you know who I'm talking about." Kenyatta's hand was planted on her hip. Rocky knew that stance. It was about to be on now. Already the people nearest them were starting to stare. "I'll bet she wouldn't have said no to your li'l offer. As a matter of fact, between then and now, she probably done already seen your name tattooed in 'bold script.'"

Why did she have to keep saying it like that? Every time Kenyatta said "bold script," she rolled her neck and cut her eyes up at him like he was some kind of vermin. Now Rocky was really in a pickle, because from the way she was extending her pause, he could tell that she was giving him time to deny her charge. She was probably hoping he would tell her it wasn't so. Problem was, he couldn't without lying. Lorna had, in fact, seen it, but only for a few seconds. The tattoo wasn't where Kenyatta was probably thinking it was, but it was close enough.

"I knew it!" she accused. Rocky had waited too long to answer, and he knew that his silence had given consent to her. "Ugh!" She turned away again.

"Wait, Kenyatta." He didn't reach for her this time. The way she was fuming, Rocky thought that if he touched her, his hand would get burned.

"Leave me alone. Don't talk to me." They were back at square one. That was the same order she had given when they first sat on the exercise bikes.

Rocky's arms dropped by his side, and he blew out a sigh as she began walking away. He was more frustrated with himself than he was with her. "Kenyatta . . . where are you going?"

She stopped and looked at him. "Somewhere where you're not." She turned to walk away again, but she paused abruptly and looked back at him once more. "And maybe on my way to wherever that is, I'll stop by and burn down your house . . . *again!*"

Chapter Thirteen

"Life was less complicated when I was a sinner."

It was Sunday afternoon, and Rocky was sharing the dining-room table with Reverend and Mrs. Tides. Following morning worship, all of his friends had decided to go out to eat or do some other fun activity with their respective families. Rocky didn't feel bad or left out. After his episode with Lorna on Friday, and the travesty with Kenyatta on Saturday, he had wanted nothing more than to spend a quiet evening at home. Then he remembered he didn't have one. Sitting at Jerome's house all by himself just didn't seem as appealing, so when Mother Tides extended the offer for him to eat dinner with her and the pastor, Rocky accepted.

The rain clouds that rolled in and out last night had rolled right back in today, and they'd brought more thunder along for the ride. Seems like lately, Atlanta had been getting rain every other week, but this weekend's storms had been a little more intense than the others. On the bright side, forecasters promised the sun would be shining in plenty of time for the Monday morning commute.

Technically, dinner was over now, but the party of three remained at the table enjoying dessert as they continued the conversation, which was started a half hour earlier. Reverend and Mrs. Tides were sipping on cups of coffee and eating slices of homemade coconut cake. Rocky didn't like coconut or coffee, so he pulled freshly rinsed black grapes from the bunches on the plate Mrs. Tides had set in front of him. One by one, Rocky pushed the grapes in his mouth and enjoyed the sweetness of the juice that burst from them as he chewed.

Mrs. Tides shook her head at Rocky's observation. "No, it wasn't, baby. The devil just wants you to think that life was better then."

"That's right," her husband agreed before blowing away steam that was rising from his freshly filled cup.

The table got quiet for a moment when a crackling noise on the outside was followed by the dimming, and then brightening of the lights on the inside. Mildred Tides had already pulled out candles and matches, just in case.

Rocky stuck one grape in his mouth and immediately grabbed another. "I didn't say it was better. I said it was *easier*, Pastor."

"How so?" Reverend Tides set down his cup.

"You name it." Rocky sighed and rolled the grape between his thumb and index finger. "Don't get me wrong. I love the Lord, but I didn't have these problems before I started loving Him."

Mildred Tides's face was a billboard of perplexity. "How on earth can you say that? You sat in jail for years, and you got there because you hadn't been loving the Lord as you should."

"I know that, and I also know that to somebody like y'all, what I'm saying don't make no sense." Rocky placed the grape he'd been playing with on the napkin in front of him. He rubbed his chin and felt prickly reminders that he'd skipped his morning shave. "I was used to that life."

"What life?" Mildred asked. "Prison life?"

"Prison life, street life, thug life—all of it. It was all I knew, and as crazy as it sounds, I could actually handle myself in all those lives better than I can in this new life." The confusion on Mildred's face had now spilled over to Reverend Tides's. Rocky had to find a way to make them understand where he was coming from. "See, it's like this. If a dude stepped to me when I was in the streets, no problem. I'd break his rib or bust his head open and keep it moving."

"And you think that's good?" Mildred looked horrified.

"No, ma'am, I didn't say it was good. It wasn't good, but it was easy, and it fixed the problem. I ain't never had to jack up the same dude twice. Crack his face; lesson learned. And if a woman had ever come at me like that Lorna did on Friday, I would have fixed that too."

Mildred looked even more horrified now. "By breaking her rib or cracking her face?"

Rocky shook his head. "Of course not, but I wouldn't have been standing there, looking like a fool, either. I would have matched her word for word. The old Rocky wouldn't have thought twice about cussing out Lorna. She stood in my face, screaming all kinds of craziness, and the best retaliation I had was to try to reason with her and make her understand why we couldn't satisfy each other and why I couldn't see her no more." Rocky sat back in his chair, clearly frustrated with himself. "She was standing there calling me a punk, only not using the word 'punk,' and with me taking it, I was proving her right."

"Son, that's not true," Reverend Tides told him. "Because you didn't reduce yourself to her level, that didn't make you a softy."

"Oh, come on, Pastor. Of course, it did. You're a man, just like I am. You know that no real man would just stand there and let somebody cut him down like that—especially not a woman."

"I beg to differ," Reverend Tides said.

"I knew you would." Rocky pulled a fresh grape, popped it in his mouth, and bit down hard. "You don't understand."

"Oh, he understands plenty." Mildred stood from the table and stacked her empty saucer on top of her husband's. Then she gathered them both and headed for the kitchen.

Rocky looked at Reverend Tides. What had his wife meant by that? Rocky held his breath. He didn't know if he would be able to take it if Reverend Tides told him that Mother Tides used to do him like that. She was the dream mother. The mother he wished he had. She couldn't have been capable. *Not Mother Tides, Jesus. Please, not Mother Tides.*

"I did four years in the military," Reverend Tides said. "Hated every single day of it. I never made rank because I was always getting thrown in the hole for misconduct."

Rocky released the breath he'd been holding, and deep lines creased the skin between his eyebrows. "Misconduct? You?"

Reverend Tides laughed at Rocky's facial expression. "I wasn't born saved, son." He patted his swollen belly. "I know you can't tell it by looking at me now, but as a young man—"

"Young*er* man," Mildred called from the kitchen, where she was loading dinner plates into the dishwasher.

"As a younger man," Reverend Tides said, barely missing a beat, "I was a skinny fella. Went to football tryouts in middle school and the coach didn't even give me a chance. Sent me home, saying I was underweight. Went to wrestling team tryouts in high school, and the wrestling coach did the same thing. Classmates picked on me all the time. In school, my teachers always called me 'Booker T.'" He paused to make way for a laugh. "I guess I have Booker T. Washington to thank for that. It was like they couldn't just call me by my first name, they had to include the middle initial too."

"Is that what 'B. T.' stands for?" Rocky had never known the names his pastor's initials were abbreviating, and he'd never thought to ask.

Reverend Tides's smile was a proud one. "Yes. Booker Taliaferro." Rocky also had never known what the *T* represented in Booker T. Washington's name. He'd just learned two lessons inside of thirty seconds. "But whereas the teachers called me Booker T, the kids called me 'Bony T.'" Reverend Tides chuckled again. "I can laugh about it now, but it wasn't funny then. When I graduated high school, I was five feet eight and weighed about one hundred thirty pounds soaking wet. I barely made weight to go into the military. It wasn't fun being the brunt of so many jokes. And yes, even the girls picked at me. The girl I asked to the junior prom turned me down because she said I was too skinny to even dance with." The pastor shook his head, and then said, "What she actually said was 'If I want to grind against a stick, I'll go to the club and be a paid pole dancer.' I really liked her, and it had taken months for me to get up the nerve to ask her, so her response hurt." Rocky couldn't relate. Getting a girl had never been his problem, not until he got saved, anyway. "I developed a complex because of all that," Reverend Tides was saying. "I always thought I had to prove myself to people. So when they did anything I didn't like or said things that I thought were offensive, my first reaction was to show them that just because I was small didn't mean they could run over me or talk to me any kind of way."

"What's wrong with that?" Now, that was something Rocky could relate to. It didn't stop the girls from liking him, but he had been small at one time too. It was the main reason he hooked up as a kid with that gang. He needed the protection that they had provided, mostly protection from his stepdad. Two nights after being attacked because of the tattoo, Rocky's new posse tripped the alarm on his stepfather's car just to lure him outside in the dark so they could jump him. There were five of them against one of him. By the time they got finished whipping up on the man, he had a busted eardrum, a dislocated shoulder, and four broken fingers on the hand he'd used to punch Rocky. His hand never did heal properly, and to this day, he still couldn't hear out of his left ear. Rocky still didn't feel bad when he thought about it. He didn't even feel bad that he didn't feel bad. If he was supposed to feel any form of compassion for his stepfather's injuries, then that was a sure sign that he was still a work in progress, and God wasn't finished with him. Rocky sat forward in his seat. "Sometimes you just gotta do what you gotta do, Pastor."

"Listen, son. When a man is truly a man, he doesn't have to prove himself to be a man. It takes far more strength *not* to fight than it takes to fight. To fight only takes the flesh." Reverend Tides poked Rocky directly on the bicep muscle of his right arm, and then simultaneously raised his eyebrows, curled his lips downward, and tilted his head in a manner that said he was impressed by the firmness of it. "That's the only kind of strength that it takes to fight. But it takes *this* strength, *this* strength, and often times, *this* strength *not* to fight." Reverend Tides pointed in the direction of his heart and his head the first two times he emphasized "this." The third time, he pointed upward.

Mildred walked back to the table, rounded it, and stood beside the chair where Rocky sat. "The same can be said for what almost happened between you and that young lady on Friday." She picked up the plate of fruit, which he had now abandoned. "It really would have only taken one major muscle to succumb to her advances, but it took a lot more than that to walk away." She placed her free arm around Rocky's shoulders, and then bent down and kissed the top of his head. "I'm proud of you, baby. Don't let the enemy fool you. You're a whole lot stronger than you give yourself credit for."

Rocky liked what Mildred had said, but the smile on his face was more a response to what she'd done. She didn't kiss him often, but every time she did, he got the warmest feeling on the inside. It was different from the warm feeling he got when Jade would place a kiss on his cheek. Jade's kisses would remind him that he was a man. Mildred's kisses would make him feel like a little boy. It was like each one erased another empty space that represented the ones he never got as a child. He'd noticed that Jade hadn't greeted him with a kiss after church today, as she normally did. Hunter must have told her what he had said. The thought almost made Rocky laugh, but a clap of thunder took his attention.

The sudden noise didn't seem to move Reverend Tides. He appeared to be deep in thought, but upon hearing it, Mildred walked out of the dining room and into the living room. From where he sat, Rocky couldn't see her, but he assumed she was looking out the window when she said, "Wow. It's really coming down out there. I'm glad we had you pull your motorcycle into the garage."

"Yes, ma'am. Me too," Rocky replied.

Reverend Tides planted his elbows on the newly cleared table space. He finally broke his silence. "Jerome told me that the main thing you were upset about when you lost your house was the fact that you also lost your job."

Rocky looked at him. "That's true."

"And why did losing your house also mean losing your job?"

He didn't know where this line of questioning was going, but Rocky had spent enough time around Reverend Tides to know that wherever it was headed, there was a lesson at the end that he was trying to get across. "Because when the house burned down, that meant I couldn't work on cars no more."

"And why couldn't you work on cars anymore?"

"Because I had to move in with Jerome temporarily."

"And since you were temporarily moving into Jerome's house, why couldn't you just temporarily move your business into Jerome's yard?"

Rocky twisted in his seat. Reverend Tides already knew all the answers to these questions. "Because out where he lives, they have these stupid rules that won't allow you to have cars that don't run just sitting in your yard."

"Is it really a stupid rule, Rocky, or is it just a rule that doesn't please you?"

Rocky shifted in his seat again, but he didn't offer a reply this time.

"They have the same rule out here in Shelton Heights," Reverend Tides pointed out. "Most neighborhoods that have Homeowners' Associations have that rule or a similar one that insures that the landscape is always clean." He looked Rocky straight in the eyes. "You see, when the area is clean, it looks better.

It's more presentable, more appealing, and the cleaner and more appealing it is, the more it's worth. What HOAs do for these houses"—he stretched his arms out over the adjoining dining and kitchen areas—"is similar to what God does for *these* houses." He pointed at himself, and then at Rocky. "The Bible tells us that our bodies are the temple of the Holy Spirit. So these bodies of ours are God's houses." Rocky still wasn't sure where Reverend Tides was going, but he didn't interrupt.

"You said that there was a time that you would beat a man who crossed you, and swear at a woman who disrespected you. When we first began speaking over dinner, you even talked about how you used to use women for your own gratification and not feel bad when you tossed them to the side afterward. Yet, last week, you had a woman who was more than willing to give herself to you, and you walked away. Not immediately and not easily, but you walked away. Am I right?"

"Yes."

"Well, you see, son, the cursing and the violence and the immorality—those things are sins. They're like junk cars. God has set rules and boundaries for the houses or the temples that make up His subdivision or His kingdom. The boundaries are not there to take away your fun. They are there to increase your property value. You're worth more now, Rocky. You're no longer the same man who spent twenty-odd years in prison. So you can't do the same things you did when you were that man. Do you understand what I'm saying?"

Rocky didn't know if it was the car analogy that helped to make it clear or not, but he really did have a better understanding. He nodded his head. "I think I do."

"You can't live in the same house you lived in when you were your former self. God burned down the old Rocky so he could move him off the old land and place him on higher ground. And this ground has a Homeowners' Association. And guess who owns your new home."

"God?"

"And you are so precious to Him that He won't allow you to invite just anything on your land anymore. I know you said you almost went the distance with Hunter's secretary, but you're still a work in progress, just like the rest of us. When gold is purified, it has to go through the fire more than once. We have to go through the process more than once, but when God gets done with us, our net worth is through the roof."

Rocky looked down at the tattoo of chain link on his arm. All he could think was that he must be worth six figures by now, because his purifying process felt never-ending.

Chapter Fourteen

"Believe it or not, I'm not at all surprised to see you. I didn't expect you to come by this early in the day, so I was a little thrown when Ingrid just buzzed me and said you were here. After you abruptly excused yourself from the restaurant on Thursday night, and I didn't see you at church yesterday, somehow, I knew I'd see you today." Jade stepped aside and allowed Kenyatta to enter into the office of her private practice. The full-of-confidence stride that Kenyatta normally possessed was nowhere to be found.

"Ughhhhhh!" was the only sound she made before dropping her Michael Kors designer tote on the floor and her behind on the leather couch that served as the centerpiece of the color-coordinated office.

When Jade lived in Virginia, prior to marrying Hunter and moving back to her hometown, she was one of three therapists who made up a partnership. Upon her relocation to Atlanta, her new husband encouraged her to launch out on her own and have the faith that God would do the rest. To demonstrate how much he believed in her abilities, Hunter insisted upon providing all of the funds necessary to purchase the office space and to get it remodeled to Jade's liking. Her liking included much of the same setup that she had enjoyed in Virginia. The walls were covered with wallpaper that was a warm shade of beige accented with a paisley pattern that was the same burgundy color as her couch.

Decorating accessories were kept to a minimum. Aside from Jade's desk and the single leather couch, there was a five-tier bookshelf, two tall floor lamps, two large abstract framed wall paintings on the walls, a water-cooler in the corner, and one mahogany coffee table that always had an open box of tissues in the center. The tissues came in handy during many of the sessions. To Jade, the room was inviting. She hoped it felt the same to her clients.

Hunter's had been great advice and a great invest-ment. Inside of a year, Dr. Jade Tides-Greene Associ-ates had turned a profit, and business continued to be on the upswing. She hadn't shared it with anyone other than Hunter, but her roster of clients had begun to include some of Atlanta's most recognized actors and recording artists. It was amazing how much of a men-tal strain it was to be who they were. If more "ordinary people" knew the facts, they might not yearn so much for the celebrity lifestyle. Of course, with them, Jade was required to come on their turf so no one, including Ingrid, her office manager, would know of the affilia-tion. At the hourly rate they were willing to pay, Jade had no problem making the adjustment. She had one on the schedule to see later this afternoon, but for now, it was one of Jade's best girls who needed her ears.

After watching Kenyatta's slow entrance and hearing her agonizing moan, Jade closed the door and stood in place for a moment. "You want to talk about it?"

"Ughhhhhh!" Kenyatta repeated, but louder this time.

The average person may not have been able to under-stand what the *"ughhhhhh"* meant, but as an educated professional and a caring friend, Jade did. Normally, when clients came to seek her services, she sat behind her desk and spoke to them, but Kenyatta wasn't just a client. Jade sat on the couch beside her. "Should we start with you or Rocky?"

Kenyatta covered her face with her hands. "Rocky is the last person I want to talk about." Her words were muffled, but Jade understood them.

"Is he really?"

Kenyatta dropped her hands in her lap, and then allowed her head to fall back against the couch so that she stared up at the ceiling. *"Ughhhhhh!"*

Jade had never seen her like this before. Kenyatta had it bad—real bad. Jade looked at her watch. It was barely eleven. "Are you taking an early lunch break today?"

"I called in sick."

"You called in sick?" Jade looked surprised.

"I needed a day off."

"Why didn't you just take a vacation day, Kenyatta? You're not sick."

"My head has been pounding ever since Saturday. I *am* sick."

Yeah . . . love sick. But Jade kept that opinion to herself. "Come on, honey, talk to me. I'm listening." She reached over and tucked a batch of hair behind Kenyatta's ear. She may have felt like "ughhhhhh," but her hair looked more like "ugh-mazing." Jade could count on one hand the number of times she'd seen Kenyatta's hair hanging free, and she wouldn't have to use all five fingers to arrive at a total.

"He said I should wear it down more," Kenyatta mumbled. "He said he likes it down and that I should wear it like this more often."

Jade's eyebrows rose. "Who said that? Rocky?"

Without directly answering, Kenyatta replied, "He told me that he likes it down, and like an idiot, when I went to the salon, I told Alejandro to give me a curl set instead of a French roll." She used her right hand to slap herself on the forehead. "Stupid!"

"Your hair is beautiful, Kenyatta."

"It would have been beautiful if I'd gotten a French roll too. Why on earth would I get my hair done the way he likes it?"

Jade sat back and leaned her head against the back of the couch too. She stared into the ceiling, just as Kenyatta had been doing for the past several minutes. "Is that a rhetorical question, or do you really want me to answer it?"

"Don't you dare" was Kenyatta's immediate reply. Jade opened her mouth to ask her next question, but Kenyatta spoke first. "How are things with you and the horse?"

Jade turned her face toward her friend and wondered what she'd heard. "Why did you ask me that? Did Stuart say something to you? Hunter told him about my crying spell last night, didn't he?"

Kenyatta crinkled her nose. "No."

"Then how did you find out?"

"Because you just told me. I had no idea until just now." Kenyatta giggled. "Crying spell? Girl, that's a hot, junky mess. You're pitiful."

Jade crossed her legs at the knees. "Oh really? You're one to talk."

Cutting her eyes in Jade's direction, Kenyatta said, "What's that supposed to mean?"

"With me, it's a horse. With you, it's a man. But the situations are very similar."

Kenyatta sucked her teeth so hard that the sound seemed to echo off the walls. "Child, please. I ain't never cried over no man, unless you count my dad, and that was because he died."

That was hard for Jade to believe. "You didn't cry when your marriage broke up?"

"Cry? Over crazy Joe? Girl, don't make me cuss. The Sunday after I finally broke free of that idiot, I shouted so hard that I got carpet burns on the bottom of my feet. I wish I would waste a tear over some man who treated me wrong."

Jade stifled a laugh, but Kenyatta's words took Jade back to her first fiancé. George Bannister broke up with her on the day of their wedding. There she was, all dressed and ready to be escorted by her dad down the aisle, when she got the news that the man who had gotten down on one knee and proposed to her hadn't even bothered to show up. It would be days later when she finally heard from him, and even then, it was by mail. He was never even man enough to talk to her and explain his disappearing act. *A letter*. The coward wrote a letter! But as badly as he treated her, it hadn't lessened the pain. Jade had cried for days. She couldn't imagine loving someone enough to be married to him, and then not feel that kind of pain if it came to an abrupt end.

Not that terribly long ago, she had counseled Jan in this very same office. At the time, Peter was serving what would become his final tour of duty in Iraq. Before he left, they'd split up after a heated argument, and Jan had valid reasons to believe that he had begun having an affair with another woman. It all turned out to be a gross misunderstanding, but at the time, she was sure that he was loving and being loved by a female soldier. Even with her believing that Peter was disrespecting her in such a manner, Jan's eyes were a broken dam of tears. When the love was real, even if the man was being callous, Jade believed tears were inevitable.

"Maybe you've never really been in love." She heard the words with her own ears when they came spilling from her lips.

"What?" Kenyatta replied.

"I know Joe was insanely jealous and excessively paranoid. And I remember you talking about how he would get mad if he saw another man look at you and would do erratic stuff like grab a knife and start stabbing the cushions on the sofa or the pillows on the bed. But I still think that if you loved him—*really* loved him—you would have cried at least a little when you were forced to make the decision to leave."

Kenyatta rolled her eyes and turned up her lip. "I cried because of a man·when I left, but Joe wasn't the man I was crying for. I was crying because leaving him meant that I also had to leave Louis."

Jade's eyes got big. Kenyatta had talked openly about how her ex-husband constantly accused her of sneaking around, but she'd categorically denied that there was ever any truth to it. But this Louis person was a new name. Jade tried to keep a straight face as she prepared herself for the reveal of the truth. "Who was Louis? Was that someone you were seeing behind his back?"

Kenyatta looked at her for a second, and then broke into a roaring laugh. "Girl, you should see your face right now." She took a minute to catch her breath. "I'm talking about Louis Vuitton. Joe was gone in his car when I sneaked away, and my brand-new Louis Vuitton was in his trunk. I had just gotten it, girl." Kenyatta shook her head at the memory. "We had just picked the package up from the post office the afternoon before, and stupid me didn't take the time to unload it from his trunk. I didn't preplan to leave him the next day. It was a spur-of-the-moment decision after he went into one of his tantrums that night. So I had to leave it behind." She wrapped her arms around her body and faked a sniffle. "I never even got to hold Louis. We would have made such a good couple."

Jade slapped Kenyatta on the knee. "Girl!"

"What?" Kenyatta said through a new laugh. "I cried for real. It was an authentic monogram canvas tote that I purchased straight from the LV Web site. That thing cost me nearly eleven hundred dollars."

"In U.S. currency?" Jade couldn't believe her ears. "You do know that you can go to the outlet mall and get that same authentic bag for less than half that amount."

Kenyatta's face contorted like she had just bitten down on a lemon covered with salt. "Outlet mall? Girl, Kenyatta King don't do outlet malls. You didn't get that memo?"

"You are a social worker," Jade pointed out. "Excuse me for stating the obvious, but social workers don't make full-price Louis Vuitton money. There's nothing wrong with the outlet mall."

"I bought that bag when I was living in Jacksonville. I wasn't doing social work then."

"So claims adjusters make full-price LV money?"

"They do when their car is already paid off and they have a husband who pays all the household bills, therefore freeing their check to use as they please. That was about the only thing Joe was good for; I'll give him that much. He paid all the bills, but the downside of that was since he paid all the household bills, he thought he owned everything in the house, including me." Kenyatta released a puff of air. "I had little or no say-so in anything. He didn't even have the courtesy or respect for me to inform me on the decisions he had made, even when they affected me. I constantly found out things on the back end, after the fact. And when I would approach him about it, he'd look at me like I was some kind of dunce. Like how dare I have an opinion about something I hadn't helped to pay for? Never mind that I was the wife and had to suffer the same consequences that he did when one of his decisions or investments went bad, which they often did. He paid the bills, so I should just be happy and satisfied with whatever." Kenyatta shook her head. "He was never physically abusive to me, but all the love I had for him was beat out of me by his constant deception, inconsiderateness, and jealousy. Why are men like that? They all seem to be one of two things. Either stupid or insensitive. Most times they're both."

"Not all of them." Jade grinned and nudged Kenyatta with her elbow.

"Yes, they are. Even Hunter." Jade was offended, but she held her tongue and allowed Kenyatta space to explain her charge. "He probably doesn't have a stupid bone in him, but he's proven that he can be insensitive. Hunter knew how much you loved Spirit, and he still sold her."

"But that was business. Selling horses is the nature of Greene Pastures." Jade repeated the same words that Hunter had told her while defending his actions.

"Business, shmisness," Kenyatta said. "You're his wife, and you're not a woman who asks for much. If my husband was balling like Hunter, I'd be in his wallet every doggone day—even if I made my own money like you do. But you don't ask him for anything, and he couldn't bypass the sale of one horse for you? Business or not, that's insensitive."

Jade lay back against the sofa again. She agreed, but she didn't want to voice it. Talking about the sale of Spirit was too painful. This wasn't the subject matter that Kenyatta had come to talk about, anyway. When Jade did a quick mental rewind of their conversation, she surmised that Kenyatta had brought up the subject of Spirit in the first place just so she wouldn't have to talk about what was really bothering her. This conversation wasn't really about Hunter doing something that had upset Jade. "So why don't we talk about whatever it is that Rocky has done that has you so upset."

"What?" Kenyatta crossed her arms in defiance and leaned back against the sofa too. "I'm not upset, and I don't want to discuss Rocky. He's a grown, rusty man. I couldn't care less what he does."

Her words sounded genuine, but Jade tested them, anyway. "I found out who the girl is that he left with on Sunday."

Kenyatta bounced into an upright position at the speed of a jack-in-the-box. "The girl that Rocky left with? Who was she? His sister? His cousin?"

She looked so hopeful that Jade almost wished she hadn't brought it up. "No. It was Lorna."

"Lorna. Lorna." Kenyatta was looking off in the distance and thinking hard. "Who is that? Where have I heard that name before?"

"Hunter's administrative assistant."

Kenyatta's eyes widened. "That trash? That's who it was?"

Jade sat up in her seat. "That's not nice, Kenyatta. Lorna's not trash. She's a little flighty, maybe. But she's not trash."

"A little flighty, my tail," Kenyatta disputed. "A little *floozy* is more like it."

"I should never have told you."

"Why? You act like I'm lying, Jade. As a matter of fact, you know better than anybody that I'm telling the truth. This is the same girl who was trying to get with your husband at one time. Wasn't she the one who was getting ready to scrap over Hunter with that other lady who used to work at the *AWC*? I can't believe you're taking up for a woman who was trying to get your man."

Jade could see right now that she needed to set the record straight. "First of all, I'm not taking up for her. I'm just not willing to demean her. And secondly, she never tried to take anybody from me. When Lorna was crushing on Hunter, he and I weren't even dating yet. So at the time, he wasn't my man or my husband. And even then, although she clearly was attracted to Hunter, she never threw herself at him or anything. It was the other lady, Diane, who was the relentless one. And after Lorna saw the way Hunter relieved Diane of her duties, she never even tried to cross the line with him. And for all we know, no lines may have been crossed with Rocky either. She could have just been giving him a ride."

Kenyatta refolded her arms across the front of her stomach. "Oh, she gave him a *ride,* all right, and I'm not talking about a ride home."

Jade wasn't expecting that response. Her jaw dropped. "What? Are you saying what you think or what you know?"

"Heard it straight from the source. He told me. On Saturday, I ran into him at the gym."

Jade sat up even straighter. "Rocky told you that he slept with her?" She didn't know why she was finding it so hard to believe. It was true that Lorna hadn't crossed any lines with Hunter, but Jerome treated the girl to lunch one day, and that $2.99 value meal was enough to grant him entrance into Lorna's private world. So if Rocky had taken her to a real restaurant that Sunday that they left together, it was a wonder they weren't married by now. "If Rocky told you that he slept with Lorna, then why on earth would you ask me if she were his cousin or sister when I first told you that I knew the girl he'd left with?"

"Okay, well, he didn't actually say those words, but I can read between the lines. Believe me, he slept with her."

Jade heard a quiver in Kenyatta's voice for the first time, and when she looked at her, she was sure she saw moisture building in the corners of her eyes as she continued to stare at the ceiling. Kenyatta's track record of never crying over a man was in jeopardy.

Jade stood from the couch, walked toward her desk, and shifted into full therapist mode. "Okay, let's start right there. You tell me what he actually said. Then maybe if we keep talking, we can find out why you've had a headache for three days, why you're wearing your hair down, why you skipped church on Sunday, and why you're sitting in my office on a Monday morning when you should be sitting in yours. And no beating around the bush, Kenyatta." Jade picked up the hourglass on her desk and flipped it over. "Your sixty minutes officially start right now."

Chapter Fifteen

Rocky sat behind the desk in his office, drinking a chilled protein shake and trying to appear busy. He had been looking at the computer screen so long that his eyes were starting to burn. The constant clicking of his mouse was probably enough to keep the pressmen, who periodically passed his open door, thinking he was hard at work, even choosing to work through the lunch hour. If they could see the face of his monitor, they would see that Rocky was on his ninth game of solitaire. He started playing the computer card game after twelve straight losses at Minesweeper. He wasn't faring much better at solitaire, but at least when he lost, he didn't have to see annoying little depictions of black bombs popping up all over the place.

Rocky wasn't hiding out to avoid work; he was doing it to avoid Lorna. When the storm finally calmed last night, and he was able to drive home without getting drenched, Rocky showered, climbed into bed, and set his clock alarm for an hour earlier than normal. The well-thought-out plan he had devised during his drive from the Shelton Heights subdivision was to get up early enough so that he could call in sick. According to the *Atlanta Weekly Chronicles* employee handbook, in order for an absence to be excusable, the person had to call in at least two hours ahead of report time. Rocky thought his scheme was solid, but God apparently had other plans. At some point during the night, their neighborhood must have lost power, because when Rocky was finally awakened by Jerome's banging on his bedroom door, they didn't have a minute to spare. Both of them had overslept, and calling in was no longer an option. If there was one thing Rocky had learned about Hunter over the past six weeks or so, it was that he didn't mix business with friendship. On the job, Hunter expected everyone to adhere to the same rules. With him still in his probationary period, Rocky couldn't afford to be late. He was still tucking in, slipping on, and zipping up stuff in the truck as Jerome sped toward the *AWC* building this morning.

In addition to praying that they wouldn't be tardy, Rocky also prayed that since his plans to call in had fallen through, Lorna would do the honors. He hoped she'd still be so outdone with him that she would feel it necessary to take the day off. His prayer that they would arrive on time was answered, but the one about Lorna wasn't. She was already there when they arrived, and her eyes had been slicing into Rocky like a meat cleaver from the time they gathered for corporate prayer until she finally left the building for her lunch break. The visual stabbing had been going on all day. It was made easier when Hunter left right after the corporate prayer to take the ninety-minute drive to Macon to get an interview with that guy at the nursing home who was Old Man Heights's kin, according to Malik and Tyler. Apparently, the information in his nursing home records proved it to be true. Since it was more personal than business, Hunter decided that he'd handle the interview himself instead of sending one of the staff reporters.

With Hunter away and Jerome in his own office, knee-deep in the responsibilities of his new position, Rocky had no buffer. His only choice was not to cross the line into Lorna's territory. She had no reason to come to the pressroom, so as long as Rocky stayed in his section of the building, he was safe. The only problem with that was there was only one set of restrooms and one break room, which all of the staff shared. By the time noon rolled around, and Lorna left for lunch, Rocky felt like his bladder would explode because of the excess water it was holding. Plus, he thought that his mouth would cough up a fur ball because of the water it wasn't getting.

It was almost 1:00 P.M. now. Lorna would be returning any minute. With the few precious moments that he had left, Rocky took long, quick strides. He needed to grab a backup cup of water and take a bathroom break. He hoped the relief would hold another four hours. Before dipping into the men's room, he took a quick peek around the corner at the area outside of Hunter's office where Lorna sat daily, just to make sure the coast was still clear and she hadn't made an early return. She wasn't back yet, but as though there was a chance that she'd hear the sounds of his footsteps and appear out of nowhere, Rocky made careful, but quick, steps back in the direction of the lavatories. As soon as he'd taken care of business there, Rocky washed his hands and headed for the break room, where he filled two cups with water just to be sure he wouldn't have to head back that way before the day's end.

By the time he made it back to his office space, sweat had gathered at his temples and at the nape of his neck. Rocky set the cups on his desk, then grabbed a paper towel from his desk drawer and used it to wipe his face. What was wrong with him? Was all this due to his new increased "property value" that Reverend Tides told him about? If so, Rocky was about ready to put a FOR SALE sign up on this new land of his and call it quits. His body wasn't accustomed to avoiding trouble and trying to keep the peace.

He sat at his desk and sighed. He couldn't put his finger on it, but something just didn't feel right. Rocky took a quick look over his left shoulder, and then his right. He was starting to get that same eerie feeling he got on occasion when he entered the mouth of Shelton Heights to visit any one of his friends. That feeling that someone was either following him or watching him. Jerome told him that he was spooking himself with all of his superstitions. Well, that made sense when it came to Shelton Heights, but he didn't have any superstitions about the *Atlanta Weekly Chronicles*. So why was he feeling it now?

The sudden ringing of the phone on his desk shook him. "Get it together, Rocky," he whispered to himself before answering. The call was coming from Hunter's office, and upon noticing it, Rocky took a breath and looked at the clock. It was ten after one. "Lord, please don't let this be Lorna. I can't handle her right now." On the third ring, he answered like he always did when he got an internal call. "Rocky speaking."

"I need you to come to my office for a minute, Rocky." It was Hunter, and his voice ushered in a sense of relief.

"Right now?" Rocky asked.

"Yeah. I know you're just coming off lunch break and are busy, but whatever you're doing, you have my permission to put it on hold."

"Okay. Be there in a sec." Rocky released a soft laugh as he moved his mouse around the computer screen and shut down the solitaire game. He'd been busy, all right.

The humor was quickly forgotten when he walked onto the main floor of the *AWC* and saw that Lorna had returned and was sitting at her desk. She was on a phone call, which was probably the only thing that prevented her from mumbling the insult that she signaled as he passed by. Rocky tried not to even look in her direction, but his eyes betrayed him. When he looked, Lorna shot her middle finger in his direction. Rocky hadn't seen anybody do that in years. They didn't even do that in prison. It made him want to laugh again, but he refused to shed his professional demeanor because of her childishness. He turned his attention away from her and continued toward Hunter's office door. When he reached the open door and looked inside, he felt his returned humor evaporate even quicker than before.

"Come on in, Rocky. Close the door behind you." Hunter was standing behind his desk. The look on his face was so solemn that it caused Rocky's stomach to tie in knots.

It would have been bad enough to have Hunter looking at him like that if it had been just the two of them behind the door Rocky had closed. But as he stood with his back against the frame, his eyes scoped the room: Hunter, Jerome, Reverend Tides, Stuart, and two policemen who were dressed in full official gear. They all wore the same expression on their faces. Rocky wanted to ask what was wrong, but something inside him said that he didn't want to hear the answer. The four men he knew exchanged looks as though each of them was wondering who would take the lead and be the one to break the news. The two he didn't know looked just as uncomfortable. This couldn't be good. Rocky braced himself for the worst.

"Rocky . . ." Stuart started to speak, but didn't get any further than saying the name. He stopped and looked at Hunter. Hunter looked at Jerome. Jerome looked at his dad.

Reverend Tides accepted the invisible baton and the responsibility that apparently came with it. He stepped toward the middle of the floor, closing some of the gap that separated all of them from Rocky. With his legs beginning to feel a bit unstable, Rocky tightened his grip on the doorknob and prepared himself for what he knew was news he wouldn't like.

"Rocky, no matter what I precede this with, it's not going to sound any better to you, so I'll just tell you." When Rocky saw Reverend Tides swallow, he swallowed too. "It's your house, son. It's gone. It burned down again."

Chapter Sixteen

Kenyatta sat at the table, clasping and unclasping her hands. The longer she sat, the more challenging it became not to display restlessness. She didn't know how much total time she'd been there, but it had to have been an hour . . . at least. The space she occupied was drab and confining. When she looked up, she saw empty white walls. When she looked down, she saw a plain brown table; its only decoration was a small Styrofoam cup of room-temperature water that she'd been offered. Even with only her inside, the space was too small. Kenyatta was beginning to feel like she was in a closed coffin. She felt hot and alone. She imagined if she yelled, all she'd hear in reply would be her own echo.

The uncomfortable temperature might have been actual, but Kenyatta had seen enough cop shows on television and had heard enough cop stories from Stuart to know that she wasn't really alone. That thing on the wall that looked like an ordinary glass mirror was actually a two-way mirror, and there were eyes on the other side of it watching her every move. Kenyatta wondered if two of those eyes belonged to her overprotective brother. If so, she knew that Stuart was going just as stir-crazy seeing her sit in the room as she was going while she sat there.

Everything had happened so quickly; recalling it all made her head spin. She had just returned home from her visit with Jade; she hadn't been inside the house for ten minutes before the banging started at her door. When she answered, there were two detectives there who questioned her for about thirty seconds, and then told her that she was being brought in for questioning surrounding a suspicious fire. The first thing that came to Kenyatta's mind was Rocky's house fire, but that had been weeks ago. The contractors were making good headway now on the rebuilding of it. Surely, they couldn't be talking about that fire, and if they were, why would they suspect her? Her questions didn't get answered until after she was brought into this godforsaken room, where she had been ever since.

Years ago, Kenyatta's mother warned her that her mouth would one day get her into trouble. Kenyatta's sharp tongue was something that Mrs. Lyons declared didn't come from her side of the family. "Of all the things you could have inherited from your daddy's people, you had to go and get their flip mouths," her mother would say. "It's gonna be the death of you, if you ain't careful. Just 'cause you think a thing don't mean you got to say it."

It had taken thirty-eight years, but Kenyatta's Judgment Day had finally arrived. She didn't even know about the second fire at Rocky's place until they dragged her into this hot room. Since being there, she had denied the insinuations a dozen times, but nobody seemed to believe her. After being asked the same questions over and over again by her relentless interrogators, it was beginning to mess with her psyche, and Kenyatta was starting to doubt her own self.

"Mrs. King, on Saturday, you were overhead in a public forum telling the victim that you were going to burn down his house. We have witnesses on standby who will testify to that fact if this goes to court. Are you denying that you said those words?" The interrogator who asked her that was a short black man who took his badge way too seriously. Kenyatta could only guess that he'd watched too many cop movies too. He leaned across the table as he talked to her, just like the characters did on *Criminal Minds* and *CSI: New York*. No doubt, it was his intention to intimidate her, but the whole while that Kenyatta was listening to him, his bushy mustache and the dried chunk of brown crud that was caught in the hairs of it distracted her. It fluttered, seeming to almost wave at Kenyatta, every time he exhaled through his nostrils. *Is that a booger?* It was huge. *Can he not feel that?*

"No, I'm not denying it," Kenyatta had answered, "but I only said that because I was angry. Do I look like someone who goes around starting fires? I wasn't actually gonna do it, and I didn't do it." She really needed him to take a few steps back. If that thing—whatever it was—finally broke free from his mustache, she didn't want it landing anywhere on or near her.

"Anger is generally the fuel that *ignites* these types of actions." When he said that, he smirked like he deserved an award for his impromptu pun. After that, he stood to full height (or at least what there was of it), which provided Kenyatta with the space needed to feel safe from unidentified flying nose particles.

Then the other one spoke. This one was a white man who was much taller than his friend. He had no facial hair, but there were enough dark curls on his head to make up for any hair that he didn't have anywhere else on his body. He was oddly handsome, and bore a striking resemblance to the guy who played David Starsky on the 1970s series *Starsky & Hutch*. Yanking out the chair that was opposite Kenyatta at the table, he turned it backward; then he swung his leg out real high, acting as if that was really necessary in order for him to straddle the seat. Kenyatta was beginning to think a part of their police training required that they watch the complete DVD collection of *Police Academy*—all seven installments. His partner remained standing with his arms folded and his legs spread apart. Kenyatta guessed that was his best attempt at looking fierce, but it wasn't working. It just made him look like somebody's growth-stunted, booger-breathing pet dragon.

The Starsky look-alike propped his arms on the back of his chair—which was now the front, since he'd turned it backward—and in a calm, but accusing, tone, he asked, "Were you also upset when you indicated that you should be considered a suspect for the first fire that initially destroyed the same home a couple of months ago?"

Kenyatta couldn't believe Rocky had told them that. The only other people in the room at the time she said that were Rocky and Stuart. Rocky had better be the one who blabbed, because if Stuart did it, he was in more trouble that he could ever imagine. She didn't care what kind of oath he'd taken as an officer of the law. There were certain lines you just didn't cross when it came to family. But regardless of which of them had spilled the beans, they both knew that she was just talking. They knew she wasn't capable of lighting fire to anybody's house. She wouldn't do that to somebody she hated; so she definitely couldn't do it to somebody she . . .

"Mrs. King?" Starsky said, snapping her from the trance that she'd been placed in when she realized what she was about to admit in her head. "Did you understand my question?"

"It's *Ms*. King, and yes, I understood the question. This *whole* thing is absurd," Kenyatta stressed. "Yes, I was upset when I said that too, and I didn't mean it that time any more than I meant it the other time."

"Do you have a fascination with fire, Mrs. King?" the standing one asked. He was trying to make her lose her calm. Why else would he insist on giving her a title that she'd just corrected? Kenyatta cut her eyes in the direction of his face as he continued his smug remark. "I'm listening to you speak, and I can't help but wonder, do your thoughts always gravitate toward starting fires when you get upset?"

Shut up, you stupid snot face! The words were at the tip of her tongue, but she clamped her teeth together to prevent them from coming out. If Stuart was on the other side of that window, looking in, Kenyatta would bet her entire bank account balance that he was sweating bullets and praying to the Most High God that she'd maintain some level of self-control. He knew her better than most, but Kenyatta knew herself better than all. She might have a smart mouth, but she wasn't anybody's fool.

Starsky spoke again. "Ms. King, we need answers that you aren't providing. You were overheard saying that you were going to burn the property in question. You were supposed to be at work today, but you called in and reported yourself as too ill to clock in. The fire was conveniently started on the very afternoon that you decided to call in sick, and when you were picked up at your place of residence, you were not the picture of an ailing woman. You were up and around and fully dressed. You appeared to have just returned home from somewhere. Do you have valid explanations for any of these coincidences?"

Kenyatta felt trapped. She was innocent, but truth be told, she could easily see why she was the prime suspect. All of this stuff was coincidental, but if she were one of the cops questioning her, she wouldn't believe it either. The last thing Kenyatta wanted to do was sound like a guilty woman who had run out of lies, but the next words out of her mouth were "I'm not answering another question before my attorney gets here."

It was then that the room's door opened and a female detective, who apparently had been watching the exchange from the other side of the glass, signaled for the pair to leave the room. Only fifteen minutes had passed, but it felt more like fifteen hours ago that they'd left Kenyatta there to share the space with dead air. The wait had been more excruciating than the questioning. Kenyatta was doing her best not to fidget or appear otherwise uneasy. The eyes on the other side of that mirror—whomever they belonged to—were evaluating her every move. She'd learned that from watching cop shows too. If she squirmed around too much, it was as good as standing in a courtroom during an arraignment and saying "Guilty" when the judge asked, "How do you plead?"

Kenyatta's heart skipped a beat at the sudden sound of the door jerking open. She hoped it was her attorney, but when she turned to her right, she noted the return of the same woman who had beckoned for the interrogators to leave. She and Kenyatta locked eyes, and then the lady said, "Okay, Ms. King, you're free to go."

Kenyatta sat frozen in place for a split second. Go? Go where? What was going on? Maybe by the time she joined the woman at the door, further instructions would be given. With her mobility returning, Kenyatta slid her chair back from the table and stood. She had been sitting in the hard wooden chair for so long that her butt was sore. She looked down long enough to straighten her dress, and when she looked back up, Stuart was standing in the doorway alongside the woman. Kenyatta wanted nothing more than to run into her brother's protective arms, but she retrained herself.

"Come on, sis. Let's go." His face was set, and she could tell that he wasn't pleased. Who could blame him? There was nothing nice about the day's events. "I have your other belongings already. Let's get you home." He placed his arm around her waist and escorted her in the direction of the exit door of the police station, and then to the parking lot.

Kenyatta said nothing, and for a long while, neither did Stuart. Her steps tensed when she noticed them heading for her brother's patrol car. She had just ridden in the back of one of those a little while ago; she really didn't want to ride in another one.

"Come on." Stuart must have felt her hesitation, because they changed directions and headed to the employee parking lot behind the precinct. Stuart used the keyless remote to unlock the doors of his Pathfinder. He held the passenger door open for her to enter, and then walked to the driver's side where he climbed in, started the engine, and turned the air-conditioning on full blast. He pressed the button to let the windows down, then closed his eyes and leaned back against the seat while they waited for the hot air coming through the vents to turn cool.

Kenyatta wondered what he was thinking. The evidence was stacked against her, but she couldn't imagine that her brother would deem her capable of this. Still, she needed to make sure he knew the truth. "Listen, Stuart—"

"Not right now, Kenyatta. Not right now." His voice was calm, but he was anything but. Kenyatta knew him. Stuart wasn't only just sitting still waiting for the air-conditioning to cool; he was trying to get his heated emotions to cool as well. When he was satisfied, he shifted the gear, pushed the button to close the windows, and they headed toward Shelton Heights.

The elapsed silence was killing her. With the subdivision sign now coming in view, Kenyatta said, "I didn't do it, Stu."

"I know you didn't."

She looked at him for the first time since they pulled out of the parking lot. "You do? You believe me?"

He glanced in her direction. "Should I not?

"Yes. I mean, no." Kenyatta shook her head from side to side like there were cobwebs inside. "I mean, yes, you should believe me. I didn't do it. I didn't."

"I said I believe you." Stuart navigated the truck into the Shelton Heights subdivision and made the turns that eventually brought them to the house they shared. "I need you to stay in the house until I get home this evening," he said. Kenyatta looked at him with questioning eyes. "I mean it, sis. You've caused enough trouble for one day."

"Are you calling me a troublemaker?" Kenyatta's defenses shot up. "I didn't do anything. I thought you said you believe me. Well, you sure don't sound like much of a believer."

"I do believe you, but that doesn't mean you shouldn't use common sense and extra caution. Now promise me that you'll stay in the house. Tyler went home with Malik today so they could work on their project, so he won't be here to keep an eye on you."

"Keep an eye on me? Keep an eye on me? *Tyler* . . . the child . . . keep an eye on *me* . . . the adult?" Kenyatta was beyond insulted. "Are you kidding me?"

Stuart's exhale was loud and lengthy. Kenyatta knew
that sigh. By nature, her brother was an understanding and patient man, but he had his limits, and his
amplified sigh indicated her toe was right on the line.
He looked at her long and hard before he finally spoke.
Though his voice level was controlled, his tone was rig-
id. "Listen, Kenyatta. I have to get back to work. I don't
have time to argue with you. Now I'm asking you for
the last time to stay in the house until I get home. If you
had done that from the beginning instead of gallivant-
ing all over the city when you were supposed to be sick,
much of this wouldn't have happened." The volume of
his voice was now on a steady increase. "As a matter of
fact, all of this could have been eradicated if you had
just gone to work this morning instead of calling in sick
in the first place. You're not sick." He pointed at himself. "*I'm* the one who's sick!" His barked-out words
caused Kenyatta's back to press against her door. "I
love you with all my heart, sis, but I am sick and tired
of cleaning up your messes. Messes that you make all
because of your hard head and your big mouth. I've
been doing it since we were kids, and I'm sick of it. You
with me? Sick. Of. It!" He made each word sound like a
sentence of its own. "Now for once in your life, can you
please do as you're told without giving lip to the teller?
Go in the house. Lock the doors. Set the alarm. And
stay there until I get home."

Kenyatta's grip on her purse was so tight that she
thought her nails would break through the leather.
Stuart hadn't taken that tone with her since . . . well,
ever. After all of that, there was still a comeback in her
mouth that wanted to be expressed. Kenyatta swallowed it. No way was she going to try and say anything
else to Stuart right now. Every day on the force was
stressful for him. He made that clear all the time. And

now she'd just taken his Monday stress and injected it with steroids.

She climbed from the truck, and quick steps delivered her to the front door. Kenyatta could feel Stuart's eyes on her as she unlocked the door and let herself into the house. She disarmed the alarm system long enough to close the front door and lock herself inside. After doing so, she set the alarm again. Everything was done in the exact order that she had been told. Kenyatta sighed and tossed her purse on the sofa. She looked through the security blinds just in time to see Stuart back out of the driveway and head back toward the mouth of Shelton Heights.

"Well, Kenyatta King," she said, looking at her reflection in the decorative mirror on the wall beside their front door, "welcome to house arrest."

Chapter Seventeen

They got him good. They had played the trump card. All this time, Rocky had been thinking that his undeclared, unmitigated respect for the U.S. Marine sergeant, who had spent twenty years in active duty, three tours in Iraq, and seven days as a tortured POW, was a hidden fact. But as he and Peter lay on the grass near the mouth of Stone Mountain Park, stretching after what had been the hardest, longest jog of Rocky's life, it was clear to him that they'd known all along.

Upon Reverend Tides's reveal that Rocky's home, which had been burned down previously, but was at the halfway mark of being rebuilt, had mysteriously burned to the ground again, Rocky became enraged and irrational. Not only was he no longer willing to trust the police to find the arsonists, he wasn't waiting on God to reveal the answer either. Rocky actually said those words.

All attempts by Hunter, Jerome, and Stuart to calm him failed. When Reverend Tides stepped in and couldn't make any headway, the men knew that the situation was critical. Rocky always listened to Reverend Tides, but not today. Between pacing the floor and punching the walls, Rocky would bark out irate answers to the questions that the two officers, who had come with Stuart, would ask. During that abnormal interrogation, one of the policemen had asked Rocky if he had enemies.

"I got more enemies than you can count!" Rocky's outburst filled the room. "That's what I've been saying from the beginning. Even when the house got torched before, didn't nobody want to believe that any of my former running buddies, or maybe some of my arch-enemies, were out to make me an example. They don't just let you leave the game like that. If you want out, you gotta be willing to pay the price. They're trying to make me pay the price."

"Calm down, sir," the policeman said. He ignored the angry slam that Rocky gave the wall with the back of his arm in response. Instead, the officer rephrased his question. He pointed to his partner, who was scrib-bling in a pocket-size, wire-bound notebook. "We've made memos of all of that, sir, but what we're trying to do is narrow the field. By chance, has there been any-one—anyone at all—in recent days who may have indi-cated specifically that he might damage your personal self or your personal property?"

"No." As soon as Rocky said it, he had a sudden recall that propelled him to spin on his heels and look at the questioning officer. "Wait a minute. As a matter of fact, yes, there has been someone. Kenyatta King."

"Rocky!" Stuart roared.

"Well, she did," Rocky insisted, challenging the looks of doubt that had overtaken the faces of his church brothers.

Stuart's nostrils flared. "That was weeks ago after the first fire, and yeah, the cause of the fire was incon-clusive, but the written report says in black and white that faulty wiring was strongly suspected to be the cause of that blaze. You know that, Rocky. Now, you can go around, all you want, all paranoid and thinking everybody is after you, but you leave my sister out of this. You with me? When she said that, I didn't take her seriously, and neither did you, so to bring it up now is just insane."

Rocky shook his head and divulged the information that stunned all of them. "I'm not talking about that time. I'm talking about Saturday. Two days ago." He flashed two fingers for dramatic effect. "I saw her at the gym, and she looked me in my face and said she was gonna burn down my house again. She said 'again,' like she did it before and a repeat performance was on the way." Now he pointed an accusing finger at Stuart. "You wanna call me insane? Yeah, I'm insane, but it ain't 'cause I'm bringing it up now. It's 'cause I *didn't* bring it up then. Naw, I didn't take her seriously, but looks like I should have, don't it?" Stuart's face dropped upon hearing the news flash. He appeared to have just swallowed one-fourth of a cat. From the looks of it, the remaining three-fourths of the feline had been divided equally among Reverend Tides, Jerome, and Hunter. They all shared the same shocked expression, and Rocky basked in the satisfaction of it.

When Stuart's brothers in blue asked him of his sister's whereabouts, it was painfully obvious that he wished he could give them the rock-solid alibi that Kenyatta was at work. But he couldn't, and everything that hadn't already gone downhill—well, it went downhill from there. When one of the officers announced that they were going to have to pick up Kenyatta for questioning, Stuart's immediate response was to lash out at Rocky. Within seconds, the two of them were in each other's faces and coming close to throwing blows. The cops restrained Stuart, and Jerome and Hunter did the same with Rocky. Once the three officers left the building, Hunter insisted that Rocky follow their lead, and he wasn't to return until he cooled off. His actions had caused a big scene, and Hunter was having no more of it. Not at the *AWC*.

Reverend Tides and Jerome sandwiched Rocky between the two of them in the cab of Jerome's pickup and made small talk as they escorted him home, like the chitchat would massage away the tension of all that had transpired. Rocky sat in angry silence wishing to God that they would both shut up. Jerome talked about the overtime he'd have to put in if he didn't get back to work soon, and Reverend Tides shared the details of some doctor's appointment that he needed to get the first lady to by five. Rocky couldn't care less about either. He just wanted them to drop him off at the doorstep and leave.

But when they arrived at Jerome's house, neither of them seemed to be in any rush to fulfill the obligations they'd voiced. Both sat comfortably in the living room with Rocky and continued to converse about regular stuff. It was as if the afternoon drama, which had transpired between the hours of one and two, had been a dream. Reverend Tides and Jerome never left Rocky alone for a moment—not even to place a phone call. So when Master Sergeant Peter Kyle Jericho came knocking at the door, the only explanation that made sense was Hunter had called him. It was second nature for Rocky's attitude to adjust when Peter removed his hat and walked in the house. He was still fuming on the inside, but whatever escape valve he'd been using to let off steam for the past hour or so had suddenly been corked.

"Go put on some gear and a pair of shoes you can run in." Peter didn't even bother with formalities. He gave the order as soon as Reverend Tides stepped aside and granted him entrance into the house.

"What?" Rocky just looked at him. He couldn't be serious. It was 80 degrees outside. Jerome had once told him that Peter was crazy. Jerome thought all U.S. Marines were crazy. Rocky had defended Peter then, but now he was left to wonder.

"You heard me. Go." Peter pointed in the direction of the bedrooms, and with him making the gesture while standing there dressed in his official military uniform, Rocky didn't see where he had any choice but to obey. He couldn't disregard the command of a man who had been forced to look at the severed heads of his fellow soldiers in the name of defending his country.

As Rocky was headed down the hall to carry out his orders, he heard Peter ask Jerome for clothes that he could change into. By the time Rocky came out wearing his Champion-brand athletic outfit and his Adidas running shoes, Peter was all geared up for the challenge too.

They headed outside. Rocky thought that they would be getting into Peter's car to drive to whatever track they were going to be jogging on, but Peter had other plans. From the time they exited Jerome's house, they hit the ground running. Rocky felt like he had been thrust in the throes of some insane form of military boot camp. Jerome's neighborhood was three miles from Stone Mountain Park, but that's where Peter informed Rocky that they were headed. They jogged the three miles to get there, and then they jogged the whole of the five-mile track, which surrounded the mountain itself.

Rocky could look at Peter and tell that he was in decent shape, but he had underestimated by far. Rocky was more than impressed at the soldier's ability to run such a long distance without having to stop and rest. They had stopped after the first three miles, when they first reached Stone Mountain Park, but that was by Rocky's request. The trek from Jerome's house to the park wasn't like running the treadmill at the gym. That stretch of roadway had been hilly at times, and he needed to catch his breath in preparation for the next five miles.

Once they were on the track, Peter wasn't extending any grace. He only allowed pauses once every half mile or so to sip water from the fountains, which were strategically placed around the track. Even then, Rocky wasn't allowed to stop moving. He had to jog in place even as he gulped down the rehydrating fluid. As far as he knew, Peter had never been a drill instructor, but he sure would have made a good one. Is this what he did to those poor high school students? This workout was challenging Rocky on a new level. He could sit in the gym and lift weights all day; he could even run for miles on the flat, rotating belt of the electronic treadmill. This all-manual run on the winding trail of Stone Mountain Park was kicking his behind, though. Both of their bodies were drenched with sweat. By mile two, Rocky had ripped off his shirt and was using it as a towel to wipe his face. They had a mile and a half to go, when Peter did the same. Their varied muscular definition was turning the heads of women left and right, but Rocky couldn't even enjoy the attention. He had to keep all of his focus on what lay ahead. Otherwise, he'd never get to the end of the road that encircled the gigantic rock that was called Stone Mountain. The last half mile was the most difficult of all, and Rocky had never been as glad to see a sign as he was to see the five-mile marker that signified the end of his punishment.

***

A good hour had passed since they finished the run. In addition to the stretches, Rocky and Peter had not only talked, but they had prayed together, right out on the grounds of the park. They were lying on their backs at the time, not in any typical prayer positions, so no one seemed to notice, but Rocky wouldn't have cared if they had. The run had cooled his hot head, and the prayer had warmed his cold heart.

One of the first things they did after crossing the "finish line" was call Stuart to see what could be done to get Kenyatta from under the microscope. There were reasons to believe she had done it, but somehow Rocky knew she hadn't. He never should have fingered her. Stuart was right. When Kenyatta volunteered to be a suspect the first time, it was because Rocky had pushed her buttons and had set her off. What Stuart didn't know was the second time, when she spouted that she was going to burn Rocky's home, that remark had been made under duress too. She was hurt by what she thought was going on between him and Lorna. She hadn't meant it, and Rocky knew it. He'd allowed his anger to get the best of him, and he needed to admit that to the proper authorities. But when he made the call from his cell, Stuart's phone rang one time, and then went straight to voice mail. When Peter called from his cell phone just seconds later, Stuart answered. It was clear that he'd intentionally ignored Rocky's call. Getting them to release Kenyatta hadn't been difficult. She hadn't been arrested; she had been taken in for questioning. They didn't have any concrete evidence to hold her, anyway.

"So are you in love with her?" Peter asked as they sat under a shade tree near one of the areas where people who drove to the mountain parked their cars.

"No." Rocky couldn't answer fast enough. He didn't need Peter getting the wrong impression. "Just because I said she makes me crazy, don't go reading more into it than there is."

"All right, all right. I was just asking." Peter held up his hands in surrender. When Rocky shook his head and released a quiet laugh, Peter looked at him. "What?"

"I don't know. I just got this picture in my head." Rocky plucked a blade of grass from the ground, and then flicked it away with his fingers. "Can you imagine me and Kenyatta together? I mean, come on. That's a homicide waiting to happen. Or a murder-suicide . . . one of the two."

"I don't know, man. You and Kenyatta. That's a lot of heat and passion, and if it's pointed in the right direction . . ."

Rocky looked out into the distance and shook his head like it wasn't even a possibility. But the thought of it made him lick his lips. He and Kenyatta. Wow! But even if he wanted, she wouldn't. It had become obvious to him that she was attracted when the whole Lorna thing set her off. If he had honed in on it then, maybe she would have been open to the possibility. But now . . . after he'd nearly sent her to jail . . . no. One thing he'd learned about Kenyatta King was that she didn't easily forgive or forget.

"You know Stu did a similar thing to Candice as you did to Kenyatta." Peter read Rocky's thoughts with perfection. "The only difference between you and Stuart is that he wasn't too proud to beg."

Rocky coughed out a laugh. "Beg? Beg who?"

"Her—that's who."

"A real man don't beg for nothing," Rocky said.

"A real man will do whatever he gotta do to get what he wants."

"Whatever. I wish I would." Rocky used his abandoned shirt to swat away an insect that had flown too close to his face.

Peter sighed. "All I can say, bruh, is that love will make you do a whole lot of stuff that you never thought you would." He delivered a light punch to Rocky's knee. "Let's head back. It's getting late."

"Don't tell me that we're gonna have to run back to the house." Rocky's eyes were pleading as he folded his still-wet shirt in his hand. "I've learned my lesson, Pete. Whatever it is, as God is my witness, I've learned it."

Peter laughed. "Well, I'm afraid we don't have much of a choice. I mean, we don't have to run, necessarily, but we got here on foot, so we're gonna have to use the same mode of transportation to get back."

Rocky couldn't do it. Even walking would be too much. He had caught his breath and the stretching had eased the tightening of the muscles in his calves, but three miles, which wouldn't be a big deal for him ordinarily, would seem much longer today after the workout they'd just had. "I'm for real, man. We have to hitch a ride or something."

"It's just three miles, Rocky."

"Jerome was right. You really are crazy. Technically, it wouldn't be just three miles. Tacked on to what we've already done, it would be eleven miles. I can't do it. That's out of the question."

Peter brushed dirt off his arms. "Well, hitching is out of the question too. But if you're that much of a wimp, you can always call your equally wimpy pal, Jerome, or you can call Reverend Tides."

If Peter thought name-calling was going to make Rocky rise to another challenge, he couldn't be more wrong: wimp, wuss, weakling . . . whatever. That military crap wasn't working anymore. "Jerome had to go back to work, and Pastor Tides mentioned earlier that he had to take his wife to a doctor's appointment," Rocky said. "Can't you call Jan?"

"She's on her nursing shift at the hospital," Peter revealed. After a thoughtful pause, he added, "There's one other option, but I'm thinking that you would probably rather walk."

"Well, you're thinking wrong, pal," Rocky assured him. "Whatever it is, I'd rather do it than walk. I'd be willing to ride the sidecar of some kid's scooter right about now."

Peter laughed at the face Rocky made. "Okay. If you're sure."

"I'm more than sure." After making that declaration, Rocky watched Peter stand to his feet and pull out his cell. He walked away as he dialed the number. That alone told Rocky that something was up, and it didn't take him long to figure it out. Peter was calling the only member of their inner circle of friends who would be available to come and pick them up today: Kenyatta.

By now, the chances were great that she was back at home. It was 6:00 P.M., and all of their other friends were either at work, or caught in rush-hour traffic as they tried to get home from work. Shelton Heights was about the same distance from Stone Mountain Park as was Jerome's neighborhood. They were just in opposite directions. Even with the surface street traffic, it wouldn't take more than fifteen minutes for Kenyatta to reach them. As beat as Rocky was, he had no qualms right now of riding with Kenyatta, but he doubted she would come, which was probably why Peter was still on the phone. He may as well give it up. All the coaxing in the world wouldn't convince Kenyatta. Not if it meant giving Rocky a ride. She'd just as soon watch his legs rot off his body, and he couldn't say that he blamed her. She'd probably never forgive him, but in his defense, what did she expect? Fire couldn't have just fallen from the sky and devoured his home. But it *was* burned to the ground, and she *did* say that she was going to light a match to it. Last time Rocky checked, two and two still equaled four.

He turned his attention to Peter again. He was off the phone now, but still walking in the distance. Rocky needed to be doing the same thing. Continuing to walk would prevent his legs from getting stiff, but walking was the last thing he wanted to do. He'd take the stiff legs right now. He'd even take being verbally massacred by Kenyatta, as long as she did it while giving him a ride home. There was no punishment—none—that would be worse than walking another three miles on hilly grounds right now.

From where he sat, Rocky had a clear view of Stone Mountain. An airplane was floating past it as Rocky looked on. He imagined that a bird's-eye view of the mountain was even more magnificent. It was huge and sturdy. As he and Peter were running the trail, they saw signs of last weekend's storms. Limbs had fallen off several of the trees, and some of them had been blown in the direct path of the trails where runners ran, walkers walked, and bikers biked. Rocky and Peter had leaped over a few of the smaller objects, but bigger ones had forced them to go around them. Debris could even be detected on some of the park benches and floating in the streams that could be seen from the sidewalks. A few years ago, while Rocky was still confined in prison, much bigger storms had swept through the city. Some people lost homes and cars due to the falling of large trees on their property. Some areas were flooded by high volumes of rain. Power was out in some communities for days at a time. Through it all, Stone Mountain still stood. None of the storms had been able to take it out.

"Upon this rock I will build my church; and the gates of hell shall not prevail against it." The recollection of Reverend Tides's message from a few Sundays ago rang in Rocky's ears. Their pastor talked about the foundations on which they built their spiritual houses, and how the choices they made could be the determining factors in whether they could withstand the storms of life. In the Bible, only the natural house that had been built upon the natural rock (concrete) could withstand the natural storms; just as only the spiritual house that was built upon the spiritual Rock (Jesus) could survive the spiritual storms.

Rocky breathed in the fresh air while he mulled it all over. How close he had come to caving in! The house fire had definitely been a storm for him, and with a name like "Rocky," the scripture connection was almost comical. Rocky buried his face in his hands and forced out a heavy breath. Living saved was hard, but he wanted to do it. He wanted to be the survivor whom Reverend Tides often preached about. He wanted to have the overcoming testimonies that his friends talked about. "God, let my spiritual house be built on the rock," he whispered. "Forgive me for my shortcomings, and strengthen my foundation. I don't want to fall. I don't want to fall."

Deafening music that was getting louder by the second pulled Rocky from his thoughts and his prayer. At first, he thought it was some ignorant teenager who had nothing better to do than ride around blasting the latest rap or hip-hop tune. As he continued to look, Rocky began to recognize the frighteningly familiar early-model Chevrolet Malibu that was headed in his direction. As it got nearer, he identified the blaring music as not rap or hip-hop, but as a hand-clapping, foot-stomping, tambourine-playing traditional gospel song.

"It couldn't be," Rocky mumbled. He turned and looked behind him.

Peter was walking toward him, sporting the widest grin. "Here comes our ride," he announced.

"Oh no," Rocky whispered. "Oh no no no no no no." He turned his face back to the edge of the roadway where the car was coming to a stop. The big, bold, sloppy white letters that spelled out AIN'T SHAMED TO PRAISE HIM, and covered the entire side of the car, erased all hopes and removed all lingering doubts. He had been wrong. There was a worse punishment than walking, and its name was Leona Grimes. Peter had called his mother-in-law.

"What y'all standing there lookin' for? Y'all come on here. I ain't got all day!" she yelled out the open window over the music.

Rocky didn't share Peter's humor. The soldier laughed all the way to the car.

"Get on in here," Leona ordered. "Y'all interrupted my Jesus time with this foolishness. I was reading my Word, which is the same thing that y'all need to be doing instead of walking around half naked." She grimaced at their exposed chests so hard that the resulting crevices in her face looked like they belonged on an English muffin. "Commandment number nine of the Ten Commandments says: 'Thou shalt not bear false witness against thy neighbor.' Do y'all know what that means? Apparently not," she snapped. "Just look at the two of you . . . just baring false witness all over the place."

Rocky looked at Peter as he opened the back door of the car and whispered, "What does bearing false witness have to do with us not wearing shirts?"

Peter wiped tears from his face that were the result of his laughter. "She thinks 'bearing' is the same thing as 'baring.'" He pointed at his bare chest. "Now, don't even ask me how the false witness part plays in, 'cause your guess is as good as mine."

Rocky huffed in annoyance as they both climbed into the backseat. Leona kept right on talking as she navigated her car back onto the street, not even bothering to turn down the volume of Shirley Caesar so she wouldn't have to yell so loud. "The only reason I'm picking y'all up is to try to save your sorry souls from hell. The sun is near 'bout ready to start going down. The Bible says, in I John 1:7, 'But if we walk in the light, as he is in the light, we have fellowship one with another, and the blood of Jesus Christ his Son cleanseth us from all sin.' Do y'all know what that means?" Rocky began repeatedly pounding the back of his head against the seat. Leona was watching the road ahead and couldn't see him, but even if she could, Rocky was sure that it wouldn't have deterred her. "That means that if I hadn't come to pick y'all up, and the sun had gone down before y'all got where you was going, y'all would have been walking in the dark and not in the light, which means that y'all would've gone straight to hell." She did a quick glance over her shoulder at Rocky. "Not that them nasty, stankin', demonic tattoos you got wrote all over your body ain't already done sealed your fate."

Peter laid his head in his own lap as he doubled over in laughter.

Rocky clenched his teeth. "I'm gonna get you for this, Pete."

Chapter Eighteen

Eight-fifteen. Kenyatta couldn't believe it was a quarter after eight, and she hadn't yet eaten dinner. No matter what she did to try and make the time pass quicker, it still crept. The last five hours that she had spent cooped up in the house felt like a lifetime. If Stuart was going to insist that she stay indoors, the least he could have done was come straight home after work. He knew how much she hated being alone for long periods of time. By nature, she was a people person, the life of the party. When he called two hours ago to say that he was going to go to Greene Pastures to join forces with Hunter in helping Malik and Tyler with their project, the considerate thing to do would have been to invite her over too. Jade was there, and Kenyatta could have hung out with her while the guys did their thing.

Stuart was punishing her. Kenyatta wasn't stupid. She knew what he was doing. At first, she thought he was just furious with Rocky for having her picked up, but these long hours alone had given her plenty of time to think, and now she had a different perspective. Her brother might have indeed been mad at Rocky, but he was mad at her too. She picked up the first clue when he went off on her upon dropping her off at home. That whole *"for once in your life, please do as you're told"* spiel was his way of telling her that if it hadn't been for her mouth, she wouldn't be in this pickle. He had called her hardheaded and bigmouthed. How rude!

Kenyatta sat on the couch and picked up the remote control. She didn't like what Stuart said at all, and she would really be furious at him . . . if it weren't so true. This was her at age thirteen all over again. That was when Kenyatta's parents made her stay home alone while everyone else got to go to the beach—all because of her mouth. If she remembered correctly, she was exiled for six hours that day. One more hour and Stuart would have tied their parents' record. He promised to bring her Chinese takeout, but as late as the hour was growing, and as hungry as she was getting, Kenyatta was ready to go into the kitchen and warm up the leftover baked chicken. If he weren't home in the next thirty minutes, she'd fend for herself.

Kenyatta curled her legs and tucked her bare feet under her body as she mindlessly scanned the channels. Thoughts of her early-afternoon drama continued to play through her mind. Not many things frightened her, but the thought of going to jail did. She couldn't imagine living anyplace where she was forced to wear unflattering clothes and shoes that had no recognizable designer's name attached to them. Just about every picture she had ever seen of women on lockdown showed them wearing their hair in those cornrow-type braids that looked okay on free women, but somehow made women behind bars look a bit too masculine. Where Kenyatta came from, they were actually called "prison braids." Some even referred to them as lockdowns. Kenyatta shuddered. To not be able to get her manicures and pedicures every two weeks . . . she'd just rather be dead. If those policemen who took her away this afternoon had locked her in a cell, she would have had to be placed on suicide watch immediately. She was a strong woman, but it took a special strength to survive jail, let alone prison.

At first, she thought the sound of the doorbell ring-ing was coming from the television. She had stopped on one of the movie channels, and Liam Neeson's char-acter, Bryan Mills, was opening the door for a visitor. It was *Taken,* by far one of Kenyatta's favorite movies. She'd watched it so much that she'd memorized almost every scene. It wasn't until Bryan had been let into the room on the television screen, and a second doorbell sounded, that Kenyatta realized there was someone at her front door. She sat as quiet and as still as possible. Her mother had taught her as a child never to open the door to anyone if she was at home alone. Even if she weren't alone, Mrs. Lyons said, if people didn't call ahead before coming for a late-evening visit, they didn't deserve to be allowed inside. Calling ahead was just common courtesy.

The doorbell rang for a third time, and Kenyatta was starting to get nervous. Most people would just go away. If no one was answering the door, that meant one of three things: either no one was at home, they were at home, but were in some compromising posi-tion that didn't allow them to answer the door, or they just didn't want to be bothered.

By the fourth ring, Kenyatta was easing her hand toward her purse. It was time to send a text message to her brother. Greene Pastures was a little bit of a drive from Shelton Heights, but if Stuart got a 911 text from her, he'd quickly find a way to erase the miles that separated the two neighborhoods.

"Kenyatta, please let me in. I know you're at home, because Stu told me you were."

Her heart stopped, then pounded, then stopped again. Was that Rocky's voice? What was he doing here? He had some nerve! She couldn't believe that Stuart would divulge her whereabouts . . . especially to Rocky. Kenyatta pressed the mute button to silence the television. She guessed this was the final slice of the punishment pie that her brother had baked just for her. First confinement to the house, then the extended alone time, now a visit from her accuser. He had saved the worst for last.

"Kenyatta, please? I want to talk to you."

About what? She didn't want to hear anything he had to say. Easing from the sofa, Kenyatta tiptoed to the door. He already knew she was there, so why was she walking on her toes? She hadn't a clue. He had now gone from ringing the bell to knocking. Should she let him in, or shouldn't she? Her mother would bust a vein if she knew that Kenyatta was even considering letting a man in her house, especially with neither Stuart nor Tyler being there.

"What do you want?" She opened the door just wide enough to look out at Rocky.

"Please let me in. Please?"

Was he begging? Kenyatta gave him a quick once-over. What a sexy mound of protoplasm! Kenyatta noted his clothing of choice. There weren't any brand names anywhere to be seen. *Umph, umph, umph.* Anybody who could wear Walmart jeans and a T-shirt from Target and make it look that good deserved an award. "This is not a good time, Rocky. I'm not in a good mood," she said.

"Five minutes," he said. "All I need is five minutes."

"Yeah? Well, all I need is two, because I only have one question for you, and I want you to tell me the truth."

Rocky shifted his helmet from his right hand to his left. "Okay."

"Who was the reason I got picked up by the police today? Was it you or Stuart?"

"Dare."

Kenyatta was baffled. "What?"

"It's this game called Truth or Dare?" he responded. "If you don't want to answer the question that requires you to tell the truth, you can opt to say 'Dare,' and that saves you from having to answer the question, and the person who asked the question would then have to dare you to do something, instead."

Kenyatta rolled her eyes. Those were not the rules of the game when she and her friends used to play it as kids. She didn't know where Rocky got his information. It must have been the prison edition. At first, she was going to challenge him on it, but instead decided to play it his way. "Fine. I dare you to tell me who had me picked up by the police. Was it you or Stuart?"

Rocky sighed. "May I come in, please?"

"You chose 'Dare,' so answer the question." The way he was trying to dodge around it, Kenyatta already knew the answer, but she wanted to hear him say it.

"It was me."

"Bye." She tried to slam the door shut, but a steel-toe boot stopped it. "Move your foot!" she demanded.

"I'm also the reason that they let you go," Rocky said. "Doesn't that count for anything?"

"Liar. My brother is the reason they let me go."

"I'm not lying. I chose not to file a formal complaint."

"Thank you. Okay? Thank you for the wonderful change of heart, but I don't want to talk to you. Good night and good-bye."

"Wait. Wait. Look." He pointed toward the ground. "I have your dinner out here, and it's getting cold." Kenyatta followed the direction of his finger and saw a bag of Chinese takeout sitting near his foot. He sweetened the pot even more. "It's shrimp fried rice, egg rolls, and hot wings. All your favorites." That darn Stuart must have told him everything.

If Kenyatta could have found a way to let the bag of food in without him being attached to it, she would have. Hunger pangs that reheated baked chicken wasn't going to satisfy wouldn't let her send him away. Rocky thanked her as he stepped inside, and she watched him walk past her and place the bags on the living room coffee table. Rocky appeared to get taller and more handsome every time Kenyatta saw him. Like at the gym last week. He really looked good that day. When she saw his bare chest, she was immediately reminded of a shirtless photo of Darrin Dewitt Henson, which she'd seen on the Internet. Rocky was more muscular and had way more tattoos than the *Soul Food* TV series actor, but there were definite similarities in the physiques.

"May I sit?" he asked.

It was only then that Kenyatta realized that she'd been staring. "Suit yourself." She tried to sound uncaring, but he had already caught her looking. She watched him remove his protective knee and elbow pads before he made himself comfortable. She joined him, sitting as far away as possible. The arm of the sofa felt as though it would pierce through the skin of her back.

"Thanks again for letting me in." Rocky placed his safety gear on the floor beside his feet.

Why was he being nice to her? "I only did it for the food." She wasn't about to fall for the okeydoke. He shook his head at her like she was a sad case, but Kenyatta didn't care. He was up to something. It started out nice like this at the gym before everything went south too. "I'm gonna go get a plate. You want one? This looks like a lot of food."

"Are you inviting me to join you?"

Kenyatta sucked her teeth. "Do you want a plate or not?" Without responding, Rocky stood and began walking toward her. Kenyatta held her breath and took a step back. What was he getting ready to do?

"Sit." Rocky pointed at the sofa. "I know where the plates are. I'll go get them."

At a temporary loss for word, Kenyatta eased back down on the sofa. She watched him disappear into the kitchen, and then listened to the clanking of dishes while he gathered whatever he was gathering. Kenyatta was nervous, but she didn't know why. Maybe it was because tonight was the first time she'd actually been alone with Rocky. She picked up the remote and turned up the volume. She needed the distraction.

"Here you go." Rocky came back, with a dinner tray balanced in each hand. He placed one on the coffee table in front of Kenyatta; then he took his to the other end, where he sat.

Kenyatta looked at her tray. He'd not only gotten a plate, but also dinnerware and a glass, which he had filled with cranberry juice. His glass had water. "Thanks," she mumbled.

"I hope that's okay." He pointed at her glass. "That's what you were drinking that other time I came over, so I took for granted that you like it." When she looked at him in silence, he added, "The day you dropped the cup and messed up your pretty dress. I see the stains came out. That's good."

Kenyatta looked down at herself. Oh God! She was wearing the same dress she wore that day! Of all the clothes she had in her closet, she had to pull out the same dress. And he had to remember it.

"That's a really nice color on you, by the way."

"Rocky, what do you want?" Kenyatta had had enough. She didn't know what kind of game he was playing, but she was calling a time-out. If the conversation was going to take a turn for the worse today, it would be on her terms. She wouldn't set herself up to be blindsided again, like at the gym. "You asked if you could come in and talk, and I'm sure you didn't come in to talk about my dress. I appreciate the food, but can you just say what you have to say and leave?"

Rocky licked his lips and nodded slowly. "I guess I deserve that."

"No. You deserve much worse." Kenyatta watched him lift his hand to his chin and rub it. That seemed to be a habit of his. Rocky picked up the remote and muted the television again. He stared at the screen for what seemed like forever. While he studied the picture on the flat-screen television, Kenyatta studied him. Rocky had such a handsome profile. It would be easy for her to be thrown off track, but she wasn't going to allow it. There seemed to be a lot on Rocky's mind, but he was stalling, and Kenyatta was growing impatient. She set her still-empty plate back on the tray. "Rocky—"

"Truth or Dare?" he suddenly said.

Kenyatta narrowed her eyes. "What?"

"Truth or Dare?"

"I'm not playing any games with you, Rocky, now if you have something to say—"

"*Truth* . . . or Dare?" He turned and looked at her that time, and his eyes said this was no game.

Kenyatta swallowed. "Truth."

The chin rubbing continued, and now it felt like his eyes were strip-searching her face. "Do you hate me?"

Kenyatta's eyes migrated to the television screen, and for a moment, she watched as Bryan Mills beat the fool out of the man who had been responsible for the kidnapping of his daughter. If she had been home alone, she would have been cheering him on. She always did when it got to this scene. "No."

"Your turn," Rocky said.

Only then did Kenyatta break her stare from the television screen. She looked at him and decided that she'd play along . . . for a while, anyway. "Truth or Dare?"

"Truth."

"Did you sleep with Lorna?"

A smile tugged at the corner of Rocky's mouth, like he was glad she'd asked. "No."

"Then why—"

"It's my turn," he broke in. "Truth or Dare?"

"Truth." That just seemed to be the safer choice.

"If you don't hate me, why are you always so mean to me?"

"Because you're always mean to me. Truth or Dare?"

His smile had widened. "Truth."

"If you didn't sleep with her, why did you tell me you did?"

"I never told you I slept with her. I told you that she saw the tattoo, and I indicated that the tattoo was in a . . . not-so-easily-seen place, and you assumed if she saw it, then I must have had sex with her."

"But if—"

"My turn." Kenyatta rolled her eyes at him for his constant interruption, but he ignored her. "Truth or Dare?"

"Truth."

He leaned forward in his seat. "So are you saying that if I took the initiative to be nicer to you, you would actually be nicer to me?"

Kenyatta shrugged her shoulders. "Yeah. I guess." He seemed to like that answer, but Kenyatta was eager to take her turn. "Truth or Dare?"

"Truth."

"If you didn't sleep with her, but she saw the tattoo, and the tattoo is in a private place, does that mean that

you had some other type of sexual interaction with
her?" Kenyatta didn't like the pause that followed her
question. He had answered all the others quickly. Was
he trying to think of a good lie to tell for this one? "You
said 'Truth,'" she reminded him.

"I know."

"And I want details," she added.

Rocky's eyebrows rose at her last sentence. He
stalled for a while longer, picking up a shrimp that sat
on top of the rice and putting it in his mouth. Kenyatta
tried to remain patient as he chewed at the speed of
molasses. The smile he displayed earlier was gone now.
After he swallowed, he looked Kenyatta square in the
eyes, and this time, she didn't look away. She wanted
to be sure she would see anything that indicated he
wasn't telling her the whole truth. "We did some making out," he said. "Some *serious* making out." Suddenly
Kenyatta wasn't so sure she wanted to hear it. "There
was a lot of touching, and some partial nudity. My eyes
saw stuff they shouldn't have. My hands touched stuff
they shouldn't have. Hers did the same. We came close.
We came *real* close. Close enough for it to be called
'sin,' but not close enough for it to be called 'sex.'"
Rocky took a breath like having to admit to the details
had been stressful. "She saw the tattoo because of the
partial nudity."

Kenyatta wanted to cry. There was no reason for
tears. He wasn't her man, so even if he had gone all
the way, she had no valid reason to take it personally.
But here she was, swallowing cranberry juice by the
mouthful to hide her pain. By the time she put the glass
down, it was empty.

"It was a weak moment," he continued. He was
looking down at his clasped hands. For the first time,
Kenyatta saw vulnerability. She wanted to reach out

and touch him, to tell him it was okay. Instead, she sat quietly and allowed him to finish unburdening himself. "This lifestyle—this Christian walk—is very different from the way I used to live. Coming to Christ brought overnight deliverance from some things, and other things have been a process. The sexual thing has been a process. I used to be very active. Very, very, *very* active." Kenyatta looked at him. That was an awful lot of "very's." Rocky lifted his eye from their downward cast. He was looking at her again. "Celibacy . . . bringing my flesh under subjection . . . has been a struggle. I've done it, but it hasn't been easy." After a lingering silence, he said, "Truth or Dare?"

Kenyatta had been so captivated by his confession that she'd forgotten that they were playing that game. "Truth."

"Why does it matter to you if I slept with her?"

"It doesn't."

"You said 'Truth,'" he reminded her.

Kenyatta stared at her clasped hands. She liked the prison version of this game better. "Dare," she said.

Rocky exhaled a soft laugh and rubbed his chin. "I dare you to tell me why you care whether I slept with her."

"I don't want to play anymore," Kenyatta said.

"I'll change the question," he offered.

"Okay."

"Why are you wearing your hair down?"

Kenyatta instinctively reached up and touched the tresses that fell past her shoulders. She'd forgotten about her change of hairstyle. "I don't want to play anymore," she repeated.

Rocky laughed again. "I'll change the question."

She cut her eyes in his direction. He was having too much fun at her expense. "What?"

"I know at one time that you were battling Ingrid for Jerome." He paused, and then seemed to brace himself for her reply. "My question is, are you still feelin' him?"

Kenyatta's heart skipped a beat, and she masked an oncoming smile by twisting her mouth and biting at the skin on the inside of it. She could tell that her answer was important to him. "That was a long time ago, and I don't think I was ever *feelin'* Jerome. Certainly not as much as Ingrid was. He made the right choice when he picked her." It was the first time Kenyatta had admitted that out loud. "Do I still think he's cute? Yes. But I'm not interested, and I have no romantic feelings for him." Rocky smiled. He must have liked her answer. She liked his smile. "Truth or Dare?" she challenged.

"Truth."

"What's your birth name?" She saw the way he looked at her. She'd surprised him with that one.

"Rocky."

"You said 'Truth.'"

"That is the truth."

Kenyatta sat up taller. "Your mother actually named you Rocky?"

He shook his head. "She didn't have to name me that for it to be my real name." He fished in his pocket and pulled out his license and placed it on the sofa between them for additional proof.

Kenyatta picked up the laminated card and looked at it. The picture wasn't flattering. It was the Grizzly Adams version of Rocky. It was amazing how different he looked without all that messy facial hair. But sure enough, the name shown was only one word: *Rocky*. "Did you legally change it?" she asked as she handed it back.

"Yes. Over twenty years ago, so it's my real name."

"I asked you for your birth name, not your real name. Rocky's not your birth name." Kenyatta cocked her head and waited for an answer.

"I don't want to play anymore." He reached for his plate. "I'm hungry, anyway." He used the remote to turn up the muted volume of the television, and then reached for the shrimp fried rice and spooned some on her plate before doing the same for himself.

Kenyatta watched him put an egg roll on both their plates; then he evenly divided the six chicken wings. After he silently graced the food, he sat back on the sofa and scooped up a forkful of rice, raised it in her direction like he was making a toast, and then put it in his mouth. It was obvious that he had no intention of answering her question. Rocky had given her two passes on questions she didn't want to answer, so Kenyatta figured it was only fair to let him slide on this one. She picked up her plate, but paused just before picking up her fork. "Truth or Dare?"

"Game's over." He fed himself more shrimp and rice.

"Okay. Well, it's not a part of the game. It's just a question that I would like you to tell me the truth about."

Rocky's eyes remained on the television, and it appeared that he was ignoring her altogether. He watched Bryan Mills flip a switch and electrocute a man whom he had tied to a metal chair with live wires attached. It was one of Kenyatta's favorite scenes too. The electrocuted man was one who had taken part in the kidnapping of Bryan's daughter. Rocky never turned away from the television, but Kenyatta knew he was speaking to her when he said, "Okay."

"When we were still playing the game, why didn't you ask me if I started the fires?"

"Because I only asked the questions that I wasn't already sure of the answers." He finally looked at her. "I already knew the answer to that one."

Chapter Nineteen

Rocky stood in the front room of a newly remodeled two-bedroom, two-bath home and tried to digest the reality that all he had to do was say the word and it was his. The real estate broker, an attractive, maturing white lady named Juliet, who was brave enough to meet them at the house at such an ungodly hour, was citing one amenity after the other and singing the home's praises. None of it was necessary. She'd pretty much had Rocky the moment the front door swung open. It really didn't matter what was said after that. At first sight, the word "sold" was just as good as plastered over the realty company's name on the sign that was planted in the front yard.

Within a few minutes, Juliet had taken Rocky and his entourage of confidants through the entire house. Reverend Tides, Mildred, and Jerome were invited along by default, since they were the ones who had orchestrated the spontaneous open house. To Rocky, the house seemed huge. The master bedroom was twice as large as the one in the burned-down house, and more than twice the size of the room he slept in at Jerome's. Even the guest room was larger than the room he slept in at Jerome's. There was an extra room in the house that Juliet referred to as a storage space, but Rocky pictured it as a home gym. It wouldn't be able to hold much more than a weight bench, free weights, and a treadmill, but that would be all he'd need. In his mind, he could picture the entire house fully furnished, and he liked what he saw.

"This is nice, isn't it, Rocky?"

He looked at Mildred Tides and nodded his answer. Then, still in silence, Rocky parted ways with the rest of them and walked through the living room into the kitchen and stared out the bay windows. There was no real scenery, only landscape and the view of other houses in the neighborhood, and even most of that was hidden by the ten o'clock moonlight. With the way Rocky felt now, it was hard to believe that just a couple of hours ago, he was railing against the idea of even giving consideration to moving into a home in Shelton Heights. It was Wednesday, his first day back at work since the Monday meltdown, showdown, and near smack-down, which had almost led to Kenyatta's lockdown.

On Tuesday, Rocky assured Hunter that he was fine to return to work on, but his boss insisted that he take another day.

"You've made your peace with me, and you've done the same with Stuart and Kenyatta, and that's all good," Hunter told Rocky over the phone late Monday night. "But before you return to the *Atlanta Weekly Chronicles,* I want you to spend a day with God. Take tomorrow and talk to Him. I'm not saying that you haven't spoken to Him and asked for forgiveness for whatever you did that you believe was outside of His will; I'm just saying spend the day with Him. And since I'm forcing this on you, I'll pay you for the day, even though you're still in your probationary period. I just think it'll be good for you."

Hunter had been right, as he usually was in these cases. Yesterday had been a day of reflection. It had been hard to keep focused, but Rocky managed. Ever since their Truth or Dare? evening, Kenyatta had been a constant figure in his head, not to mention his heart. He hadn't seen or spoken to her since they bid each other good night on Monday, but all through the day on Tuesday, he wanted to hop on his motorcycle and drive to Kenyatta's job. The strong desire to see her kept visiting him every few hours, but Rocky would dismiss the idea time and time again, reminding himself of the assignment Hunter had given. This was a day to spend with God.

Prayer was first on Tuesday's agenda. Rocky set his alarm clock, just as he would have if he had been going to work, but when it chimed, instead of jumping up and heading to the bathroom to shower, he rolled out of bed and onto his knees. It was something that Jerome repeatedly challenged the brothers of the Hope for Men ministry to do as a means of strengthening their spiritual lives. Rocky had never applied it before yesterday, but he remembered feeling empowered when he got up from his knees, like nothing could happen during the day that God wouldn't equip him to handle.

After prayer, Rocky washed his face and brushed his teeth, still avoiding the shower stall. It didn't make sense to take a bath just yet, because he had the urge to work out. His initial intent was to head to the local gym for an hour of weight training and a half hour of cardio, but by the time he had changed his clothes, he had also changed his mind. Rocky and Jerome walked out the front door together, but as Jerome hit the road in his truck, heading toward the AWC, Rocky hit the road in his running shoes, heading toward Stone Mountain Park. His legs carried lingering soreness from Monday's eight-mile jog with Peter, but Rocky pushed through it. Once he conquered the first three treacherous, hilly miles that delivered him from the house to the park, he was good to go the distance. But his plans were revamped again, once he reached the point that would have marked the start of his five-mile run. Rocky was reinforcing the knot in the shoestrings of his running shoes when he overheard two men who walked past him talking about readying themselves to climb the mountain. *Climb the mountain?* Intrigued, Rocky fell in line behind them and followed at a distance, hoping that they would escort him to the place where climbing was the order of the day.

The men led him to a trail on which others were already walking. Rocky had never walked up a mountain before, and his heart pounded, not in fear, but in anticipation of the experience. It was a much shorter distance than the five-mile run would have been. Walking the trail that led to the top of Stone Mountain was only 1.3 miles, but every step of it was an uphill climb. Overhearing the words of others who were also taking on the challenge, Rocky learned that everyone who reached the top got firsthand knowledge of what it felt like to stand nearly 1,700 feet above sea level. Once he made it, he was in awe. From the top of the mountain, Rocky could see miles and miles of the city below. Without moving from his spot, he could shift his eyes one way and view downtown Atlanta, and shift them another and glimpse mountains in North Georgia. He was sure that he was seeing stuff that was fifty miles away from where he stood, maybe even farther. He wished he had a camera and made a mental note to have one the next time he did this. It was phenomenal, and he was viewing it all from *upon this rock.*

Rocky looked up into the sky. It almost seemed so close that if he jumped high enough, he could touch the heavens. It was impossible, but that was the impression it gave. The elevation made him feel closer to God and so, so far away from whatever was happening below. Rocky looked out over the cityscape. Somewhere down there, someone was dealing with the road rage that often accompanied Atlanta's morning rush-hour congestion. Somewhere down there, a husband and wife were at the height of a domestic dispute. Somewhere down there, a drug deal was going down, and maybe even going bad. Somewhere down there, a prisoner, just like the one he once was, was peering through the slit in their cell's wall and longing for the chance to be free. Somewhere down there, there was a house that had now been burned to the ground two times within three months, with no definitive reasons as to how or why. But as long as he stood at the top of the mountain, none of it could affect him. Rocky was above it all.

"Upon this rock I will build my church; and the gates of hell shall not prevail against it."

Reminders of Reverend Tides's sermon made Rocky not ever want to come down, but he had to. There were more things on his agenda that needed to get done, and unlike on Monday, he didn't have a ride back home, so he needed to get moving. Not that he wouldn't have taken walking over *that* ride, anyway. Rocky still couldn't believe Peter's warped sense of humor. If he were Peter, instead of laughing, Rocky would be worried. That Christian Cocoa Puff was Jan's mother. For all Peter knew, whatever was wrong with Leona Grimes might be hereditary, and it just might be only a matter of time before his wife would be just as batty.

The trek back home consisted of more walking than jogging, but that just gave Rocky more time to meditate. The breeze of Tuesday's early morning was a thousand times more inviting than Monday's mid-afternoon temperatures had been.

After finally reaching home and showering and shaving, Rocky had done something that he thought would take weeks for him to gather the will to do. He saddled his motorcycle and visited the latest ruins of his home. Just as he had done for many days after the first fire, Rocky parked his Harley-Davidson in the driveway and sat on the edge of the property and looked at the devastation. Just this past weekend, he had been at the same site, chatting and laughing with the contractors, and feeling good about the high probability that he would be back in his home before the end of the year. "After Thanksgiving, but before Christmas" was what one of the builders had told him. "Merry Christmas to me," Rocky had responded, and the two of them laughed together. Now everything was gone again. Nothing remained. Even the builders were gone, and they had taken all of their machinery with them. It looked, once again, like a wasteland. More papers had to be filed, another investigation had to be launched, the burned material would have to be removed once more, and at some point, rebuilding would begin . . . again.

"Lord, are you trying to tell me something?" Rocky was looking up into the sky as he whispered the words. He wished a plane would suddenly appear and use its exhaust to write the answer overhead.

Rocky didn't know what to think anymore. Was there really someone out there who was trying to teach him a lesson? Was he being made an example? Had he become Exhibit A of what happens when one leaves the game? None of the guys Rocky knew were cowards. They wouldn't throw a rock and hide their hands. If they were responsible for torching his house, they would have made themselves known by now—even if only to him. Rocky had sat on the edge of the property for what felt like forever and tried to make sense of it all. All of his current friends seemed to want to believe it was a coincidence. Could it be? Maybe it was faulty wiring the first time, but what were the chances that back-to-back blazes on the same property were both accidental? Neither scenario—the one about the gangsters or the one that faulted happenstance—made good sense to Rocky.

He was making preparations to head back to Jerome's when the school bus pulled up at the stop across the street to drop off the neighborhood kids. Only then did Rocky realize he had been sitting there for two hours. He was just about to put on his helmet when he saw a vaguely familiar face headed his way. It was the boy who'd given him the liquor two months ago.

"Why yo' house keep burning down?" No hi, no hello . . . nothing. The boy craned his neck to look up into Rocky's face while he waited for an answer.

"I don't know."

"My daddy says you a playa, and that's why it keeps catching on fire."

Rocky was taken aback for two reasons. First of all, he wouldn't have guessed that the boy even had a daddy, at least, not one who was active in his life. He'd just assumed when the boy's mother so generously sent him the cold drink, she was a single mom on the hunt to net her kid a dad. Secondly, unless the boy's father knew him, Rocky didn't understand why the man would make that kind of assumption. Especially in front of his child. "What's your daddy's name?" Rocky held his breath. If the boy had said Eric or Tyrone or Lance, or any other of the real names that belonged to "Nose Face," "Smoke," or other crew members, Rocky's Tuesday was about to turn sour.

"Autley Dennison."

Rocky knew no one with that first or last name. "Does your daddy know me or something?" He was still curious as to why the man would draw such a blind conclusion.

"Nope," the boy said. "But he said he know a woman was the one who did this." He pointed toward the burned property.

"Did your dad see a woman out here? Did he see who did this?" A bit of fear and doubt threatened to creep into Rocky's heart, but he willed it away. No . . . Kenyatta didn't do this, and he wouldn't let anybody make him think she did.

"Nope," the boy repeated. "But he said only a ho would do some mess like this." Rocky's eyes widened, but he didn't have time to say anything before the kid continued. "He said if you had jerked around some dude, he would just shoot you and get it over with. Only a woman would set fire to your house, 'cause that's the kind of stuff they do."

"Well, I'm sure he's the expert," Rocky said, strapping on his helmet. He opted not to even reprimand the boy for his degradation of women. What good would it do? As long as the boy was going home to a father like that, Rocky felt a correction would be useless. "You probably should run along home now. But tell your dad I said thanks for the helpful information. I'm sure it will be highly useful in solving the mystery. Oh . . ." He dug his hand in his pocket and pulled out a bill. "I found out that I didn't pay your mama enough for that drink she gave me. Take that to her, and tell her I said thanks again." He watched as the boy trotted off with a satisfied smile. His mother wouldn't see that five any more than she saw the ten.

***

"There you are. You're being too quiet, son. What do you think? Do you like it?"

The voice from behind him pulled Rocky back to the present, and he broke out of his stare into the darkness and turned to look at Reverend Tides. Juliet, Mildred, and Jerome were standing behind the pastor. All of them looked equally anxious to hear his answer to the question that had been posed. "Yes," Rocky said. "This is nice. Very nice. Way more than I expected."

"And what about that price?" Jerome made a three-sixty as he turned to get a full scope of the living-room space behind where they all stood. "It's ridiculous, man. The price is just ridiculous!"

"Oh no," Juliet said, whipping around to face Jerome, and then turning her face back toward Rocky. Her expression teetered between panicked and offended. "No no no. It's not ridiculous. Interest rates are at their lowest right now. This is the absolute best time to buy a house, and especially one here in Shelton Heights. The price is not ridiculous at all. It's fabulous. I think it fabulous. Don't you think the price is fabulous, Mr. Rocky?" She had insisted on putting the title there ever since she was informed that he only had the one name. Initially, when Juliet asked for his last name, and Rocky told her he didn't have one, the lady had smiled and said, "Oh. Are you mononymous?" It was a good thing that Reverend Tides was in the room, because Rocky thought she was trying to make a pass at him. Reverend Tides answered with a yes on his behalf, and then explained to Rocky later that it was a term used for people with only one name.

Rocky had felt pretty stupid at the time, but now that he had one up on her, the score was even. "'Ridiculous' means *outstanding,* ma'am," Rocky clarified over Jerome's laughter. "At least in this case."

"Oh." Juliet released an uncomfortable giggle and raked her fingers through her short, graying hair. "Oh. Well, yes. Yes . . . it is ridiculous." Her face had turned crimson, and she all of a sudden sounded ill at ease. "And you want to know what else is ridiculous? The fresh coat of paint on the walls, and the brand-new carpet on the floors. Not to mention that this kitchen comes fully furnished with a brand-new stove, dishwasher, and refrigerator. Now *that* is what I call ridiculous. Don't you think that's ridiculous too?" Poor thing. Now she was babbling. By now, Jerome had excused himself and had gone to hide his laughter in the bathroom down the hall.

Mildred Tides changed the subject, probably to keep the woman from drowning in her own pool of embarrassment. She pointed out toward the living room. "That carpet really is a very nice color. What do you call that?"

"Yes, yes, it's very nice," Juliet said while putting her glasses on and looking at the paper attached to the clipboard in her hand. "Columbus Blue," she announced. "It's called Columbus Blue." She led the way back into the open space and spread out her arms like Barker's Beauties used to do on *The Price Is Right*. "Is there anything else I can show you, or perhaps any other questions that I can answer for you, Mr. Rocky?"

He wished she would stop calling him that. "Uh . . . no. I think I've seen enough."

"Do you need some time to think about it?" Reverend Tides asked him. "It's late, and I know you're tired. This was print day at the *AWC,* and it was a long one for you. Plus, I know about your . . . *cautions* about the neighborhood. You don't have to rush, and you don't have to feel obligated just because Mother Tides and I set up this spontaneous meeting for you. I really just wanted you to see the quality that you can get for your money. If you want to take a few days to think about it, I'm sure I can talk to the right people who will give you that, and not make the house available to others until the set deadline has passed."

Rocky could certainly understand why his pastor thought he might need more time to think. After the fit Rocky had pitched when he and Jerome stopped by the Tides's house for dinner on the way from work, it made sense to think that he would need time.

While they enjoyed dinner, Rocky mentioned his decision to move out on his own. He'd come to that decision on his ride back to Jerome's after viewing the remains of the home in which he once had lived. During that ten-mile bike ride, he resolved that he didn't want to be a boarder at Jerome's for another four months, or however long it would take for another investigation to be complete and the house to be rebuilt.

"Somewhere out there, there is a home—one with two bedrooms—that I should be able to afford, now that I have steady work," he'd concluded.

The thought had barely left Rocky's mouth when Reverend Tides began telling him that he should move into Shelton Heights. He'd had a dream on Sunday night, the night before Rocky's house had become charred rubble again, that Rocky had moved into the infamous community. Reverend Tides said not only did he dream of Rocky's relocation there, but in the dream, Rocky had moved into the largest house in the subdivision. Reverend Tides described it as having the appearance of a mansion. Rocky's response was to laugh and ask his pastor what he'd eaten before going to bed that could have triggered such a far-fetched dream. Reverend Tides laughed too, but he insisted that there was some meaning to it.

"Maybe it means I'm getting ready to die and go to heaven." Rocky laughed. "What you saw must have been my mansion in the sky."

"Baby, don't say that." Mildred saw no humor in it.

"Rocky, don't miss your blessing by being narrow-minded," Reverend Tides warned.

"I don't mean to be narrow-minded," Rocky explained. "I do want to move, but not out here. There are a gazillion houses in metropolitan Atlanta. Shelton Heights has some nice houses—I'll give y'all that—but if I got crazy stuff happening to me somewhere else, ain't no tellin' what would happen here."

Reverend Tides shook his head. "You're insulting the Lord, son. Don't you serve the Almighty?"

"Yes, but so do you, and it didn't stop you from being kidnapped a few years ago, and halfway starved to death while you were chained up in some deranged dude's basement," Rocky blurted out. "And it didn't stop Pete from being captured as a prisoner of war and coming deathly close to being beheaded. And it didn't stop Stuart from being stalked and threatened by his crazy ex-wife. So what does serving God have to do with it?"

"We're all still here, aren't we?" Reverend Tides said. "My offender is in a psych ward. Most of Pete's offenders were massacred. Stuart's offender is doing time. Yes, we went through those things, but every one of us survived, and we came out as stronger men of God than we ever were before what we went through."

Rocky put down his fork, which wasn't easy, considering the fact that Mildred Tides's veal parmesan was the best he'd ever had. "I understand what you're saying, Pastor, but my life has been hard enough. My house burning down twice was something that was out of my control. Trouble found me, but at least I did all I could to avoid it. I didn't go looking for it. If I go looking for a house out here, that's as good as saying I'm looking for trouble. Where I was living, it ain't got no track record of meteorites falling out of the sky and killing people, and kids making the mistake of taking their own eyes out with BB guns, and bears trampling through people's homes in the middle of the night, or pastors being kidnapped by members of their own church."

"He wasn't a member." Mother Tides was quick to correct Rocky's statement. "His name wasn't on the church roll, and he never paid tithes. He wasn't a member. He was a habitual visitor."

Rocky wiped his hands with a napkin. "The point I'm getting at is that all that stuff happened to people out here. Y'all can't deny that weird stuff happens in Shelton Heights."

"He's superstitious," Jerome mumbled through a mouthful of food.

"I am not," Rocky contested. "I'm just *cautious*, that's all."

Even after all that, Reverend Tides convinced Rocky just to be open-minded enough to look at one of the available houses. Then he made one phone call, and within half an hour, they were meeting Juliet at the front door of the home that had changed Rocky's tune. It was a far cry from the description of the mansion that Reverend Tides had dreamed about, but Rocky loved it.

"I don't need time to think about it," he told Reverend Tides. Then looking at Juliet, Rocky added, "What do I have to do to seal the deal?"

Chapter Twenty

This was normally the night Kenyatta joined her sisters for Women of Hope, but the unsigned note she had found attached to the front door when she got home from work on Thursday changed all that. The simple one-liner said: *Kenyatta, please check the voice mail on your home phone.* It was followed by a series of twenty numbers that were as foreign to her as was the neat penmanship that had been used to write them.

Ordinarily, she would have parked her car in the garage and entered through the connecting door, but since she planned to leave for the church meeting in a little while, Kenyatta had parked in the driveway and was using the front entrance. The note raised her awareness, and she caught herself looking around to scope her surroundings before folding the slip of paper in her closed hand and letting herself inside the house. Once she was inside, the very first thing she did was to lock the door and reset the alarm. The knowledge that someone had been at the front door sticking an anonymous note on it made her feel uneasy. It also intrigued her.

Kenyatta didn't even bother to put her belongings down before making a beeline to the telephone that sat on the shelf of the entertainment center. The upright AT&T unit was more for show than anything else. With the convenience of their cell phones, the landline was rarely used. Kenyatta punched in the code to retrieve the messages and was alerted by the automated voice that four of them were in cue. For a while, it seemed that none of them were of any concern to her. The first message was from her mother asking Stuart to give her a call. The second was from some charitable organization soliciting donations for a clothing drive. The third was her mother again, scolding Stuart for not returning her previous call. When the fourth message began, Kenyatta's ears came to attention.

"Hi, Kenyatta, it's Rocky. I tried to call you at work about thirty minutes ago, but you'd already left. I would have called your cell, but I don't have the number, and your bigheaded brother wouldn't give it to me." Kenyatta smiled at the annoyed tone Rocky used when he said that part. "I didn't want to just show up at the house and put you on the spot or nothing, so I figured I'd call this number and stick a note on the door to make sure you got the message, 'cause I remember Tyler saying one time that he didn't even know why y'all had a home phone, 'cause nobody ever used it." Kenyatta smiled at that too. It was the truth. "Anyway, I was wondering if you'd consider . . . I don't know . . . going out with me tonight?" The strap of Kenyatta's handbag slid from her shoulder and the whole thing dropped to the floor. What did he just say? "I got something I want to show you, but you have to go out with me to see it. So, will you? I left my number at the bottom of the note. I tried to code it so if anybody else saw the note, they wouldn't be able to figure it out." Rocky laughed at himself. "Every other number on the paper is a good number. So take the second, fourth, sixth, and so on, and you'll have my number. Call me . . . please . . . and let me know if I can come by and pick you up. I know tomorrow's a workday. We won't be out late. Promise. Talk to you later. I hope."

When the machine prompted her to save, erase, or play the message again, Kenyatta chose option number three. She had to be sure she'd heard it right the first time. Had Rocky just asked her out? The instant replay proved that he had. Once she got beyond the initial shock, excitement crept in. In a million years, she never would have thought he would ask her out. Kenyatta wasn't naïve. She knew that there was some chemistry between the two of them. And if she'd had any doubts about it before, they would have been erased when he asked her how she felt about Jerome. But still . . . she never would have expected an invitation from him, and for certain, not this soon. It was just three nights ago that, for the very first time, they'd started a civilized conversation that was still civilized when it ended.

Kenyatta looked at the twenty-digit number on the paper that had still been folded in her hand. Clever. She reached for her purse and pulled out her cell, but stopped shy of dialing. If she called from her cell, her number would appear on his caller ID. Sure, she wanted him to have it, but she wasn't sure that she wanted him to know that she wanted him to have it. Not yet, anyway. Kenyatta tucked her cell back in its place, and then reached for the cordless phone that was on the stand in front of her. She was pressing the final number of his area code when she stopped again. She should probably wait. Of course, she was in a hurry to call him, but she wasn't in a hurry to let him know that she was in a hurry to call him. Not yet, anyway.

I know. I'll take my bath first; then I'll call him. Kenyatta reasoned within herself that a good long soak in the tub was just what she needed in order to relax. And this was the best time to take advantage of it.

Stuart had his own private bathroom, which was attached to his master bedroom, but Kenyatta was forced to share the second one with Tyler. Sharing a home with her brother would be nearly perfect if there wasn't that bathroom issue. Having to pick up behind her sloppy nephew, especially the dirty socks that he habitually left in the middle of the bathroom floor, was a constant aggravation. Kenyatta didn't understand why the boy kept his bedroom so neat, but he didn't see the need to do the same for the restroom.

While Kenyatta ran her bath, she pinned up her hair with a butterfly clip, and then stood over the sink and pampered her face. She removed the makeup she'd been wearing all day, gave her skin a deep cleansing, then followed up with exfoliating, toning, and moisturizing. In her family, skin complexion varied. Her two older sisters were fair-skinned, she and her younger brother were brown, and Stuart was dark. Very dark. Family members would often refer to him as their mother's tar baby. He was in his teens before the family realized they had been offending him for years. Stuart had long outgrown that complex now. Somewhere along the way, that dark skin of his had turned to his advantage. He loved his hue, and so did the ladies.

Regardless of their skin's shade, though, Kenyatta and all of her siblings had enjoyed flawless skin all their lives. They didn't even go through the normal skin woes that puberty was known for causing. When Kenyatta's middle-school and high-school friends were waging war against pimples with every skin cleanser and cream that promised a miracle, Kenyatta was barely washing her face at all. Every morning she'd wipe her skin with a warm cloth and go about her day. It wasn't until she hit thirty that she started coddling her skin. It wasn't about waging war on acne; it was about waging war on aging. Kenyatta had determined that she wasn't going down without a fight. She rarely revealed her age, opting to keep people guessing, instead.

Her bath wasn't as long as she would have liked it to be. Kenyatta wanted to make Rocky wait, but she didn't want him to wait so long that he assumed she wouldn't call. If he made that assumption, he might make other plans. Kenyatta didn't want that. It had been a long time since she'd been on a date. She got invitations all the time, but few of them were accepted. At her age, she didn't see the point in going out with a man who didn't have the potential or a prayer of being *her man*. It was a waste of time. Maybe that was the real reason that she felt so flustered right now. She was accepting Rocky's invitation. Did that mean she saw him as having potential?

She emerged from the bathroom wrapped in an oversize cotton towel. It only took her a few minutes to choose an outfit. He hadn't given a clue of where they would be going. So after moisturizing her body from head to toe, Kenyatta chose something versatile, not too dressy and not too casual. A silk burgundy twinset by Bob Mackie, black slacks by Salvatore Ferragamo, and burgundy pumps from Anne Klein. Her full-length mirror told her that she was ready for anything, whether Rocky chose dinner and a movie, dinner and dancing, or something totally different. All that was left was to fire up the curling iron and touch up her hair. Kenyatta walked from her room to the living room. Now would be a good time to make the phone call. By the time Rocky got dressed and reached her, she'd be fully ready.

"Hello?"

Kenyatta almost laughed when he answered on the first ring. Talk about anxiety. Apparently, she'd had him worried, and she liked the idea that for the past hour or so, Rocky had been on pins and needles wondering if she would accept his invitation. "I got your message." She tried her best to sound calm, lethargic even. That way, he'd think that she'd just walked in the door from work and the answer of whether she'd take him up on his offer was still up in the air.

"I'm glad you did," Rocky replied. "So how much time do you need?"

Kenyatta pulled the phone from her ear and looked at it, like the phone itself had said the words. "How much time do I need for what?"

"To get ready."

Oh no, he didn't. "I haven't said I was going anywhere."

"I know. But I bought a new, shiny helmet for you and everything. You have to."

"A new what?" He couldn't possibly think she was going to ride on his motorcycle. They'd take her car. The motorcycle was definitely out of the question.

"A new helmet," he repeated. "Open the door."

"What door?"

Rocky laughed like she needed special tutoring. "The front door of the house, Kenyatta. I'm at your house."

Without properly ending the call, she set the cordless phone back on its stand and walked to the front door to look out the peephole. Sure enough, he was there. That arrogant cuss! He hadn't been on any pins, nor had he been on any needles. Rocky was so certain she'd go out with him that he'd already arrived. And speaking of already arrived—just how long had he been there?

"How long have you been here?" Kenyatta's thoughts were made verbal as soon as she opened the door.

Before he answered, Rocky's eyes did a thorough scan of her selected outfit. The red helmet that had been trapped near his left armpit, between his arm and his side, was removed and now dangled in his right hand. For a short while, words seemed to escape him. "I, uh . . ." Rocky licked his lips and started over. "I, uh . . . I've been here for about twenty minutes."

"But you were supposed to wait for me to call you." Kenyatta felt the onset of an attitude. She placed her left hand on her hips, and her right foot was starting to tap. "What made you so sure I was gonna say yes?"

His eyes were locked on hers now, and the smile he offered was one she'd never seen before. It was shy and boyish. It was endearing. "I wasn't. But in Reverend Tides's message last Sunday, he said sometimes when we ask for the impossible things . . . you know . . . the things that we really don't think we qualify for or deserve, we have to ask for them in faith, and then act like it's already done." Rocky shifted his feet a little. "I just thought I'd try it out."

Kenyatta suddenly felt some kind of different. It was a feeling that she couldn't define and wasn't sure that she wanted to. She also wasn't sure how to respond to what he'd just said. The longer she stood there and returned his gaze, she found that Rocky's eyes were beginning to hypnotize her. Kenyatta turned away and walked deeper into the house. No verbal invitation was extended for him to follow, but Rocky took the liberty, anyway, and he closed the door behind him. When Kenyatta found her voice, she said, "I just need to do something with my hair real quick. I'll be right back." Her eyes fell to the helmet he held in his hand. The color was pretty, but she hoped he didn't think for a moment that she was going to put that thing on her head. Just so there was no misunderstanding, she added, "I'll get my keys too. We can take my car."

"Thanks, but I'd rather take my bike, if you don't mind."

Kenyatta looked at him like he was crazy. She *did* mind. Never in her life had she been on a motorcycle, and she didn't want to start today. And she knew he saw her outfit because she made good note of him checking her out when she first opened the door. This outfit did more than *look* like it cost a lot of money. Maybe he didn't understand. "No, really," Kenyatta said. "We can take my car."

"Thanks, but I'd rather take my bike, if you don't mind." He said it just like he'd said it the first time. It was literally like someone had pressed rewind, and then pushed play. Kenyatta opened her mouth to protest further, but when Rocky started strutting toward her, her voice lodged itself in her throat. He got within inches of her and stopped to place the helmet on the sofa beside where they stood. In the middle of inhaling, Kenyatta's breathing was placed under arrest when she saw both his hands headed toward her face. She felt the air become lodged in her chest, and she reached for the back of the sofa, hoping that holding on to it would soften her fall if she passed out from lack of oxygen.

As it turned out, Rocky was aiming for her hair, but that still didn't stop her insides from quivering. He gathered her loose curls in his hand and gently pulled them toward the back of her head. His fingers did a quick massage of her scalp in the process. If Kenyatta didn't know any better, she'd swear that he was trying to check for lumps or tracks. Was he trying to find out if her hair was *her hair?* "Why don't you wear it back in a bow, like you had it at the gym that day?" His voice was barely above a whisper. Either that or Kenyatta's blood was rushing to her head and stopping up her ears. "If you wear it back, you can wear the helmet and not be concerned with it messing up nothing." He paused for a minute, like he was giving her time to consider his suggestion; then he said, "What do you think?"

What did she *think?* She'd already lost the ability to talk, hear, and breathe. How on earth was she supposed to be able to think under these conditions? He backed away, putting some needed space between them. Then Kenyatta backed away too. When she felt sure that her legs were strong enough to support her weight, she released her hold on the sofa then turned and walked back toward the bathroom. Not only did she have to do something with her hair, but she also needed to replace the makeup she'd washed away during her shower. But first things first. Before any of that, she had to find a way to exhale the air that was still trapped in her chest.

Chapter Twenty-one

"The tighter you hold on, the safer you'll feel," Rocky said over his shoulder just before revving up his Harley-Davidson. As soon as the motor roared, Kenyatta squeezed harder. Rocky savored the feel of her arms around his waist, and then used his foot to make it roar again. This time, he could feel her nails pressing against his flesh. The fabric of his shirt served as a barrier between Kenyatta's fingers and his skin, but he could still feel the sharpness of her manicure, and it was giving him far more pleasure than pain. Rocky reeled in his senses. It was time to stop taking advantage of her fear. "We're getting ready to start moving now," he announced to her. "It's gonna seem like we're going real fast, 'cause we don't have the doors and windows that cars have. I promise you, you won't be in any danger, okay?"

"I'm scared." She was whimpering. "I've never liked motorcycles. I don't trust these things."

"Do you trust me?" He looked over his shoulder at her and watched her head bob up and down in reply. Whether she really trusted him, Rocky didn't know. But to see her indicate that she did was enough to satisfy him. "Good," he said. "Don't worry. You're safe with me." Kenyatta nodded again, but she immediately pressed the face of her helmet into his back as they prepared for takeoff. Rocky grinned, and then he guided his motorcycle into the street.

The ride from Stone Mountain to its neighboring suburban town of Lithonia was really just a strategy to spend more time with Kenyatta. It was also a ploy that Rocky used as a means to show her a little of his life. He was as passionate about riding as she was about shopping. Rocky took his first motorcycle ride at the age of six. He recalled it so well because it was the only clear, good memory he had of spending time with his father. Rocky was in kindergarten at the time, and his dad came riding to the school on a new bike he'd purchased. School had just been recessed for the day, and all the kids were fascinated with the shiny, loud machine. Rocky felt like "Student of the Month." All the boys wanted to be his buddy after that day because they hoped a friendship with Rocky would win them the same opportunity that he was getting: a ride on the back of a motorcycle.

Rocky's dad hoisted him up on the seat and told him to hold on tightly. When Rocky told his dad how afraid he was, he got the same response that he'd just given Kenyatta. "Don't worry. You're safe with me." Neither of them wore helmets or any other kind of safety gear that day, but his dad said they were safe, and Rocky believed him. It turned out to be the thrill of Rocky's life, and right then and there, he decided that the day would come when he'd have a bike of his own. It had taken years to live that reality, but here he was . . . and today he was sharing the experience with Kenyatta.

Rocky had put some real thought into the plans that he had cooked up for tonight, but all that was on the agenda was dinner. He didn't want the evening to end too quickly, so as sunset rested on the city, he rode like the wind. The longer they rode, the more relaxed Kenyatta became. Her opened eyes and relaxed grip were two distinct telltale signs.

"Where are we going?" They had slowed to a stop behind a line of other vehicles, which had been interrupted by a traffic light, when Kenyatta asked the question.

Rocky turned his head and looked at her. She had her chin resting comfortably on his left shoulder. He smiled. "That helmet looks really cute on you. Do you know that?" He could see her face light up behind the clear protective shield.

"Don't avoid the question," she said. "We've been riding for twenty minutes. Where are we going?"

Rocky thought she was having fun, but now he wondered if he should be concerned. "You're not enjoying the ride?"

"Actually, I am. Very much." She kind of shifted the position of her hands at that moment, and Rocky thought he'd jump out of his skin. The movement felt too much like a caress. There was no way she didn't feel how every muscle in his torso had contracted beneath her touch, but Kenyatta kept talking as though nothing had happened. "I haven't eaten since early this afternoon when my coworker Carter insisted upon treating me to lunch. I should have known better than to agree to it. All she ever eats is that green stuff that grows around the bottom of trees, so we ended up at some health food sandwich shop. I had a tofu salad that tasted like newspaper shredding."

Laughing, Rocky said, "So what you're telling me is riding is fun, but you're ready to eat."

"Exactly, so I hope we're headed in the direction of somewhere that serves food."

The traffic light changed. "We are now," Rocky said as he lifted his feet from the ground. When they approached the next intersection, he pressed the gas pedal hard and made a sharp turn to the left, which caused the cycle to lean. Kenyatta screamed and squeezed him so tightly that Rocky thought she'd break his ribs. He laughed out loud, and then hollered over his shoulder, "Just hang on and ride, baby girl. I got you."

They rode in silence for the next ten minutes, and then Kenyatta spoke again. "Are we going in circles?" The only thing that surprised Rocky about her question was that she hadn't asked it sooner. The scenery had started being familiar five minutes earlier. He knew that once Kenyatta noted it, the cross-examination would begin. "If we were gonna eat over here in Stone Mountain, why did we ride all the way to Lithonia?"

"I wanted to go the scenic route," Rocky replied over his shoulder.

"Where are you taking me?"

"The same place I'm taking me."

"Okay, then. Where are you taking you?"

Rocky took his left hand off the handlebar, and used it to tap her on the thigh. "No backseat driving, please, ma'am."

Another five minutes passed, and then: "We're headed right back to Shelton Heights," Kenyatta observed aloud. The subdivision's sign was only a few hundred feet away. "Are you taking me back home?"

Rocky said nothing as he turned into the neighborhood and began navigating his motorcycle up and down the streets. Finally he delivered them to the driveway of a dimly lit home. "I want you to meet somebody," he told Kenyatta while climbing off his Harley-Davidson and helping her to do the same.

She looked around. This house and the house she shared with Stuart were on opposite ends of the large subdivision. "Who is it? Who lives here?"

"You'll see." He hung both their helmets on the handles of the cycle, and then he placed his hand on the small of Kenyatta's back and led her to the front door.

For dramatic effect, Rocky rang the doorbell, and the two of them stood together in silence for a short while.

"I don't think the owners are home," Kenyatta said. "You must not have told them that you were coming by. You can't just spring up at people's houses at eight o'clock at night."

"Maybe *you* can't, but I can." Rocky put his hand in his pocket and pulled out a key ring and began unlocking the door.

"What are you doing?" Kenyatta's whisper was frantic. "You've got a key? How did you get a key?"

When the door opened, they were greeted by darkness and the smell of something delicious. Rocky flicked on the switch that would turn on the floor lamp nearest the door. He didn't want too much light—just enough that would allow him to see the evolution of Kenyatta's expression once reality sank in. From her current look of utter perplexity, she was still a long way from figuring it out.

"What's going on? Who lives here?" She looked to him for a reply, but instead of answers, Rocky only gave clues.

His hand remained on her back, and he led her farther into the sparsely furnished living room. Other than the tall lamp that he'd turned on, there was only a flat-screen television that stood on a stand against one wall, and a black blanket that was spread in the middle of the floor, with floor pillows on top of it.

"Rocky? . . ." Kenyatta's face said that she still wasn't getting it.

"Come here." Rocky released her back and took her hand in his. That was a first. He'd never held her hand before. However, when he felt Kenyatta's fingers return his grasp, he knew she had no qualms with his forwardness. But when he led her to the blanket, she stiffened. Rocky immediately understood her hesitation. A blanket. Pillows. Low lighting. He could only imagine where her mind was traveling. "Trust me," he whispered. Then he extended his free hand in the direction of the floor. "Sit. Please."

He helped her arrange the pillows in a way that she would be comfortable, and when she was seated, he walked into the kitchen and began preparing their plates. It was a simple meal; one of the very few that he knew how to prepare. Smothered fried chicken, yellow rice, and green beans, which he'd heated right out of the can. Rocky returned to the living room, balancing a bamboo bed tray in each of his hands. Kenyatta had removed her shoes and had them sitting on one side of her next to her handbag. On each of the trays were their meals on paper plates, with napkins, plastic dinnerware, and individual packets of hand-sanitizing cloths on the tray beside the plates. When he set one of them in front of her, he watched her face and could tell that the lightbulb was slowly turning on.

"Rocky, what on earth—"

"Shhh. I'm not done yet." With a grin on his face, Rocky headed back to the kitchen. He was smiling because Kenyatta was smiling, and if she was smiling, that had to mean he was doing something right. Most guys probably wouldn't have been overly concerned about such trivial matters, but Rocky was. Being romantic didn't come naturally, and he'd worried all afternoon whether what he was doing was right.

In his lifetime, Rocky had had a lot of women. Not girlfriends. Not wives. Not relationships. He wouldn't even call them lovers, because love had absolutely nothing to do with it. They were just women. From the time Rocky lost his virginity at the age of fourteen while in a group setting at an unauthorized house party, all he had ever identified women with was sexual gratification. It wasn't about romance, and it definitely wasn't about love. It was just about doing it, and being done with it until it was time to do it again. That's all his mother had been good for in any of her relationships, including her current one. She'd been married to the same jerk now for over thirty years, but she'd never been any more to him than she had been to the men before him. Rocky didn't have a father whose loving actions he could mimic. This position that he felt himself applying for in Kenyatta's life was one for which he was grossly underqualified. He had no education or experience to bring to the table. But he was submitting his résumé, anyway.

As he filled two long-stem glasses (the only "real" dishes he had in the house other than the cookware he'd borrowed from Jerome) with cranberry juice, Rocky kept thinking how fortunate it was for him that his kitchen came fully furnished. Juliet had been right. Those were great amenities to have. They had helped him to pull off this homemade dinner date on such short notice. He never would have had the time to shop and purchase a stove or a refrigerator in enough time to christen his first full day in the new house with this special dining experience.

"Thank you. This smells good," Kenyatta said when he placed her glass on her tray. Then when he slipped his feet from his shoes and sat behind his tray across from her, she finished her earlier question. "What's going on, Rocky? Why are we here, and how did you get a key to get in?" She leaned forward and whispered, "We are here legally, aren't we?"

Maybe Rocky should have been offended by her insinuation, but he wasn't. "No crime in a man being in his own house, is it?"

"His . . . own . . . house?" Kenyatta repeated the words slower than he'd initially said them, but it was obvious that she still hadn't connected all the dots when she followed up with, "Who is *his,* and where is he? Whose house are we in?"

Rocky reached for her hands, and after a moment's hesitation, she obliged. With his head bowed, he said, "Lord, thank you for this food that we are about to eat, and thank you for the home—*my* home—that you allowed the food to be prepared in. And thank you for my first houseguest, Kenyatta. And please let her like this food I cooked. In Jesus' name. Amen."

Rocky raised his head, and after a few seconds, he released Kenyatta's hands. She stared at him as he stripped open his sanitizer packet and pulled out the wet napkin to wash his hands. He pointed at her packet. "That's the best I could do for tonight. My water won't be turned on until tomorrow, but if you insist on soap and water, I have some bottled water in the kitchen and you can take it in the bathroom and use it to wash and rinse over the sink if you want."

"This is your house?" Her silence was finally broken.

"Yes. I signed the paperwork this morning, and I started moving in this afternoon." He looked around the dimly lit space. "I still have a long way to go, and Jerome said I could stay with him for as long as I needed, but I decided to move in right away, which might not have been the best move to make, seeing as I don't have no furniture and no running water." Rocky looked back at her. "But I have air, and I have electricity, and I have . . . you . . . here as my first dinner guest, so I'm good."

Kenyatta turned her face away from him without responding. At first, he didn't know what her reaction meant, or how to find out what it meant. But the more she kept her face turned away from him, the more Rocky realized that Kenyatta was having an emotional moment. His words had moved her. They had moved him too. When Rocky said that last part, he felt a distinct warming in his chest.

When she insisted upon keeping her face turned toward the blackened flat-screen television, Rocky placed the wet napkin back on his tray. Using his hands and knees, he crawled around until he was in front of her again. He stared into her moist eyes for a moment, and the dim light didn't hide the movement of her neck when she swallowed. Rocky used his left hand to caress her right cheek, and then tilted his head to the side and kissed her left cheek. He let his lips linger there for a short while, and then turned his head so that his cheek could brush against hers. A gasp could be heard in the air, but Rocky wasn't sure whether it was his or hers. One thing he knew for certain, though; he was going to have to wrap up her plate and let her take her food to go. She wouldn't be able to stay in the house with him much longer. Not if they wanted to do what *was* right versus what *felt* right.

Against his cheek, hers felt as silky as the fabric of the burgundy top she wore. Yeah, he was going to have to take her home, but before he did, there was one more curiosity that he had to satisfy. Rocky pulled away just long enough to look into her eyes again; then he took a leap of faith. When Kenyatta saw him closing in, she caught her breath and jerked slightly away. She opened her mouth like she wanted to say something, but without a sound, she closed it again. Upon seeing her reaction, Rocky licked his lips and narrowed the gap between them once more. "It's okay, baby girl. I know my limits. It's just that . . . I think a cat's got your tongue, and I'm 'bout to go in and get it back for you. That's all."

Chapter Twenty-two

"Are you gonna answer that?" Kenyatta heard the question, but she didn't hear it at the same time. "Earth to Kenyatta! Are you gonna get the phone or not?"

"Huh?" Kenyatta snapped her face to the left, and an image of Carter slowly came into focus.

"Never mind." Carter entered Kenyatta's space, reached across her desk, and picked up the receiver. "Kenyatta King's office."

Kenyatta stared at her coworker. Had the phone been ringing? She'd been so caught up in her thoughts that she hadn't heard a thing. Happenings—sounds, smells, and tastes—from last night were still fresh and foremost in her mind. The tastes that were most vivid had nothing to do with dinner. It was all about Rocky and his lips. Kenyatta had never been kissed like that before. She used to think her ex-husband was an exceptional kisser; now he wasn't even a decent one. She'd downgraded Joe to middling, at best. No wonder Rocky had been with so many women. Whenever he kissed them, their clothes probably just dropped off on their own accord. Kenyatta took a breath and looked at her computer screen. That was the same electronic client file she was looking at before she took her lunch break four hours ago.

Hardly any work had been completed today, because all she could think about was Rocky and the phenomenal evening that she'd shared with him. Apparently he wasn't feeling the same way. Otherwise, he would have called her. It was almost four o'clock, and not a peep had been heard from him since he walked her to the door of her home last night. It was that darn Stuart's fault. When she opened the front door, he was sitting in the front room, looking at them like they were teenagers, and Kenyatta had missed her curfew. It was only ten when she got home. Circumstances required that they cut the evening short, but not before Rocky slipped her a key to his front door.

"I'm bad with keeping up with extra keys. I just need somebody to have one, just in case." That's what he'd said, but with the way he was looking at her, Kenyatta was left to wonder if he was hoping she'd arbitrarily use it one night to let herself in.

Lord, help us. Kenyatta knew it was going to take the strength of the Almighty to keep them doing what was right in His sight. She'd heard some of the single Christian women in their Women of Hope meetings talk about the struggle to keep their relationships holy, and in the past, Kenyatta had scoffed at it. As far as she was concerned, if a woman *really* knew the Lord, her mind would never even go there. This thing with Rocky was teaching Kenyatta a new lesson.

"Let me take your name and number, and I'll have her give you a call at her convenience," Carter was saying. She switched the phone from one ear to the other, grabbed a pen from Kenyatta's collection, and pulled a slip of notepaper from the cube that sat beside the pencil holder. "Uh-huh . . . uh-huh . . . uh-huh," she said as she scribbled. "I didn't catch the last name." Pause. "Oh. Okay. So it's just Rocky?"

Kenyatta jolted out of her chair and began trying to grab the phone, but Carter whacked her hand all three times.

"All right, sir. I'll give her the message," she said in as normal a voice as she could manage while someone was grabbing at air, trying to take the phone from her hand. "You're welcome. Bye."

"Carter!" Kenyatta was furious. "Why didn't you give me the phone?"

"Listen, hun, you ain't gonna make me look like I'm crazy. I had already told the man that you weren't in the office. What would it look like for him to all of a sudden hear you on the other end just as soon as I say his name? That would make both of us look unprofessional."

Kenyatta wanted to strangle her. "That wasn't a business call, so professionalism wasn't a factor."

"Really, now?" Carter rushed to the door and closed it. "Talk, hun, talk. Who is he? Where'd you meet him? How long you been knowing him? Is it serious? Give me details, and talk slow."

Sounding like an old-school tape recorder whose speed was dragging, Kenyatta said, "None . . . of . . . your . . . business." Then in a normal tone, she added, "Was that slow enough for you?" Carter was a nice girl, but she was just too phony. She killed Kenyatta when she switched into a mode of trying to pretend they were best girls.

"So you're not gonna tell me?"

"No, Carter. Now, can you please leave so I can return the call?"

Carter tossed her hair over her shoulder. "I should have just let it ring till he hung up." She stopped at the door and looked back at Kenyatta. "You keep this up and I'm gonna take you off the rotating list I have of people that I invite when I feel like treating somebody to lunch."

Kenyatta placed her hand on her hip. "Good. No . . . *great*. Whatever is the worst thing that I can do that would guarantee my ban—can we pretend I just did it?"

Laughing like she had just heard the best joke ever, Carter opened the door to make her exit. Just before closing it, Kenyatta heard her say, "You are so funny. Oh my God. I just love your sense of humor. Talk to ya later, hun."

There was just no offending her. Kenyatta sat back down and slid the notepaper closer. Just looking at Rocky's name and number sent her heart into overdrive. She picked up her telephone and took a deep, cleansing breath before dialing.

"*Atlanta Weekly Chronicles;* how may I direct your call?"

Kenyatta was caught off guard by the female voice on the other end. Why had Rocky given her the office number instead of his cell? Lorna was the receptionist there. The voice had to belong to her.

"Hello? Is anyone there? How may I direct your call?" she repeated.

Kenyatta swallowed. "Yes, I'm sorry. Hi. May I speak with Rocky, please?" The dead air that followed assured Kenyatta that it was, indeed, Lorna.

"Who is this?"

"Excuse me?" Kenyatta was blindsided yet again; not so much by what Lorna said, but by the tone in which she'd said it. All of the professionalism that had initially been in her voice had been dismissed.

"Who . . . is . . . this?" She said it like Kenyatta belonged on the short bus.

Kenyatta rotated her head in an attempt to ward off the kinks that growing tension was threatening to allow in. Surely, Lorna didn't just talk to her like she had trouble understanding English. *Stay calm, Ke-*

nyatta. Stay professional. If she were going to obey her thoughts, she'd have to speak to someone else. "May I speak to a manager, please?"

"If you wanted to speak to a manager, why did you ask to speak to Rocky? You don't want to speak to no manager. Who is this?"

Heifer, say what? Natural instincts brought Kenyatta to her feet. She gripped the edge of her desk and clenched her teeth. She wanted to take it there so badly, and she would have, if she didn't fear that her actions might jeopardize Rocky's job. Hunter was his friend, but Hunter didn't play that, and Kenyatta knew it.

When Kenyatta didn't respond fast enough, Lorna spoke again. "This is a business, *Miss.* We don't take personal calls here. If you want to talk or *do whatever* to Rocky, do it on his own time and his own dime."

"May I speak to Mr. Hunter Greene, please?" Kenyatta had had enough.

"How 'bout you speak to Mr. Dial Tone." Apparently, Lorna had had enough too, because the next sound Kenyatta heard was a click, followed shortly thereafter by Mr. Tone.

Kenyatta stared in disbelief at the telephone that she held in her hand. The words that were beginning to line up in her mouth were so ungodly that, at some point in the last thirty seconds, it seemed her tongue had vacationed in hell and brought back souvenirs. She slammed the phone back on its cradle, then walked the floor behind her desk as she talked to herself. After a good pep talk and a few paces, she reached for the telephone and dialed. It was answered on the second ring.

"Dr. Jade Tides-Greene's office; how may I help you?"

"Hi, Ingrid. It's Kenyatta."

"Hey, Kenyatta. Happy Friday. How are you?"

Kenyatta rolled her eyes. This was not the day for chipper small talk. "Maybe for you, Ingrid, but I've had much happier Fridays. Can you just put me through to Jade?"

"Um . . . sure. Hold on."

While she waited, Kenyatta used her free hand to cover her eyes. Ingrid didn't deserve that. She'd have to apologize to her later.

"Kenyatta?"

"Jade, hi. Listen . . . I know Ingrid told you that I just bit her head off for no reason, and I did. I'm sorry, and I promise I'll tell her that later."

"Be sure that you do," Jade said, sounding like somebody's mama. "What's going on?"

"Never mind all that. I need Hunter's desk number at the *AWC* right now."

"Well, I know you don't expect me to give you my husband's direct contact information while you're sounding like you're looking for somebody to kill. You're going to have to give me more insight whether you want to or not, sister. So tell me what's going on?"

Kenyatta released a heavy sigh. This was wasting time that she didn't have to spare, but she knew Jade wasn't going to budge an inch until everything made psychological sense. Knowing it would be a losing battle to try and fight her on it, Kenyatta conceded and gave Jade a quick rundown of what had transpired.

"Okay," Jade said. "I can see this is not the best time, so I'll check in again with you this weekend to get the update on what's going on with you and Rocky. I already know that the two of you had a date, and that's the reason we didn't see you at Women of Hope last night, but with this telephone war that just went down between you and Lorna, I'm going to need details. But for now, just sit tight. I happen to know that Hunter is out of the office right now, which means if you call his desk, it will roll over to Lorna, anyway. He went to the school to hear Malik and Tyler give their presentation today."

"Oh yeah," Kenyatta said. "Stuart was going to that too. I'd forgotten all about that."

"Here's what I'll do," Jade said. "I'll call the paper and talk to Rocky and let him know you're trying to reach him. That way, he can call you back."

"If you call and ask for Rocky, that chick that's working the desk is gonna know that you're calling for me," Kenyatta reasoned.

"And?" Jade challenged. "The *AWC* belongs to me and my husband. What do I care if she knows why I'm calling? I am authorized by the company's founder to fire her, or any other employee, on the spot, and I'll use that authority if she gives me any grief when I call."

Kenyatta smiled and secretly hoped that Lorna would give Jade grief. "Okay. I'll wait for his call. Thanks, girl."

While she waited, Kenyatta drummed the desk with her nails, and the drumming got more intense as she relived her conversation—if it could be called that—with Lorna. Last night when she and Rocky were kissing, and talking . . . and kissing some more, Rocky was adamant in his declaration that there was nothing between him and Lorna. Not only did he have no heart attachment to her, but according to him, the feeling was mutual. To Kenyatta, though, the exchange she'd just had with Lorna didn't sound like one in which the party on the other end of the line had no feelings for him. Lorna had flipped out just at the sound of a woman asking to speak to Rocky. To Kenyatta, that didn't sound like detachment.

When her telephone rang, the drumming of her nails finally stopped. "Kenyatta King speaking." She figured she'd keep it business-like, just in case.

"Hey, Kenyatta King. How are you?"

The sound of his voice immediately massaged away some of the tension that had begun mounting. "I'm not sure yet." She was being truthful.

"Jade told me what happened," Rocky said. "I'm sorry you had to deal with that."

"Why didn't you just give me your cell number?" Kenyatta had to ask. The question had been hanging in the back of her mind from the start of her call with Lorna. She'd read somewhere that one of the first signs of an untrustworthy man was his refusal to supply his personal phone number.

"I left my cell at home. When Jerome came by to pick me up, I thought I had everything, but I realized en route that I'd left my phone home, and we didn't have time to go back and get it. I've never left my cell anywhere before. I guess my mind . . . I guess it was on a lot of things this morning."

Kenyatta smiled a little. She knew the feeling, but she couldn't lose sight of the real issue. She didn't want it to seem like she was grilling him or that she was some kind of insecure nag, but if there was going to be any kind of relationship between her and Rocky, she needed to know she could trust him; that he was being totally truthful with her, and she needed to know that *before* things got too serious. "Are you sure nothing happened between the two of you other than that one night of groping and . . . whatever?" She didn't like talking about it.

"Yes, I'm sure. I told you everything, Kenyatta."

"Then why is she acting like there was more?"

She could hear the frustration in Rocky's voice. "I don't know. I've been trying to figure that one out myself. She's been giving me the eye and the finger every day since it happened. I'm just doing my best to avoid her until it all blows over." When Kenyatta didn't respond, Rocky added, "You do believe me, don't you?"

"I really want to, Rocky." Kenyatta sighed, and then said, "Can I tell you something that even my closest friends don't know?"

"Yes."

She hoped she didn't live to regret this revelation. "I know I come across as a really confident person, but I have some esteem issues." Rocky said nothing, so she continued. "I've always battled with my weight. It's not that I think I'm fat; I don't. But these hips and thighs—"

"Mmm . . . tell me about it."

Kenyatta couldn't help but giggle. "Stop it, Rocky. I'm serious."

"So am I. Baby girl, your hips are incredible, and now that I'm a safe distance from you, and you can't clobber me, I'm gonna admit that when we were bike riding and you asked me a question about where we were headed . . . When I patted your leg and said no backseat driving, I was really copping a feel. And let me say this: ain't nothing wrong with your thighs."

Kenyatta was blushing so hard that even her feet felt warm. "Will you stop it and just listen to me?" When he didn't reply, she took it as a cue to continue. "In every relationship that I've been in or *tried* to be in, I've lost to the other woman. My only win was Joe, and he turned out to be borderline psychotic, so it looks like the only way I can get the man is if he's not worth getting. In my teen years, I determined that my second-place finishes were largely because I didn't *put out* like a lot of the other girls did. Seems like all that the boys in high school wanted was sex, and since I wasn't giving *it,* I wasn't getting him. As I've gotten older . . . Well, really since I was in my twenties when I began really developing the shape of the women on my daddy's side of the family, I've always attributed my losses to my body type, because the women who win are always thinner."

"Like Ingrid?" Rocky said.

Kenyatta couldn't deny it. "Yes. Like Ingrid, like Lorna, and like a long list of others that stems as far back as college." She couldn't deny her next words either. "I really like you, Rocky. You're turning out to be a lot different from what I first thought. I used to hate everything about you, and now it's the total opposite." He was still quiet, and Kenyatta could only hope that she wasn't making a fool of herself. "And last night, well, that meant something to me. Kissing is very personal, and just because I go on a date with a man, that doesn't mean there's a kiss on the way. I went out with Jerome several times, and he never even kissed me—not on the lips, anyway. I don't go around letting everybody do that, and certainly not in the way that you did it." Kenyatta had had dental exams that were less thorough.

She stopped to take a breath and wished Rocky would break in and say something, but he didn't, so she kept going. "So that's my big secret. I struggle with self-esteem issues—so much so that sometimes I talk bad about other people so that I can feel good about myself." She wiped a tear from her left eye. "Like, I told myself recently that the reason Jerome picked Ingrid over me was because she wasn't as educated or as pretty as I am." Kenyatta's voice cracked. "I even said that Jerome didn't deserve me; he was threatened by my education level and my independent personality. I knew that wasn't why, but saying it made me feel better." She released a heavy sigh. "I can't even believe I told you that. I haven't admitted self-esteem issues since I told my mom about it nearly twenty years ago." When Rocky's silence continued to reign, she sighed and said, "You must think I'm an awful person now."

"Deon Simon Rockford."

"What?" Kenyatta sat up straight and grimaced at the futility of what Rocky had just said.

"You just trusted me with something you hadn't told anyone in nearly twenty years, so I'm doing the same. That's my birth name, and I haven't told anyone that in twenty years."

"Deon? Like Deion Sanders?" The name "Rocky" fit him better, as far as Kenyatta was concerned, but she liked his given name too.

"Different spelling, but you say it the same way."

"So why did you change it?"

Rocky released a soft laugh—one that Kenyatta was sure meant that he would tell her, but definitely didn't expect her to understand. "I changed it twice, actually. My mother gave me my father's first and middle names. His first name was spelled capital *D*, apostrophe, capital *O*, small *n*."

"*D'On?*" Kenyatta wrote it on the same slip of paper on which Carter had scribbled Rocky's number. She liked it spelled that way. It was unique.

"Yeah. And although I never had his last name, everybody would call me 'Li'l D' because his nickname was 'Big D.'" After a pause, Rocky said, "Even long after he was out of my life, I was still being called Li'l D. So on my eighteenth birthday, I dropped the middle name altogether and changed the spelling of the first name to *D-E-O-N*. Like that was somehow gonna magically put an end to the branding of Li'l D." He laughed a little. "Of course, it didn't. It still starts with a *D*. So a

few months later, I changed it to Rocky." He paused,
and with another laugh, he said, "Your brother called
me Simon not too long ago, and it almost set me off. I
thought he'd somehow found out what my real name
was, but he was actually comparing me to Simon Peter in the Bible. I should have known better than to
think he'd found out my birth name. That name has
been buried for a long time. Anybody who got to know
me after the age of eighteen only knows me as Rocky.
Aside from y'all, that list is mostly made up of cops,
crooks, and one-night stands."

Kenyatta pushed that last part out of her mind and
relaxed against the high back of her chair. "So you
changed your name because you didn't want to share
the same name as your dad?"

"Yes."

"Why not? Was he mean or abusive?"

"No. Actually, it was the exact opposite. Whenever
he was around, he was nothing but nice. The problem
was, he was rarely around. He was born in the West In-
dies—Jamaica, to be exact. As I understand it, though,
he lived in the States for most of his life. As a kid, I
wanted more than anything to be close to the man everybody called Big D, but I couldn't, because he never
stayed around long enough." Kenyatta's heart went out
to Rocky. She could tell that this was a sensitive subject
for him. "I think the last time I saw him, I was seven or
eight. I can't remember a whole lot about him, but for a
while, I thought I'd be as tall as he was."

"Your dad was tall?"

"Six-nine." Rocky said it like it came with a blue rib-
bon. "I was actually a short dude for a while, but when
I turned eighteen, I shot up like a tree. I grew like six
inches that year, and I kept growing, even as an adult. I
was six feet when I went to prison, and now I'm six-five,

so five inches came after the age of nineteen. When my father moved on without me, I always wondered what I'd done to make him leave." In her line of business, Kenyatta couldn't count the number of times she'd heard that one. Children always thought it was their fault when parents abandoned them. "I learned later that my mother was the one who made him leave. She told me herself that she gave him an ultimatum. He either had to marry her and make us a real family, or get the you-know-what out of our lives. I guess he chose the you-know-what. About two or three years into my prison sentence, my mother called and told me that he died in a freak accident. He had gone to Jamaica for a visit and was out swimming somewhere when he got swept up in some hard currents and drowned. I think a couple others drowned too."

Kenyatta's heart sank. She hadn't had the best luck with men in her life either, but the one man she could always count on until the day he died was her father. She couldn't imagine never having had him as a mainstay in her life. "I'm sorry, Rocky." It was all she could think to say. "So the man you told me about last night . . . the one who punched you the day you got the tattoo . . . that was your stepfather?"

"Yes. He was the abusive one. My mom had five kids total. So I have four half siblings, and I have no relationship with them."

"What do you mean?"

"My mother's husband was a pimp and a drug lord. Not by profession, but by action. I dropped out of school and started selling drugs after I joined the gang, and he was cool with it, as long as he got a cut of the money I got paid. My older half sister—my mom had her by a different guy—she dropped out of school in the eleventh grade after she found out she was pregnant.

Rumor was that she was pregnant by our stepfather, but we never knew, because he pretty much tossed her on the street. Last I heard, she had joined one of those cults where they live on a compound in the desert somewhere. And while I was in prison, I got word from my mama that my younger siblings had dropped out of school too. Right now, one of my brothers is in jail up north somewhere. The other one sold drugs like I did, but he got killed in a drive-by ten or eleven years ago. And as for my youngest sister . . . she started turning tricks at fifteen and disappeared at seventeen. The general consensus is that she's probably dead too."

Kenyatta was wiping silent tears as she listened to Rocky unload his heart. For most of her life, she'd looked down her nose at just about anybody who did time. As far as she was concerned, nothing in life could be bad enough to turn a person to a life of crime. But as she listened to Rocky, her heart was pricked. Sure, there was always another option. A person didn't have to turn to drugs, prostitution, or other corruptions, but if he wasn't shown other options—if somebody didn't take the time to introduce him to Christ—how would he know?

Rocky must have heard her sniffle, because he next said, "I'm not trying to get your sympathy, Kenyatta. I don't want you to feel sorry for me. I really said all that so you'd know that you're not the only one who has wondered if you're as good as the next person. You're not the only one who didn't feel like you were worth loving or being taken care of. Everybody's probably been there, and we all say different things and act different ways to cover the hurt. When I was locked up, I was angry almost every single day. On a good day, I worked that anger off in a weight room. On a bad day, I worked it off on somebody's face or limbs.

"But one of the things I'm noticing about myself since I've been saved is that God is taking away the anger, and He's making it so I can forgive some people. I've forgiven my dad for abandoning me. I've forgiven my stepdad for making my life a living hell. And I've forgiven my mom for allowing it. Granted, I don't regret that decision not to move back home with them when I got out of prison until I got back on my feet, but I forgave them. I think I've even managed to forgive the people who have burned down my house."

Kenyatta used her shoulder to balance the phone against her ear. She was using both hands to hold her compact mirror and refresh the makeup that her tears had disturbed. "Your mother invited you back home?"

"Yeah. When I first got out. They moved to Tampa, Florida, a few years ago, and she says that since her husband has gotten older—he's in his sixties now—that he's not abusive anymore. He's got arthritis really bad in the fingers on his right hand, and he's deaf in one ear too."

"Wow. I guess the aging process wasn't really all that nice to him."

Rocky hesitated, and then said, "Yeah. I guess not."

A grin crossed Kenyatta's face as she prepared the question that had crept in her mind. "So . . . can I call you Deon?"

"Not if you want me to answer."

"What about Li'l D?"

"Kenyatta . . ."

"What about—"

"Can I call you 'Ke-Ke'?" Rocky asked.

"No."

"'Ya-Ya'?"

"Ewww!"

"What about 'Ta-Ta'?"

Kenyatta cringed. "Okay. Okay. I'll call you Rocky."

"Thank you." He laughed.

After a brief silence, Kenyatta said, "But you can keep calling me 'baby girl' if you want."

"Oh yeah?" She could hear the smile in Rocky's voice. "You like that?"

"Yes. That's what Special Agent Derek Morgan calls Penelope Garcia on *Criminal Minds*. It's a TV show."

"Well, you'll have to forgive me for not being into shows about policemen or criminals, but whoever Penelope Garcia is, if she can be called baby girl, so can you."

Kenyatta's mind recalled something else that Rocky had said moments earlier. "You've really forgiven the people responsible for your house burning down?"

"I had to," Rocky said. "Not forgiving them was killing me." He released a chuckle. "There are people who live in that neighborhood who believe a woman burned my house."

Kenyatta sat up straight. "They saw someone?"

"No. They say it's the trademark of a scorned woman."

Kenyatta looked at her nails. She could hardly wait to get to the salon tomorrow to cover that new growth. "Well, after what you said happened between you and Lorna, do you think maybe she's capable of that?"

Chapter Twenty-three

"Oh, Rocky, come on. You can't be serious." Hunter sank in the chair behind his desk. "I thought you said you were done with this witch hunt. You were able to get out of your contract for the old house; God has given you a new one. Can't you just be grateful and move on?"

Rocky remained standing in the same spot where he had been ever since he first entered Hunter's office and brought up the subject matter at hand. "I *am* grateful, man. But if there's any chance that—"

"But that's just it. It's not possible. Lorna was at work that day, remember? She was here right along with us."

"And that was my first thought too," Rocky said. "That's why when Kenyatta first said it, I told her that it couldn't be so. I was thinking that Lorna had an alibi . . . and I was it. I saw her here, just like everybody else did, so I'd have to testify against my own charge."

"Exactly."

"But wait." Rocky held up his hand to stop any further interruption from Hunter. "Everything went down after the lunch hour. Lorna left for lunch, and was gone for the full hour. When she came back, she flipped me off and gave me a look that had *payback* written all over it."

"Sit down, Rocky." Hunter motioned toward the seat in front of his desk, and Rocky sat. "And Lorna is sitting outside this office, so please keep your voice down.

My office walls are thick, but if you get loud enough, you can be heard on the outside. I don't need for her or any of the other workers to hear this."

Rocky sat back in his chair and folded his arms. Maybe Lorna needed to hear it, because if she burned down his house, she might want to get a head start on her escape. He'd forgiven the arsonist, but if he found out who he or *she* was, justice still needed to be served.

"Listen," Hunter continued, "I'm not saying she didn't give you looks and gestures that might make her an even better suspect, I'm just saying I don't think she did this. First off, when Stu and his boys came by here to inform you of the fire, the structure had already gone up in smoke, for the most part. If you strike a match on a house at noon, I don't think the whole house would be engulfed by one."

Rocky scooted forward in his chair. "It wasn't a whole house. Technically, it was half a house, since they were only halfway complete with the rebuilding. And as far as the timing is concerned, she could've dashed gasoline on it or something to make the fire spread quicker—like Angela Bassett did in that chick flick she played in with Whitney Houston."

"*Waiting to Exhale*—you actually watched that?" Hunter asked.

"Did you not just hear me say that Angela Bassett was in it? Yes, sir, I surely did."

"Point taken." Hunter chuckled. "But the gasoline idea is a bust. That would have been far too easy for authorities to figure out. You think we'd be sitting here all these days later with no answers as to how that fire got started if your place was doused with gasoline?"

Rocky sat back in his chair again. His new suspicion seemed so cut-and-dried before he entered Hunter's office. "Look, Rocky. I don't want you to think I'm taking sides with Lorna. I'm not. If you had told me that she was creating a hostile work environment for you, I would have long ago put an end to this. I don't allow that from any of my staff."

"I hadn't said anything because you and Jerome swore that it would blow over. You said that she was a *man-eater* and would get over it, just like she got over her one-night stands with every man."

"Shhh!" Hunter looked toward the door.

Rocky lowered his voice. "Well, it hasn't happened, and it can't be because she's in love with me or nothing. We had one dinner . . . just one before our little feel-me-up session. There's no way she has an emotional attachment to me, but every day I walk by her, she gives me that look that if she were a cat, I'd be looking like pinstripes."

Hunter crinkled his nose. "'Pinstripes'? You'd be looking like pinstripes?"

"Yeah." He bent his fingers like they were claws and made angry cat-fighting noises that drew laughter from Hunter. "Glad you think it's funny," Rocky concluded.

"I'm sorry, man." Hunter sobered. "I don't mean to laugh at your calamity, but if you'd stayed away from her, like I tried to tell you, none of this would have happened."

"Yeah, well, hindsight is twenty-twenty," Rocky mumbled.

Hunter rubbed the back of his neck like he needed a massage. "I'll talk to her about her behavior and her attitude the first chance I get. I can't have her going off on every female who might call here for you. This time, it was Kenyatta, and that was bad enough. Next time, it could be an actual client. I don't care how mad she is with you, she can't do stuff like that." Hunter leaned forward and placed his elbows on his desk.

"And speaking of Kenyatta, what's going on with that? When Stuart and I met at the school this afternoon, he told me the two of you had a date last night?" Hunter's sentence sounded like both a statement and a question, all in one.

"Dang, did he tell everybody? When Jade called me today to tell me that Kenyatta was trying to get in touch with me, she told me that she knew too. I just figured that Kenyatta had told her, but she said she got it from Stu. Is there anybody that he ain't told yet?"

"Well, it is news to some, but I knew it would end up at a church altar." When Rocky stretched his eyes, Hunter said, "That's right. It was either going to end in a funeral or a wedding. Either way, somebody would be at the altar. I'm glad it's going in the wedding direction."

"Man, you way ahead of the game."

"Am I?" Hunter challenged.

Rocky sighed and smiled. "I like her, okay? I like her a lot. Kenyatta's got me in a place I don't think I've ever been."

"In love?"

"No." Rocky wasn't about to admit it. Not yet, anyway. "She's got me in a place where I want to be in a real relationship. I like the way she makes me feel."

"In love?" Hunter repeated.

"Will you cut it out? I like her. Can we leave it at that? We haven't made it official yet, but I plan to ask her out again. When I do, I'm gonna ask her if she'll be my lady. And we'll see where God takes it from there."

"I like the way you put that," Hunter said. "See where God takes it. That's the way to do it, man. Keep Him first."

Rocky nodded. "I think I'm picking up a few pointers from you and Jade . . . and Jerome and Ingrid . . . and

Stuart and Candice . . . and Reverend and Mrs. Tides . . . and Malik and Kyla." Rocky laughed. "I have a lot of role models."

Hunter laughed with him. "Yeah, well, don't let my bride hear you say that. She hates it when people speak of Malik and Kyla as though they're a couple. She says they're too young. They're fifteen and sixteen. I've told her that she's gonna have to let Malik grow up. She still sees him as that ten-year-old kid he was when she came into our lives. The boy is taller than she is now, and the way I see it, if Kyla is the one he ends up with, we should count our blessings. She's a good Christian girl and has the best of parents."

Rocky couldn't resist. "Her grandmother's got crickets chirping in her head, though, and it might be hereditary."

Hunter laughed. "Let's hope not. I just think it's good when you find that right one, and the earlier you're blessed to do that, the better. It can save you a lot of heartache." Hunter took a thoughtful pause. "I wouldn't trade my son for nothing, but if he could have been pushed out of Jade's womb instead of the one from which he came, that would have been awesome."

Rocky looked at his open hands. "Man, I don't have enough fingers and toes to count how many wrong choices I made in women. I'm just thankful that I had sense enough to protect myself. Ain't no telling how many seeds I would have planted if I hadn't. It would have been ridiculous. Kenyatta wouldn't have wanted nothing to do with me." Rocky crossed his legs. "And you know, at first, I thought that idea of keeping yourself till you get married was ridiculous. I mean, *really* ridiculous. And I thought that, up until last night. Last night when I was with Kenyatta, and we were being affectionate, it felt good to have those limitations. It felt good to know that I'd have to go the distance if I wanted to go the distance. You know what I'm saying?"

"Yeah." Hunter wore a smile of experience. "Having to work for and wait for a prize sometimes makes it even better. I know what I'm talking about. I mean, it's so good that God had to mean for it to be this way."

"Well, I'm holding Him to that," Rocky said. "I want to have that same smile one day." He pointed at Hunter's face.

"You will," Hunter guaranteed him. Then he said, "I think the reason *she's* holding a grudge with you is because you messed up her track record." He dipped his head in the direction of the area where his secretary's desk was located on the other side of the wall. "Lorna's not accustomed to a man turning her down. She's broken down the best of them, and after she gets what she wants, she moves on. I'm sure if we ever dug deep in her mind and in her past, there's probably a reason she has such little respect for herself. I've heard the chats around the watercooler. She's always the aggressor. She's always the one who calls the shots, and because of her . . . *skills,* men fall in line to try out for her team. They play the game by her rules, and she always wins. But with you, she didn't score. She shot; the ball went around the rim a few times; but when it finished circling, it didn't fall in her direction. She missed the basket. You messed up her streak. You were right there on the verge, but you said no. You were probably one of only a few to do that. Maybe you were the first. You won, Rocky. You overcame something that at one time was your absolute strongest weakness."

"Upon this rock I will build my church; and the gates of hell shall not prevail against it." Rocky rubbed his chin as the thought filtered through his mind. "Never thought of it that way," he admitted. "So what

do I do to stop her madness? Is she gonna be clawing at me forever?"

"Not if she wants to keep her job," Hunter said. "That kind of behavior won't be tolerated here. She's going to have to accept the loss and move on, or she can refuse to accept the loss and *move on* literally." A knock at the door took Hunter's attention. "Come in."

Jerome walked in with caution and looked at both men. "Closed door? This must be serious."

"Not anymore. You can leave the door open," Hunter said; then he looked to Rocky for a second opinion.

"It's cool."

"I'm not even gonna ask," Jerome said as he walked to Hunter's desk and handed him a finished copy of the weekend's paper. Rocky was going to have to get an extra copy for himself. One of the staff writers had done a small piece on the back-to-back house fires last week, and this week, they had written a follow-up that shared the testimony of Rocky's new home. Rocky had already read it in rough draft form; plus, he pulled out that page as they were printing it on Wednesday, but he was looking forward to reading it again as part of the complete publication. Jerome was tapping the paper that Hunter had just laid on his desk. "Let's talk about something good, like that feature you did on Old Man Heights's brother."

Hunter looked down at the week's front-page story. It was about a hostage situation that had taken place Tuesday on the eastside of the city. It had ended peacefully, but not before the passing of six hours of negotiations. "Thanks, brother-in-law. But let me be the first to admit that this was the first, and probably last, time I'll ever interview an Alzheimer's patient. Whew! I think Old Man Cecil Heights and Old Man Shelton Heights shared the same brain."

"But Shelton Heights is dead," Rocky pointed out.

"And so is the brain" was Hunter's reply. "After talking to Cecil, I have to wonder if Shelton was *really* of sound mind and body when he wrote his will."

Jerome laughed, and then sat in the chair beside Rocky. "Well, I hear that the boys did a bang-up job on the presentation. Stuart was a proud papa when he called me on his way from the school this afternoon."

Hunter clapped his hands in a soft applause. "They did an exceptional job, and I've decided to feature them in next weekend's paper. I made sure that the chief of police and our mayor were there to hear it. Everybody was in awe at how a pair of fifteen-year-olds was actually able to find out that Shelton Heights really had a brother."

"So does that mean that all that dough and property that he left behind goes to the guy in the nursing home?" Rocky wanted to know.

"Not hardly." Hunter shook his head. "There are two big problems that anybody who makes that argument would have to take on. One, Cecil is ninety-eight years old, and not only is he mentally feeble, but physically, he's got one foot in the grave and the other on a banana peel. And if and when he passes, we'll be back at square one, because his wife passed away thirty-five years ago, and his daughter passed away twenty-two years ago. Both of them died of breast cancer. I guess breast cancer ran in her side of the family, like Alzheimer's runs on his side. And number two, the will specifically says that everything goes to this nonexistent son of his. So even if Cecil was well, I don't think he'd get it."

"Are you sure the son isn't real?" Rocky said. "I mean, nobody knew the brother was real until it was proven that he was. Maybe there's a son too."

"No, there's no son. We checked live birth records and everything."

Jerome laughed. "Malik and Tyler had Hunter and Stuart all caught up in the hype. They were burning the midnight oil right along with the boys. Checking live birth records." He laughed again. "Who does that for a school project?"

"It was more than a simple school project; it was a history competition," Hunter said. "If they win locally, they'll advance to state competition. They'll walk away with a nice chunk of money if they go all the way to national and win it. I think they have a good chance."

"Well, if nothing else, it gave you a lot of information you needed to write the article," Jerome said, "and you deserve your own award for the way you wrote it and called Cecil Heights senile without actually calling him senile. That's some creative writing right there."

Hunter grinned. "Thanks, man."

"What words did you use?" Rocky said. "I might need to borrow a couple of them for the 'housewarming' at Greene Manor tomorrow." He made quotation marks with his fingers as he emphasized the word. "You know Jan's mother is gonna be rolling up there in her Ain't-Shame-to-Praise-Him Mobile."

Jerome laughed. "Man, you stupid. Why you gotta go for the long name? Most of us just call it the God-Is-Good Mobile."

"The 'God Is Good' sign is on a tag attached to her front fender. That one doesn't define her as a nitwit. But to have 'Ain't Shame to Praise Him' painted on the side in big old block letters is insane. Especially when it's painfully clear that she got a paintbrush and did it herself."

Hunter shook his head. "Ms. Leona might come, and she might not. For some reason, she seems to avoid coming to the ranch. But regardless of if she comes, tomorrow is a special day, and I need you to be on your best behavior." He pointed at Rocky. "Wear long sleeves to cover your tattoos, if you have to, in order to shut up the crazy lady. Don't mess it up."

"Man, I ain't wearing no long sleeves," Rocky said. "The calendar might say it's fall, but the temperatures ain't started talking yet. If she got a problem with my tats, she can stay home. Shoot. I'm the one with the new house, so it's my housewarming, right?"

Hunter nodded. "Yeah . . . right."

"Excuse me. Hunter?"

All of the men turned to see Lorna standing in the doorway with her purse over her shoulder. Rocky was the first to turn his face away from her. He was in a pretty good mood right now and didn't want Lorna killing it with her hateful glare.

"Yes, Lorna," Hunter replied.

"I just wanted you to know that I'm leaving. There are four or five extra copies of the paper on my desk, in case you want to take those with you."

"'Preshate it. Is everybody else gone already?"

"Dontavious and I are the last ones. I'm giving *him* a ride home so he doesn't have to catch MARTA." She said it like it was supposed to hurt Rocky's feelings or make him regret missing out on what somebody else was going to get.

"Okay. Have a good weekend. See you Monday," Hunter said.

"Bye."

As soon as they saw the two silhouettes pass the window on the outside, Jerome turned to Rocky. "I'd say she just got over you, pal."

Chapter Twenty-four

Rocky had been tired for the past two hours, but drowsiness was just beginning to creep in as he turned over on his new mattress. It wasn't too soft and it wasn't too firm. It was just the way he liked it. The house was coming together, bit by bit, but he wasn't going to rush it. The most pressing thing was to get a bed. It had been moved up to the top of the list this morning. The floor he'd slept on last night reminded him too much of the thin mattresses he was forced to sleep on in prison, and Rocky didn't want to do it again tonight. Jerome agreed to go with him to purchase a bed when they left the office this afternoon. It was the perfect plan, since Jerome had a flatbed pickup truck with the room they needed to transport the furniture. He had stayed around long enough to help Rocky bring the pieces in the house, and then he was gone. A date with Ingrid was on the calendar for tonight, so that left Rocky to assemble the bed by himself.

His heart desired to see Kenyatta again tonight, but circumstances wouldn't allow it. She had switched the date of her standing Saturday hair appointment to this evening in order to clear her calendar for tomorrow's housewarming. Kenyatta had joked that she needed to take her pillow and pajamas with her, because she was sure, with it being a Friday, the busiest day of the week for her beautician, she'd be there all night. Rocky reasoned that it was probably best that they spaced out their dates, anyway. Peter had been right that day they jogged around Stone Mountain. He'd all but said if Rocky and Kenyatta ever got together, it would be like lighting a fire under a pot of grits. They did, in fact, have that heat and passion that Peter spoke about, and if both of them weren't mindful of the flame, the likelihood of a boilover was great. They would have to be careful . . . and prayerful so that the enemy wasn't allowed to use their strong affections against them. God would not be pleased if . . .

Rocky turned over again. This time, because he thought he heard a noise. As he lay quietly in the bed, staring up at the ceiling, only stillness surrounded him. It was probably nothing. He just wasn't accustomed to sleeping in such quietness, and because of it, even the silence was becoming perceptible. At his old house and at Jerome's, Rocky had always slept with the television on in the bedroom. So far, the only set he'd purchased for this house was in the living room. Last night, he'd slept on the floor in there so that he could have the noise of the television. Tonight it was too quiet. He was tempted to get up and transfer the set to his room, but he didn't feel like getting up. Putting together his bed had worn him out after an already busy workday. Besides, he shouldn't be so addicted to watching television in bed that he'd have to go through all that trouble. Rocky smiled at his own contemplation, then turned back over to his favorite position of lying on his stomach.

Just when he felt himself drifting, Rocky heard it.
Click.

He'd know that sound anywhere. It was a gun, and somebody had just cocked it. Rocky's first thought was to pretend he was asleep. If the intruder was there to rob him, he'd soon see that Rocky's most prized possession in the mostly empty house was the flat screen in the living room. The robber would take it and run, without the worry that the victim had seen his face.

But whatever the identification of this predator, he wasn't prowling like a burglar. Rocky could feel his presence. Hear him breathing. He was standing directly over him. This one wasn't here to rob him; he was here to kill him. *Beautiful . . . just beautiful.* Two nights in Shelton Heights and already his life was over. Why had he listened to Reverend Tides? Why did he have to be in such a hurry to move out of Jerome's? At least there, he was safe from the curse. Using slow movements, so as not to be viewed as threatening, Rocky slowly turned over. He raised his hands to show that he had no weapon.

"Who are you? What do you want? My wallet is on the floor in the corner. You can take all I have."

"You think money can buy you anything, don't you?" The man immediately became enraged; yelling like Rocky had just spit in his face instead of offered him cash. "Is that what you think? Is that what you think?"

"Just take whatever you want then. I just moved in, and I don't have much, but whatever you want, you can have."

"That's the rule you live by, ain't it? Just take whatever you want. Is that what you do? Take whatever you want?"

Rocky's mind raced to figure out who the man in the shadows was. He must have known him, because he knew Rocky as a crook. Drug dealing had been Rocky's specialty in his street days, but he'd been a pretty skilled thief too—taking what he wanted, when he wanted. The voice wasn't familiar. He was trying to sound like a tough guy, but despite the angry edge, the

intruder's tone was similar to Michael Jackson's. He
definitely didn't sound like one of Rocky's boys from
back in the day, but he could easily be one of their flun-
kies who had come to carry out an order. Rocky shook
his head. He always knew that even though he was now
a changed man, there was a good probability that his
past would catch up with him eventually.

"Is that what you do? Just take what you want?"
the man repeated. "Well, you done went and took too
much now. Don't nobody mess with my woman," he
said. He followed that with a mouthful of vulgarities,
and then said, "You done messed with the wrong one."

"Mess with my woman"? It was Joe. The darkness
of the room prevented him from seeing the face, but
with Rocky's involvement with Kenyatta, there was
no other possibility. Kenyatta apparently didn't know
what her ex was capable of. She'd told Rocky that he
was verbally abusive, but he had never raised a hand
to hit her. Well, maybe he'd never hit Kenyatta, but he
was about to kill Rocky, and Rocky had no defense. No
gun. No knife. Not even a blunt object that he could use
to change his doom. In a fair fight, Joe wouldn't have
a prayer of winning, but with a gun pointed to his face,
Rocky was the one who needed prayer.

"You think you can just move into one neighborhood
and have your way with women, and then just move to
another one and do the same thing?"

Have my way with women? Rocky hadn't had a
woman in six months. *That* he knew for certain. If he
was going to be accused of having been with one—and
definitely if he were going to be killed for being with
one—he at least wanted to be guilty. "I haven't had my
way with anybody. We only had one date."

That seemed to anger the man more. "Oh, you gon'
look in my face and tell me that you went out with my
wife?"

Look in his face? In the darkened room, Rocky could barely see the man's silhouette, but he could see enough to determine that this one couldn't be still for a moment. The entire time he talked, he was rocking from side to side. But no matter which side he rocked toward, the gun remained pointed at his target. Rocky tried to reason with him. "She's not your wife anymore, man. You're divorced. And I know you didn't really want the divorce, but—"

"Is that what she told you? Is that what she told you?" he bellowed. Then he strung a few creative vulgarities together to describe her.

Rocky didn't appreciate that. "Hey!"

"Hey, what?" Now he was dancing around like Muhammad Ali, still holding the gun as he bounced. "Oh, it's like that? Oh, it's like that? You gonna defend her now? You think she your woman, so you gonna defend her?"

Okay . . . Kenyatta had told Rocky that Joe was crazy, but he didn't know she had meant clinically. Unless Kenyatta, Stuart, and everyone else he knew had been lying to him, Kenyatta and Joe were definitely divorced, and they had been for some years now. Obviously, the divorce was something that Joe still couldn't accept. Insanity had a way of doing that to a person. When a man had common sense, he could be talked out of murder. When he was genuinely mad, it was a wrap. Rocky kept his eyes open, but he began to pray silently. The Lord's Prayer was always the first one to come to mind; probably because it was the first biblical passage that he learned once he gave his life to Christ. It had seemed appropriate for a regular everyday prayer, and it seemed the same now. Rocky might not have been able to choose how he was going to go, but he could choose which words would be the last in his mind when he went.

The man reached up and switched on the lamp beside the bed, like he wanted to be sure that Rocky could see his fancy footwork. It also allowed Rocky to see his face. He wasn't a bad-looking man, but he wasn't what he would have envisioned as Kenyatta's type. Joe was skinny, by Rocky's definition. He was shorter and thinner than he would have expected Kenyatta to be attracted to. He also looked younger than he had expected. This guy looked to be in his early thirties at the most. Rocky would have expected Joe to be in his mid-forties.

What a way to die. With the manner in which Rocky had lived most of his life, he'd always known there was a chance he'd die in some violent way. In the middle of all of the catastrophic things that were going on with his old home, there were days when Rocky visualized being snuffed out by one of his old crime buddies, or maybe even by one of the many former inmates whom he'd beaten in prison. But to be gunned down by some insane dancing idiot? This was ridiculous! Although Rocky wouldn't be leaving behind a widow, he imagined that his funeral would be just as absurd by the time the string of drama queens he'd fooled around with got finished performing. He shook his head at the thought of it all.

Joe finally stopped bouncing, and all that aggressive movement had made him winded. But even that didn't stop him from pointing the gun in the direction of Rocky's face. "And you all up in the newspapers. Last week, you didn't have a house. This week, you got one in the beautiful community of Shelton Heights. Well, whoop-de-freakin'-do for you, big newspaper article man! Since you wanna live in it, you shouldn't mind dying in it." He was sweating bullets. It was far more perspiration than his hopping around should have rendered. Rocky had seen that look before. Hyperactive. Sweaty. Irrational. Maybe Joe wasn't crazy, after all. Maybe he was high, or needed to be high. Kenyatta never described him as a drug user, but a lot could have happened in the years since they'd been apart.

"Yeah. You messed with the wrong one this time," the man reminded him. And then with a scowl, he added, "And you gon' use my son as a go-between?" Now Rocky was confused. What son? Kenyatta didn't have a son. "That's just dirty. That's just dirty," Joe insisted. "You ain't no man. You a punk. Only a punk will use another man's boy. That's *my* boy; you hear me? My flesh and blood. I might ain't got much, but I got that one. I *made* that one. That no-good trick of mine—you might've gotten her. But I'll kill you before I let you get my son."

"What son?"

"Shut up!" the man yelled in a tone that raised the scale of his voice by two octaves. Yeah. He was about as high as a hot-air balloon. "Don't be tryin' to play me, nig. You gon' deny it? Huh? You gon' deny it? I got the proof. I got the proof. See?" He dug in the pocket of his jeans and pulled out two crumpled bills and flung them on Rocky's lap. "Fifteen dollars. That's all that cheap ho charged you? Well, you the fool. You oughtta got change back, 'cause she ain't even worth that much!"

Rocky's mouth dropped. This wasn't Joe. This was the daddy of that kid—the boy he'd given the money to for payment for the drink. This man thought there was something going on between Rocky and the boy's mother, a woman Rocky had never even met. "Wait, man. You got it all wrong."

"Shut up! Just shut up!" He was about to start talking in second soprano now. "I don't wanna hear nothing you got to say." The gun was so close to Rocky's face now that Rocky could see clear down the barrel. "I'm through talking to you, nig. All you need to be saying is good-bye."

Why did he have to move out here? The thought of having to die now brought Rocky far more sadness than fear. His mind went to Kenyatta, his church, his friends, his job, the GED, which he was just weeks away from getting. There was so much he wanted to do that he hadn't done yet. So much he wanted to say that he hadn't said. But it was too late for all of that now.

When Rocky saw his killer's trigger finger make a move in preparation to close the deal, he shut his eyes and held his last breath. He wasn't afraid of death, but he didn't care to see the ejection of the bullet that would introduce him to it either. In his years of drug dealing, alley brawling, grand larceny, and cop dodging, Rocky had heard many a gunshot. But none had ever been as piercing to his ears as the one that drowned out the sound of the prayer ending *"Amen"* in his head.

Quiet.

Rocky opened his eyes to see blood spattered all over his bedcovers and even on his wall, but he felt no pain. He'd been shot before, and he knew the burn of a bullet. Why wasn't he feeling anything? When he looked up, he didn't see his assailant standing in front of him anymore. *Am I in heaven?* A deep, agonizing groan brought Rocky's eyes to the floor beside his bed. There he was. The man who once stood over him with steel pointed in Rocky's face now lay in a pool of blood . . . dying. But what happened?

The sound of a breathy exhale drew his eyes to his bedroom door. "Kenyatta!" She stood frozen in place, still aiming the gun in the direction of where the man once had stood. Rocky snatched off his covers and ran to her. She appeared to be in shock . . . shocked by her own actions. Rocky didn't know what to do. He wasn't supposed to be this close to a gun, but he needed to get it out of her hand before she harmed herself.

"Kenyatta. Baby girl. It's okay. Put it down. Just— just toss it over there on the bed." In slow motion, she did what he said; then she turned and looked up at him. Kenyatta's eyes were beginning to flood, and it didn't take long before the tears overflowed and spilled down her cheeks. Rocky reached for her face and began wiping her tears with his fingers. The man on the floor moaned again. Rocky supposed the right thing to do was to call the police, report the incident, and get the man some help. He would do that in a minute, but right now, he had to make good on a deathbed promise. "I love you." He wiped away more of her tears, and then repeated his sentiment before covering Kenyatta's mouth with his own.

Chapter Twenty-five

It had been a long, full day. The place Rocky called Greene Manor stayed alive with adult interaction, and Greene Pastures did the same with the children. As devastating as it almost was, Friday night's dramatic ordeal didn't spoil Saturday afternoon's plans. If anything, it enhanced them. It gave everybody more to talk about, and it gave them all more reasons to celebrate. Rocky's life had been spared. Kenyatta would not be charged, and the man who was struck in the side by the bullet from her gun would not die from his injuries.

The police had shown up very shortly after the shooting. The assailant's wife had called and reported her suspicions that her irate husband had gone to search for the man who had been featured in the paper. She admitted to telling him that she and Rocky were having an affair, and she had her son corroborate that Rocky had sent her money. The woman had done it to get back at her husband for having an affair of his own. She didn't think he would take it that far.

Everything was calm now as the adults shared the sofas of Hunter and Jade's massive den while a marathon of reruns of *Sanford and Son* played on the television. Few of them were actually watching. Tyler, Malik, and Kyla had opted to grab seconds of ice cream and cake and retreated to the entertainment theater room, where they could watch music videos on the big screen. From the current scene, there was no indication that just an hour or so ago the estate had been filled with laughter, cheers, and tears. *Happy* tears.

Everyone, with the exception of the true honoree, had been let in on the secret that the occasion that had been masked as a housewarming for Rocky was really a surprise party for Jade, whose birthday was only five days away. She screamed when the secret was finally exposed, and she cried when she was blindfolded and taken out into the yard to see her gift. Hunter's not-so-subtle hint was that it was parked outside and ready for a ride. Jade was excited about the thought that Hunter had bought her a new car, but what she got was worth much more than she expected. It was almost more than her heart could handle.

Upon catching a glimpse of Spirit standing at a distance in their front yard, Jade's breaths came so hard that they all thought she might pass out. She couldn't even speak. Eventually she responded by jumping into Hunter's arms, wrapping her legs around his waist for added support, and planting about twenty kisses on his face, forehead, and lips. Then she jumped down and sprinted toward the horse amidst the cheers of her well-wishers. Rocky saw Hunter wipe a tear at the sight of his wife's joy. He commented that it was worth having to spend twice as much to get Spirit back from the buyer as it had cost the buyer to purchase her.

"Let's face it, guys," Jerome had said, speaking to the men who stood there as onlookers, "we're never gonna beat him." He pointed at Hunter. "The best we can ever hope for is the silver, 'cause he's always gonna bring home the gold."

Shortly after they celebrated Jade's special day, it was Rocky's turn to be surprised. He was the only one who wasn't told that the housewarming wasn't a total smoke screen. Because of the gifts that his friends actually presented, Rocky would be able to use a large portion of the insurance money for other things. Cookware, dinnerware, and glassware could all be scratched off his "needs" list. Bath towels, toaster, microwave, a George Foreman grill—all those could be crossed off too. Reverend and Mrs. Tides presented him with a family Bible. They said every home needed one.

Thanks to the huge flat-screen television Hunter and Jade had gotten him, Rocky could permanently move the smaller set he'd purchased into the bedroom. Kenyatta had bought him two sets of complete bedding. One had a motorcycle theme; the other displayed the logo of the Atlanta Falcons. Rocky felt like a big kid when he saw them, and he couldn't wait to put them to use. Kenyatta had really gotten a ribbing from the others for buying dressing for the bed, but Rocky knew her intentions were pure. She had seen all of the blood that had splattered on his covers last night. She knew what he needed.

Now as they all shared the den, Rocky looked across the room at Hunter. He was sitting on a La-Z-Boy, with Jade sitting in his lap, and Leah sitting in hers. Leah was asleep, but her parents were nuzzling one another, and every now and then, they would exchange words that were spoken too softly for any of the others to hear. Rocky imagined that they'd be glad when the company left. Unfortunately, though, nobody seemed to be in a hurry.

All of the couples sat in pairs. Even Reverend and Mrs. Tides were sitting together on a love seat. She was knitting, and he was reading the current edition of the *AWC*. No kissing and hugging going on there, but nonetheless the love wasn't lost in the picture. Although Rocky and Kenyatta weren't being as affectionate as Hunter and Jade, he sat with his arm around her, while her head rested on his chest. Rocky wondered if she could hear the way she made his heart drum. As she relaxed against him, Rocky could still smell whatever line of products had been used on her hair last night. Kenyatta had gotten it styled in a down fashion again. Rocky knew she did it just for him. He kissed the top of her head, and she looked up at him and smiled. He was going to have to marry this one. Kenyatta was the truth. She had put a bullet in a dude for him. It didn't get any more real than that. Her saving his life had been the main topic of the afternoon, and the fascination continued.

Mildred Tides looked up from her knitting. "You sure are brave, child," she told Kenyatta. "Even if I knew how to shoot a gun, I'd be so scared that I probably couldn't do it."

"Yes, you could, Mother Tides," Kenyatta said. "If it came down to somebody shooting Pastor, or you shooting that somebody, you'd do it."

Rocky grinned. Kenyatta had just used a scenario that pit person number one against person number two, when person number two was about to harm or kill the most important person in person number one's life. That spoke volumes as to how she saw him. Rocky held her more tightly.

"How did you even know the guy was there?" Candice asked.

Rocky had heard this story already. "Oh, y'all are gonna love this," he announced while loosening his hold on Kenyatta so that she could sit up straight.

Kenyatta covered her face like she was embarrassed, but she removed her hands when Rocky nudged her. "I didn't know he was there," she admitted. "I just knew somebody was there. I was coming home from the salon, and I just wanted to pass Rocky's house, so

I took the long route through Shelton Heights. When I approached his house, I didn't see his motorcycle, because it was in the garage, but I saw a strange car parked along the side of the road in front of his mailbox. I was gonna let it slide, but curiosity got the best of me." She covered her face again.

"Long story short, she thought I was in there with another woman." She was taking too long to tell the story, so Rocky thought he'd cut out whatever other preliminary details she had planned to share.

Sounds of "ooh" filled the room.

"Anyway," Kenyatta said while she flashed her palm in Rocky's face. "First of all, y'all should know that we had talked a couple of hours earlier, and he had told me that he was gonna turn in because he was tired. So why would somebody be at his house if he was so tired?"

"You right. You right," Candice said. "I'm with you, girl."

"Thank you," Kenyatta said while Stuart gave Candice a sideways look. "Anyway, he had given me a spare key to his house, which, as far as I'm concerned, gave me the green light to go in the house whenever. So I got out of the car and rolled right on up to the front door to see who this was that was all up in my man's crib at that time of night." Her neck rolled, and she got "Amen's" from just about all the ladies in the room. Rocky couldn't help but laugh. He was entertained by her dramatics and tickled pink that she'd called him her man. "When I first walked in, I was hearing this kind of high-pitched voice that was talking and sounding kind of out of breath. And add to that, I was hearing this *thump, thump, thump, thump* noise too. That's when I pulled out my gun."

Rocky felt the need to add a little narration. "The guy that was holding the gun on me was jumping around and acting crazy. He was real high."

"Well, before I got to the room door, I had figured out that it was a man, and Rocky was in trouble. I stopped in the hallway to get the gun ready, and when I did that, I started being able to make out what was being said. I wanted to pull my cell and dial 911, but then the man would have heard me and probably would have shot Rocky right then and there, so I just had to do what I had to do."

"Were you scared at all?" Jade asked.

"I was terrified. I've had that gun ever since I left Joe, because I knew that he wasn't letting me go without at least trying to get me to come back. He'd never been physical with me before, but he had the tendencies, so I didn't want to take any chances. I've had the gun for a few years, but that was the first time I'd ever shot it outside of when I was learning to shoot. I thought I'd killed him. I'm glad I didn't, because I don't know how I would have handled it if I'd actually killed him."

"Jesus," Jan said. "At the next Women of Hope meeting, let's be sure to warn all the single sisters not even to think of approaching Rocky." She looked at Kenyatta. "You actually would have shot the woman if you had walked in there and found out that the thumping and heavy breathing was them messing around?"

"No, I wouldn't have shot her," Kenyatta said.

"She would've shot me," Rocky said, wearing a wide grin.

"And you're smiling about that?" Peter frowned. "Bruh, she just told you that she would have *shot* you. Mind you, the two of you have just started dating. That doesn't scare you?"

Rocky ran his hand through Kenyatta's hair. "No."

"Y'all haven't figured out yet that Rocky actually likes the over-the-top kind of girl?" Hunter asked.

Kenyatta looked at him. "Who you calling 'over-the-top'?"

Hunter laughed. "Woman, look at you. Your neck is about to come unscrewed."

"That's all right, baby girl, don't listen to them," Rocky said. "The only one in the room that it matters to loves it." He accepted the kiss that Kenyatta gave.

"So let me get this straight, Kenyatta." Jerome scooted forward on the couch. "All this time that you've been threatening to kill all of us, you really have had a gun on your person?"

"Yes," she said, "so watch yourself. You'd betta treat my girl right or you're outta here." A wide grin plastered itself across Ingrid's face. Rocky imagined that was the nicest thing Kenyatta had ever said about her.

"Yeah, well, from now on, a good gauge to know whether or not she's carrying it is to see if Rocky is anywhere near," Stuart said. "Kenyatta has paperwork that permits her to carry a gun, but Rocky has paperwork that prevents him from being anywhere around one."

"Thank you for that public service announcement, Officer Lyons," Rocky said. "Broadcast my business to the world, why don't you?"

Stuart defended himself. "Like there's anybody here who didn't already know. Nobody here is gonna be looking down their noses at you. It's not like Ms. Leona is here."

"Hey!" Jan shot back.

Peter raised his hand as though he were in a classroom setting. "Ooh . . . ooh! I know why she's not here. I know. I know."

"Stop it, Pete," Jan said. "See? Before we left home, I asked you real nice not to go there."

"Oh, come on, bay. Let me tell it."

"She's probably not here 'cause I'm here," Rocky said.

"Nope." Peter was so anxious to tell it that he was bouncing. "It's not you. Believe it or not, it's Mr. Perfect." In a dramatic sweeping motion, Peter stretched his arm toward Hunter. That was enough to get everybody begging Peter to tell it, and their cries of "aye" overshadowed Jan's single "nay." Peter held up his hands to silence everyone. "Okay. Hold on. Hold on," he said. "Get this. She's not here, because Psalm 100:3 says: 'Know ye that the LORD he is God: it is he that hath made us, and not we ourselves; we are his people, and the sheep of his pasture.'"

Hunter fell back against the chair. "Please, Pete. Please say it ain't so."

"What ain't so?" Murmurs of that question ran around the room.

"Sorry to disappoint you, Hunter, but it is so. My dear mother-in-law is not here because you are violating the Word of God by having horses in your pasture instead of sheep." Laughter had replaced all the questions. "Her exact words were—"

"Pete!" Jan tried to shush him again, but again to no avail.

"Her words were 'That boy got all that money, but ain't none of it gonna be enough to pay his way outta hell, if he don't get rid of them horses and get some sanctified sheep on his land. *Thus* saith the Lord.'"

Rocky hugged Kenyatta more tightly against him as they both laughed. Rocky didn't know which was funnier; what Leona had said, or the way Peter looked and sounded as he tried to mimic her. Especially when he said the word "thus."

"She did not say, 'Thus saith the Lord,'" Ingrid said.

Peter held up his right hand. "As God is my witness."

Jade spoke up. "Tell Ms. Leona, I love her and all, but I just got Spirit back. I'll beat an old lady for speaking against my baby."

Candice said, "Have you-all ever thought about medicating her?"

"I say, let Kenyatta shoot her" was Jerome's suggestion. Kenyatta nodded like all she needed was permission.

"Y'all better stop talking about my mama, I know that much." Jan's finger scanned the room, pointing at all of them.

"Seriously, though," Hunter said, "I think she qualifies for that rest home that Cecil Heights is in. There were people there that actually have *more* sense than Ms. Leona." He caught the pillow that Jan tossed at him.

"Well, I know this much," Reverend Tides said as he folded the pages of the newspaper he seemed so engrossed in reading. "The *AWC* keeps getting better and better each week. And that was a very interesting article on Cecil Heights."

"Thanks, Reverend Tides." Hunter beamed at the compliment. "It's amazing how he got tucked in a nursing home all the way in Macon, Georgia, and to the world, it was like he'd disappeared off the map. His mind is really gone, too, because when I was talking to him about Shelton, he had forgotten his brother was dead. It was like I reminded him of it as we were talking. My heart went out to him because he got real sad for a minute there. But then when he started talking again, he was saying stuff that actually validated what Old Man Heights had in his will, and we know for a fact that he was crazy when he wrote it. He had no offspring."

"I thought about that, honey," Jade said. "I think what happened is that Shelton Heights said that stuff so much to his brother that Cecil, in his depleted mental state, started to believe it. If a person has a mental disability, whether it's retardation or Alzheimer's, they can be made to believe that contrived situations and even fictional people exist."

"That makes sense," Mildred said.

"Makes a lot of sense," Hunter agreed. "And I'm sure the state will be glad that Klyvert was just a figment of an insane man's imagination."

Rocky looked at Hunter. "Who?"

"Klyvert. That was the name Old Man Heights gave his 'son.'" Hunter used his hands to put the word in invisible quotation marks.

"What's the matter?" Kenyatta asked when Rocky continued to look confused.

"Nothing. I've just never heard that name before."

"You and nobody else either," Hunter said. "He made it up."

Rocky's skin suddenly felt clammy. "No. I've heard the name before. I've just never heard it outside of where I heard it."

"Klyvert? You actually know somebody named Klyvert?" Jerome asked.

"No. I mean, yes. I mean, I knew someone who had that as a last name, not as a first."

"That—that . . . is a last name." Hunter's speech had slowed. Nobody else was talking at all. "Who do you know with that last name?"

Rocky stared at Hunter. The world was full of coincidences. This had to be one of them. "My—my dad."

Hunter nudged Jade off his lap and stood. He took slow steps toward where Rocky sat. "Have you read the article?"

It felt like Rocky's throat was closing. "No. I hadn't gotten around to it yet. All I've read so far was the article on me and the new house."

"What's your father's first name?"

Rocky looked around the room. Everybody appeared to lean forward in their seats as they anticipated his answer. He felt like he was on some kind of game show, and the answer to this question decided whether he'd win or lose. "D'On." The moment the name came out of his mouth, the room erupted.

"Are you serious?" Hunter walked to Reverend Tides and grabbed the paper he'd just finished reading. "You're not jerking me around, right? You honestly have not read this column?"

Rocky's heart felt like it was going to knock a hole in his chest. "No. Why?"

Hunter opened the paper to the article and placed it in Rocky's lap. He pointed to the name in the story. They'd spelled it wrong, but there it was in black and white—Cecil echoing the fact that Shelton Heights had had a son, and his name was D'On (or as they had it spelled, Deion) Klyvert.

"This must be a different person." Rocky felt overwhelmed. "My grandfather's name wasn't Shelton Heights. I've heard the name 'Shelton Heights' for years. Everybody knows about the man and the myth and the housing community. Even in prison, they know. Don't you think if my grandfather's name was Shelton Heights, I would have connected some dots?"

"What's your grandfather's name?" Kenyatta asked.

Rocky looked at her, and the truth dawned on him. "I don't know. I've never known."

"Then how do you know his name wasn't Shelton Heights?" Hunter asked.

Rocky looked down at the article in the paper. He stared at the printed photo of Shelton Heights that was there. Were his eyes deceiving him? Rocky was beginning to see similarities. His mother always used to tell him that he had his grandfather's good looks. Now Rocky was seeing eyes and lips that matched his.

"And there it is." Everyone turned to look at Reverend Tides. He stood. "There's the mansion that I dreamed about. I dreamed you moved into Shelton Heights, and the house you occupied was the largest in the subdivision. It was a mansion, and it all makes sense now."

"Whoa." Jerome's eyes were the size of quarters. "This means Rocky owns Shelton Heights?"

"Well, if all of this pans out to be true, which I have no doubt that it will," Hunter said, "it's his father who owns it, but Rocky would be an heir."

"What if his father is dead?" Kenyatta asked. Rocky looked at her. He would have asked it first, but his mouth was temporarily paralyzed.

"Whoa," Jerome repeated. "Rocky, dude . . . you *own* Shelton Heights."

"Oh! This is the big one. You hear that, Elizabeth? I'm coming to join you, honey!"

Rocky's eyes gravitated to the television set. The timing of the scene couldn't have been more perfect. He watched as Fred, on *Sanford and Son*, stumbled around his living room, gasping for breath, and holding his chest as he pretended to have yet another massive heart attack. The picture on the television screen was how Rocky felt. He wanted to get up and do the same thing.

"'Upon this rock I will build my church; and the gates of hell shall not prevail against it.'" Reverend Tides smiled as he said the words.

Kenyatta squeezed Rocky's hand. "Baby, you own Shelton Heights."

Jerome suddenly jumped from his seated position and crossed the floor of the den, making quick steps.

He stopped in front of all Rocky's housewarming gifts that had been lined up alongside the wall. Finding the bag he'd brought, Jerome snatched it up. He walked back to the sofa and crinkled his nose in exaggerated fashion. "Buy your own darn toaster!"

Epilogue

Rocky stood at the top of Stone Mountain and looked down on the city. A full month had passed since so much about his own identity had been revealed. Much of it was questionable at first, but it had since been verified. D'On Klyvert, father of D'On Rockford, aka Deon Rockford, aka Rocky, was, indeed, the son of Shelton Heights. Hunter said that the reason he, Malik, and Tyler were not able to locate live birth records for D'On Klyvert was because they were looking for records in the States, whereas D'On Klyvert had been born in Jamaica. Cecil had told Hunter that the child had been born in Georgia. Must have been another Alzheimer's moment.

From what they could gather in the days after Jade's party, Rocky's dad probably never knew who his biological father was. He'd lived his entire life not knowing his net worth. Not knowing his property value. It was also concluded by the amateur Sherlock Holmeses that it was very possible that Shelton Heights had no idea where his son was. The Jamaican whom he had impregnated was most likely a minor who had given up her son, which was how D'On Klyvert ended up in the States. All Old Man Heights knew was that he had a son out there somewhere. He probably longed for him and loved him, which is why he showed it the only way he knew how—by leaving everything to his son and his son's family.

The part about the old man being a warlock had no substantiation. Even in the presentation that Malik and Tyler were now preparing to take to state-level competition, they stated that there was no valid proof that Shelton Heights was a witch. All of that had been gossip that was rooted in the way the old man became a recluse, and how strange things began happening once he died. Shelton Heights had been murdered in the middle of the night, right on the grounds of the entryway into the Shelton Heights subdivision. It had been long believed that the people who murdered him probably only intended to rob him, but they became angered when they found out he had no money on his person. Everybody knew he was rich, so it stood to reason that he would have something of value on him. But he didn't. The murder of the old man had been gruesome and violent. With all of the folklore surrounding him, the killing, and the timing of all the questionable things that began happening to the people who lived there, the subdivision, as beautiful as it was, almost became a ghost town. The rent and mortgage amounts had to be lowered drastically to get people to take the chance at living there. That's when the rumors started of him being a witch, and his spirit was terrorizing the people who took advantage of the low-cost housing.

In his later years, when his mental state began to deteriorate, Shelton began to look like a homeless vagabond, in spite of his wealth. Rocky had to laugh when he saw one of the photos that depicted a bearded Shelton Heights. He looked like an unshaven hermit, and when Rocky looked at him, he saw himself. Maybe that was why he hid behind a beard for so long. He was lonely, sad, and depressed, and the beard masked that and made him look tough to the other inmates. It was

just like Kenyatta's story of how her belittling of people
was a mask to make her feel better about herself. Rocky
smiled into the breeze that brushed against his face. He
and Kenyatta were going to make a good couple.

His full inheritance hadn't been released to him yet,
but Rocky knew that after everything was handled by
the law team that Reverend Tides suggested, his life
was going to be different. The funny thing was that he
didn't want it to be. "Filthy stinking rich" was the way
he had always viewed Hunter and Jade. Now Rocky's
wealth was about to be even filthier and more stinking.
The thought was almost frightening—that he would go
from a gang-fighting, drug-dealing, prison-dwelling
convicted felon to the man God was now molding him
to be. Now, more than ever, he was glad for the new circle of friends he had. He wanted to remain grounded,
to never forget from where he had come. Rocky had no
doubt that his friends wouldn't let him forget.

He would be happy to have all the money he'd ever
need to provide for himself, his future family, and even
to give to charities and to his church. But he didn't want
the core things in his life to change. Hunter laughed
when Rocky told him that he wanted to keep his job at
the *Atlanta Weekly Chronicles*. Jerome laughed when
he told him that his same Harley-Davidson would continue to be his vehicle of choice, even though he would
buy a car so as to end the cycle of bumming a ride to
work and church. Even Kenyatta laughed when he told
her that he still wanted her and no one else. He had
silenced her laugh with a kiss, and by the time he released her lips, he had made a believer out of her.

They'd had a long talk a few nights ago, and Kenyatta
had come up with a theory of her own about all that
had happened to Rocky. She thought it was too much
of a coincidence that Shelton Heights's estate was only

weeks away from being released to the state when the havoc began with Rocky. Reports blamed faulty wiring as the "probable cause" for the first fire, and said that lightning during the storm had "likely" struck the structure the second time. None of the findings were conclusive.

Kenyatta believed that all of the crazy things that had happened to people connected to Shelton Heights in the past were because the old man's spirit was not at rest. She thought it was possible that even with Alzheimer's, he was in the process of trying to find his son at the time of his death, and because of the ill timing of it all, he couldn't rest. When he finally realized that his son was dead, but that his son had a son, the spirit of Shelton Heights's mission became to make the identity of his grandson known. A part of the way he wanted to do that was to get Rocky to move into Shelton Heights. Kenyatta believed that it was the old man's unsettled spirit that torched the home. She said the eeriness would stop now. Shelton was at peace. Everybody had a theory. Only God knew the truth.

It was time to get back to work. Rocky's lunch break was coming to a close. Holding his face toward the sky, Rocky whispered a prayer. He didn't know about Kenyatta's theories or any of the speculations that he'd heard from his friends. He had heard more than his share in the past month, but Rocky chose not to live by any one of them. He didn't want to believe that all would be well because the spirit of his biological grandfather, who had been dead for years, was finally at rest. Instead, he wanted to believe that everything would be well because the Spirit of his Heavenly Father, who lived both now and forevermore, was watching over him. And because Matthew 16:18 said it would be so.

Reading Group Discussion Questions

1.   Rocky made promises to God while in prison that he tried to dodge fulfilling once he was released. Have you (or someone you know) been guilty of making vows to the Lord when situations were unfavorable, and then reneging on them once deliverance came?

2.   It seemed that most of the men viewed Hunter as the "leader" among them, and the women viewed Jade as the same. Why do you believe that was the case? Do you think they were the ones with the greatest qualifying leadership characteristics? If not, who would you have chosen?

3.   Rocky had a great weakness for women even after giving his life to Christ. How do you feel about that? When a person becomes a born again Christian, should they still have the same carnal struggles that they had before the life change?

4.   What about Kenyatta's esteem issues? Do you believe true Christians battle with such issues to the point of trying to make others look bad to pacify their own shortcomings?

5.   Leona Grimes criticized Rocky for his tattoos, saying that they were sinful and that Christians should not have them. What are your thoughts about Chris-

tians and body art? Should it be totally avoided and/or removed once a person becomes born again?

6.   During a heart-to-heart discussion with Reverend and Mrs. Tides, Rocky made the observation that living the life of a sinner was easier than living the life of Christian. Do you agree or disagree . . . and why?

7.   Hunter's assistant (Lorna) was known to be loose and was often described as a "man-eater." Do you think that Hunter (a man who viewed his business as a ministerial tool) was justified in keeping such a person as a part of his staff, or should he have released her because of her off-site behavior?

8.   Rocky had several idiosyncrasies that were a direct result of his stint in prison. He avoided public transportation because that's what he was on at the time he got arrested. He didn't particularly like sharing a home with his best friend, Jerome, because they had also shared a cell together. "Law and Order" type shows were not his favorite because of his personal dealings with the law. Is it possible that he should have had some type of professional counseling after being released into society? Should all people who experience lengthy stays behind bars get professional counseling once released?

9.   From the moment Rocky heard Reverend Tides preach the "Upon This Rock" message, it stuck with him and resurfaced in his memory at different times throughout the story. Why do you think that was?

10. What was your take on the reasons for the back-to-back fires that consumed Rocky's first home? In the past, all of those types of unexplainable happenings had taken place within the Shelton Heights subdivision. Rocky's home was located elsewhere in the city, yet misfortune plagued him. Could Kenyatta's theory have been true? Could the spirit of Old Man Shelton Heights have orchestrated the disasters as a way to force Rocky to move into the infamous community so that all the other pieces of the puzzle would also come together?

11. How do you feel about ghosts? Do you believe (on any level) that they exist and that the unsettled spirits of deceased people can reside among the living and haunt or even help those who are left behind? Is it unchristian-like to believe in such phenomena?

12. When all of the mysteries of Rocky's true identity were uncovered, the aftermath of it all placed him in a different station in life. Even so, Rocky vowed that he'd still keep his same job, his same primary mode of transportation, and his same lady friend. How realistic is it that he will continue to maintain those things once he is able claim all that is his? Do you think he will really be able to stay grounded considering his background?

13. Who was your favorite character? Why?

14. Who was your least favorite character? Why?

15. If you could rewrite any part of this story, would you? If so, which part would it be?